CONGO INC.

GLOBAL AFRICAN VOICES
Dominic Thomas, *editor*

I Was an Elephant Salesman: Adventures between Dakar, Paris, and Milan
Pap Khouma, *Edited by* Oreste Pivetta
Translated by Rebecca Hopkins
Introduction by Graziella Parati

Little Mother
Cristina Ali Farah
Translated by Giovanna Bellesia-Contuzzi
and Victoria Offredi Poletto
Introduction by Alessandra Di Maio

Life and a Half
Sony Labou Tansi
Translated by Alison Dundy
Introduction by Dominic Thomas

Transit
Abdourahman A. Waberi
Translated by David Ball
and Nicole Ball

Cruel City
Mongo Beti
Translated by Pim Higginson

Blue White Red
Alain Mabanckou
Translated by Alison Dundy

The Past Ahead
Gilbert Gatore
Translated by Marjolijn de Jager

Queen of Flowers and Pearls
Gabriella Ghermandi
Translated by Giovanna Bellesia-Contuzzi
and Victoria Offredi Poletto

The Shameful State
Sony Labou Tansi
Translated by Dominic Thomas
Foreword by Alain Mabanckou

Kaveena
Boubacar Boris Diop
Translated by Bhakti Shringarpure
and Sara C. Hanaburgh

Murambi, The Book of Bones
Boubacar Boris Diop
Translated by Fiona Mc Laughlin

The Heart of the Leopard Children
Wilfried N'Sondé
Translated by Karen Lindo

Harvest of Skulls
Abdourahman A. Waberi
Translated by Dominic Thomas

Jazz and Palm Wine
Emmanuel Dongala
Translated by Dominic Thomas

The Silence of the Spirits
Wilfried N'Sondé
Translated by Karen Lindo

IN KOLI JEAN BOFANE

CONGO INC.

刚果股份有限公司

Bismarck's Testament

俾斯麦的遗嘱

Translated by MARJOLIJN DE JAGER
Foreword by DOMINIC THOMAS

INDIANA UNIVERSITY PRESS

Published with support from
the John Gallman Fund for New Directions

This book is a publication of

Indiana University Press
Office of Scholarly Publishing
Herman B Wells Library 350
1320 East 10th Street
Bloomington, Indiana 47405 USA

iupress.indiana.edu

Original publication in French
© 2014 Actes Sud
English translation
© 2018 by Indiana University Press
All rights reserved

The paper used in this publication meets the
minimum requirements of the American
National Standard for Information
Sciences—Permanence of Paper for Printed
Library Materials, ANSI Z39.48–1992.

Manufactured in the United States of America

Cataloging information is available
from the Library of Congress.

ISBN 978-0-253-03190-7 (paperback)
ISBN 978-0-253-03191-4 (ebook)

1 2 3 4 5   23 22 21 20 19 18

to the young girls, the little girls,
and the women of Congo
to the UN
to the IMF
to the WTO

The new state of Congo
is destined to become one of the most
important enforcers of the work
we intend to accomplish. . .

Chancellor Otto von Bismarck,
at the closing of the Berlin Conference,
February 1885

Contents

Foreword

In Koli Jean Bofane's *Congo Inc.: Bismarck's Testament*: The Limits of Empathy and the Postcolonial Scramble for Africa

Dominic Thomas

In Koli Jean Bofane's first novel, *Mathématiques Congolaises* (2008), transported his readers on a journey into the confusion and disorder that have become so endemic to depictions of the Democratic Republic of the Congo (DRC). The "two Congos"—the Republic of the Congo (capital Brazzaville) and the DRC (capital Kinshasa)—sit face-to-face on the banks of the eponymous Congo River. The *Global African Voices* series has already published (or will be publishing) several works by Sony Labou Tansi (*Life and a Half* and *The Shameful State*), Alain Mabanckou (*Blue White Red*, *The Tears of the Black Man*, and *The Negro Grandsons of Vercingetorix*), Wilfried N'Sondé (*The Heart of the Leopard Children*, *The Silence of the Spirits*, and *Concrete Flowers*), and Emmanuel Dongala (*Jazz and Palm Wine*), authors who hail from the Republic of the Congo. In Koli Jean Bofane's *Congo Inc.: Bismarck's Testament*, first published in France in 2014, will therefore be the first novel in the series focusing on the DRC. Thanks to Marjolijn de Jager's truly remarkable translation and uncanny ability to capture the essence of the original text, readers will be able to appreciate why different juries, having awarded In Koli Jean Bofane the Grand Prix littéraire de l'Afrique noire for his first novel, also selected *Congo Inc.: Bismarck's Testament* for the Grand Prix du Roman Métis and the prestigious Prix des Cinq continents de la Francophonie.

The subtitle—*Bismarck's Testament*—in what is a hypnotizing, mesmerizing, daring, and deeply disquieting novel, harkens back to the era when Germany's first chancellor, Otto von Bismarck (1815–1898), convened the Congo Conference (also known as the Berlin Conference) in 1884–1885. It was of course at this conference that the fourteen signatory powers negotiated the terms of the General Act, an initiative that triggered what became known as the "scramble for Africa." However, the General Act also simultaneously granted legitimacy to the ambitions of King Leopold II of Belgium, who imposed his rule over the Congo Free State from 1885 until 1908, at which point it became the Belgian Congo up until political independence in 1960. This territory also comprised the northern region along the equator and the city of Mbandaka, where In Koli Jean Bofane was born in 1954. Adam Hochschild's book *King Leopold's Ghost: A Story of Greed, Terror, and Heroism in Colonial Africa* highlighted the brutalization and exploitation of the "native" population in the relentless and unchecked drive to extract the country's resources.[1] Similarly, in his monumental study *Congo: The Epic History of a People*, David Van Reybrook underscored how "today, the Congo Free State is notorious not so much for its vague borders as for its crushing regime. And rightly so. Along with the turbulent years before and after 1960, the year of independence, and the decade between 1996 and 2006, that period is seen as the bloodiest in the nation's history."[2]

In Koli Jean Bofane does not shy away from controversy; he makes a concerted effort to provide the reader with a near exhaustive inventory of the damning history of the region while emphasizing its key geostrategic importance—beginning with the Berlin Conference and then straddling both world wars, on to Hiroshima and Nagasaki, the Vietnam War, the sanguine history of decolonization and genocide, and culminating in the nefarious activities of multinationals:

> The algorithm Congo Inc. had been created at the moment that Africa was being chopped up in Berlin between November 1884 and February 1885. Under Leopold II's sharecropping, they hastily developed it so they could supply the whole world with rubber from the equator, without which the industrial era wouldn't have expanded as rapidly as it needed to at the time. Subsequently, its contribution to the First World War effort had been crucial, even if that war— most of it—could have been fought on horseback, without Congo, even if things

had changed since the Germans had further developed synthetic rubber in 1914. The involvement of Congo Inc. in the Second World War proved decisive.

The final point had come with the concept of putting the uranium of Shinkolobwe at the disposal of the United States of America, which destroyed Hiroshima and Nagasaki once and for all, launching the theory of nuclear deterrence at the same time, and for all time. It contributed vastly to the devastation of Vietnam by allowing the Bell UH1-Huey helicopters, sides gaping wide, to spit millions of sprays of the copper from Likasi and Kolwezi from high in the sky over towns and countryside from Danang to Hanoi, via Huế, Vinh, Lao Cai, Lang Son, and the port of Haiphong.

During the so-called Cold War, the algorithm remained red-hot. The fuel that guaranteed proper functioning could also be made up of men. Warriors such as the Ngwaka, Mbunza, Luba, Basakata, and Lokele of Mobutu Sese Seko, like spearheads on Africa's battlefields, went to shed their blood from Biafra to Aouzou, passing through the Front Line—in front of Angola and Cuba—through Rwanda on the Byumba end in 1990. Disposable humans could also participate in the dirty work and in coups d'état. Loyal to Bismarck's testament, Congo Inc. more recently had been appointed as the accredited supplier of internationalism, responsible for the delivery of strategic minerals for the conquest of space, the manufacturing of sophisticated armaments, the oil industry, and the production of high-tech telecommunications material.[3]

Pillaged, plundered, looted, despoiled, embezzled, stripped, ransacked, ravaged—each and every one of these synonyms remains pertinent to the unquenchable transgenerational thirst for Congo's natural resources. The process of assigning accountability is not restricted to external predators, to the succession of foreign or outside forces on the ground; rather, In Koli Jean Bofane's scene is truly apocalyptic, a dramatic staging of biblical proportions, one on which the attention also turns to the local vultures who gather in multitudes to devour the festering, putrid carcass and who share the blame and culpability for the deleterious consequences of their choices.

The DRC is one of the largest and most densely populated countries in the world. The military dictator Mobutu Sese Seko introduced a process of renationalization known as "zaïrization" in 1971, renaming the country the Republic of Zaire. The political instability that had become characteristic of the early years of postcolonial transition—and that included the assassination in 1961 of the first democratically elected leader, Patrice Lumumba—subsequently defined the rule, from 1965 to 1997, of Mobutu himself, a much-satirized dictator who became the embodiment of corruption, degeneracy, and wickedness. Indeed, critic Nicolas Michel aptly described *Congo Inc.: Bismarck's Testament* as "a heady mixture of political erudition, cruel irony," a work in which "the Congo's extravagance had found its match in In Koli Jean Bofane."[4] What remains incontrovertible in the novel is the seamless continuation between the colonial and postcolonial "scramble"—namely, the ongoing despoliation of resources by multinational corporate interests coupled with, nourished, and sustained by corrupt governance. What ensues is widespread civil conflict, human rights abuses, and environmental degradation.

Witness to this devastation is the novel's main protagonist, a young Congolese Pygmy named Isookanga. However, anyone who comes into contact with him soon learns not to underestimate this central figure because of his stature. Connected to the outside world from his rural village setting thanks to a telecommunications tower installed by Chinese business operatives, Isookanga devotes his days to making the necessary preparations for his exodus to the capital and megalopolis, Kinshasa, "the place of concentration and fission is Kinshasa, laboratory of the future and, incidentally, capital city of the nebula, Congo Inc." Certainly, mobility and relocation are not in and of themselves new in the library of francophone sub-Saharan African literature, a library that proudly displays the emblematic stories of Fara in Ousmane Socé's *Mirages de Paris* (1937), Laye in Camara Laye's *The Dark Child* (1954), Tanhoe in Bernard Dadié's *An African in Paris* (1959), Samba in Cheikh Hamidou Kane's *Ambiguous Adventure* (1961), Joseph in Daniel Biyaoula's *L'Impasse* (1996), or Massala-Massala in Alain Mabanckou's *Blue White Red* (1998). All of these protagonists were seduced by the colonial project and postcolonial opportunities they perceived in Europe, by what Christopher L. Miller has described as the inherent "francocentrism," the symbol of upward mobility and the promise of advancement.[5] However, Isookanga's migration is internal and he remains within the borders of the nation-state.

Media attention has tended to concentrate on the movements of migrants and refugees traveling across the Aegean and Mediterranean seas over the past few years, and we have witnessed a toughening of European Union policy that has resulted in stricter control, selection, and regulation over who is permitted to enter and remain in what has increasingly been referred to as Fortress Europe. Images have featured hundreds of people boarding unseaworthy crafts in desperate attempts to cross these seaways, all too often concluding with tragic human losses. Arnaud Leparmentier and Maryline Baumard have discussed the findings of a 2015 study conducted by the International Organization for Migration (IOM) that points to burgeoning numbers of both economic migrants and asylum seekers coming from the African continent. These can be explained by a broad range of push factors that involve declining economies, political unrest, civil conflict, human rights abuses, and, of course, serious environmental concerns; the supply nations all have in common one or more of these elements. However, as the aforementioned study also reveals, of the 32 million or so Africans who have been displaced, internal and intra-African population dislocation movement remains far more significant.[6]

Isookanga's rural exodus or flight takes him to the capital, a common pattern as urban centers continue to proliferate. Like so many of his fictional (and real-life predecessors), the adventure is one that will take him from innocence to insight and initiation as the logical outcome of harsh life lessons. By the time he sets out, his knowledge of the outside world has been attained from the endless hours he has devoted to the online game *Raging Trade*. Under the avatar "Congo Bololo," which translates as "bitter" or "sour" Congo, and to the soundtrack of American rap music, he takes on ruthless adversaries. "The first-aid kit," we learn, "that contained the stealth weapons he'd managed to accumulate throughout his sessions with the game wouldn't suffice; his adversaries were daunting. He didn't know what they were up to— those rapacious American Diggers, Skulls and Bones, Uranium and Security, the Goldberg & Gils Atomic Project, all of them making sure he'd get his just desserts, he knew that—but Congo Bololo hadn't spoken his last yet. He was going to crush them, methodically, one by one." Journeying alongside Isookanga, we discover the striking correlation between the online game and the challenges confronting the DRC on the larger geopolitical landscape of globalization. The colonial enterprise may very well have been premised upon the insatiable accumulation of goods and the pursuit for profit, but analogous mechanisms unambiguously remain the order of the day. When asked by his uncle "'but what is it exactly that you want to do?'" he does not have to think twice before responding, "Globalization, computer technology, Uncle." Uncertain as to what the future will hold, his determination overrides any concerns he may harbor: "Would the now established globalization drive people to veiled behavior even in everyday life, to a ghostlike secrecy? [. . .] Isookanga wasn't sure of it yet, but what mattered for now was that he was finally in downtown Kinshasa, the capital."

Shortly after his arrival, Isookanga meets Zhang Xia, a Chinese man endeavoring to resolve his own complicated personal issues. Zhang Xia becomes a mentor of sorts, sharing words of wisdom with the somewhat disoriented young man: "'Experience is a lantern that only sheds light on the path you've already walked.'" Their interaction is far from unusual in a city in which the Chinese presence is by now a long-standing one. In *Sur les ailes du dragon: Voyages entre l'Afrique et la Chine*, Belgian author Lieve Joris had recorded her travels between Africa and China and described the extraordinary flow of goods and people between these two regions of the world.[7] Trade relations between China and the DRC have grown exponentially in recent years, most notably in terms of mining operations and infrastructure development and investment; this has taken place in the context of a relentless pursuit of Congo's riches, such as timber, cobalt, and tin. Conclusions and reports of this nature abound: "the DRC will remain the destination of choice for Chinese mining investors in the coming years, thanks to the country's low production costs and the largest undeveloped high-grade (2–3% compared to global average of 0.8%) copper deposits in the world."[8]

Isookanga remains steadfast, resolute, announcing, "'You know, I'm not that interested anymore in what goes on in the forest or with my people. I'm a man of the future who goes along with his time. Me, I'm globalizing.'" His uncle Old Lomana, however, sees things quite differently, and it will take some time for Isookanga to see through the prism of triumphant globalization. Old Lomana has observed how the eco-balance has been disturbed and the wildlife driven away: "'Something's happening in the ecosystem, Isookanga. Parameters are in the process of changing radically.'" For him, the intrusion of new technologies and of "'the telecommunications pole'" installed by "'those barbarians'" are to blame for the disruption of the natural environment, and

> since it had been put up, that bit of metal had brought nothing but trouble. First of all, it had caused harm on the level of social peace, because it had its detractors among the majority of the Ekanga population as well as its supporters, who were thrilled to finally join the modern world. Although one could ask in what way the antenna could possibly be of service to them—phone whom? surf what?—they would defend the iron tower as if it were a member of their own family. Then there was the matter of subsistence; sustenance had turned on its heels. Now they had to go for miles to flush it out. Some people simply didn't look any farther than the end of their nose.
> And his own nephew Isookanga was one of them. Nothing but nonsense. Modernity, modernity. Can you eat modernity?

Initially, at least, these concerns are secondary to Isookanga, who had started "to defend ideas that had nothing to do with the Ekonda and the preservation of their biosphere." Only gradually does he begin to open his eyes and see how the city epitomizes the futile greed of the times: "Everything was working out well for everyone in this conflict. Nothing ideological or political about it. It was simply a matter of being in control of the largest reserve of raw materials in the world, and may the best man win." Only then can he begin to identify with the kinds of exchanges such as the one that takes place between Chiara Argento and Celio: "'There are far too many interests in Congo, Celio. They all want to line their pockets. It's the only purpose of the rebellions; all of our reports prove it.'"

In Koli Jean Bofane's novel reckons with the harsh realities confronting the DRC (and elsewhere, of course, in the region and on the African continent), including the embedded corruption. This analysis is anchored in fiction, but the fictitious space ultimately resembles all too much the contemporary reality. *Congo Inc.: Bismarck's Testament* is dedicated "to the young girls, the little girls, and the women of Congo," but also (ironically?) to the IMF, WTO, and UN. This is a world fashioned by violence, a world that tests the limits of empathy and understanding, a deeply troubled world. As the Cameroonian philosopher and political scientist Achille Mbembe has argued, "In a world set on objectifying everybody and every living thing in the name of profit, the erasure of the political by capital is the real threat. The transformation of the political into business raises the risk of the elimination of the very possibility of politics. Whether civilization can give rise at all to any form of political life is the problem of the 21st century."[9] Yet, somehow, in the face of genocide, ethnic cleansing, civil conflict, disease, coercion, and gender-based violence, out of the horror, mutilation, dismemberment, hacking, burning, and rape, In Koli Jean Bofane's novel strives to delineate the contours of a universe in which fiction can address the indignation and gradually pave the way for moral imagination.

Acknowledgments

The author wishes to thank the following:

- The Federation Wallonia-Brussels for its support
- Mao Tse-Tung for his speeches, especially the one devoted to the Mulelist Rebellion of 1964, which inspired Zhang Xia
- Confucius for his thoughts, some of which have been used here
- Isabelle Rabut for her advice on proper names and her translations into Chinese

The translator would like to express her sincere appreciation of Dee Mortensen, editorial director at Indiana University Press, for her unwavering support of, and enduring encouragement for, the translation of this novel. Profound thanks to my husband, David Vita, as always, such a careful and enthusiastic first reader of my work.

Indiana University Press would like to thank the Federation Wallonia-Brussels for support for the translation.

CONGO INC.

1

LANDS AND TIMES
土地和时间

"Fuckin' caterpillars!"

For more than an hour the exasperation the innocent little bugs had been causing Isookanga had stimulated his senses, enabling him to make his way more quickly through the forest, avoiding low branches, creating gaps in the foliage with the same determination as an icebreaker's bow at a time of global warming. Between the towering trees, cathedrals resting on their gigantic root foundations, the young man's outline seemed insignificant. He was dressed simply in shorts made of pounded bark. From time to time the canopy would open shafts of light that made the dangling moisture droplets shimmer. Insects danced in their midst, competing for space with ferns of the Pleistocene era, lianas dangling down from nowhere, and dying trunks fighting against decay. In this tangle of life and death, while the sap struggled to rise, implausibly colored orchids were smugly showing off in the drizzle, saturated with fragrances of fluids, the odors of organic waste, and of the spray animals left behind to mark their territory.

The screeching of parrots and toucans from the treetops couldn't compete with that of the monkeys, masters at disturbing the peace. A cuckoo tirelessly repeated a monotonous, two-note song, echoed back through the clutter of vegetation. Not much chance of hearing the large wild animals, except occasionally through the vibrations a solitary elephant would make on the ground or when a wild boar scraped its skin against the roughest bark it could find.

On the ground and below, in the kingdom of porcupine and armadillo, ant and scolopendrid—venomous centipedes—invisible, sprawling empires were ceaselessly being built and demolished under the iron rule of greedy and omnipotent sovereigns that reigned over populations without light.

"This really isn't the time, shit! Skulls and Bones Mining Fields are threatening me from every side, Kannibal Dawa has dropped me like a hot potato, that bitch from Uranium and Security keeps taking points away from me, and in the meantime, what am I doing? Couldn't eat corned beef like everyone else? Open a can of sardines? Caterpillars! And right this very moment, too! Yesterday, yesterday, always yesterday! That's what the ancestors said! That's what tradition demands! 'Nephew, instead of starting that video game of yours, better go and catch me some of those little invertebrates in the forest, and make it snappy!' Why not keep up with the times and make some progress, for God's sake? Feed yourself and start thinking like the rest of humanity. Fucking uncle! Just because he's chief of the Ekonda?[11] Yeah, chief of the caterpillars is more like it!"

Isookanga's rage had now peaked. As he came bolting out of the forest he called out to a boy, balanced the burlap sack with the small creatures on his shoulders, and ordered him to drop it off at the other end of the village at Old Lomama's. Then he hurried over to his hut. He quickly took off his tree bark shorts, pulled on a pair of Superdry JPN jeans and a T-shirt emblazoned with the image of Snoop Dogg, draped a chain with a rhinestone pendant with the letters "NY" around his neck, and slipped into blue flip-flops. Now he was ready to join the video game session that had started at least fifteen minutes earlier. And those fifteen minutes gave the other players a great advantage; staying in the game was a form of lobbying those bastards embarked on what could make you lose points in no time at all.

---

1. The representatives of the Ekonda clan, who are part of the Mongo people, are small in stature and sometimes called Pygmies.

Congo Inc.

In front of his LCD screen, using the name Congo Bololo,[2] Isookanga flew over a landscape controlled by an attack helicopter to locate possible enemies. Something moved behind a clump of trees; he would send off rockets to flush out a convoy of reinforcements. The young man was having a field day, shooting from his keyboard like a veritable psychopath, balls of fire exploding from every direction. On the side of the Toyota pickup trucks trying to get away he recognized the colors of that bastard Kannibal Dawa.[3] In the hallways of the UN, Kannibal Dawa was the strongest perhaps, but he was no match for the missiles of Congo Bololo in the field of operations. Isookanga fired off a few bursts of large-caliber shells, just to increase the damage. At that moment, without any warning, the boy he had sent to Old Lomama came through the door, raising the curtain that served as a closure.

"Old Lomama *azo benga yo!*"[4] he announced, slightly out of breath.

"Fucking shit! Can't they leave me alone! What does the uncle want now?"

"I don't know, man—he just said for you to hurry up."

With a heavy heart the young man had to resign himself to pausing the program, thereby freezing the virtual universe in which he was immersed.

● ● ● ● ●

"*Kota!*"[5]

Cautiously Isookanga took two steps inside Chief Lomama's hut. "*Losako,*[6] Old One."

"*Elaka Nzakomba.*[7] My son, I have to talk to you. I, who am your uncle, I'm saddened. When I think of it . . . What haven't we done for my sister's son ever since she got it into her head to go running around the country doing business? Haven't we shown the necessary enthusiasm for your education?"

"Yes, Uncle."

Isookanga knew the litany well. He was used to it. The most important thing was coming.

2. Bitter Congo. This term comes from the name of a very bitter medicinal plant, said to cure numerous pathologies, which must be mixed with water and drunk in large quantities.

3. The *dawa* is a fetish, a gris-gris or talisman.

4. "Old Lomama is calling you."

5. "Come in!"

6. A Mongo greeting to which the response is a personal saying.

7. The response here is "Everything depends on God."

"Haven't we done everything within our power to provide for your well-being?"

"Yes, Uncle."

"Did we ever demand any thank-yous for any of it?"

"No, Uncle."

"Why, then, my son, are you discarding our customs?"

"But, Uncle . . ."

"Be quiet! More than twenty-five years old and what have you accomplished? You bring shame upon me! First, you descend upon us one fine day with a device in your ears like a doctor. We couldn't talk to you anymore. You were indifferent to everything. What were you listening to? Isn't the voice of the ancestors enough for you anymore? When the thing broke, we were treated to that cannabis smoker you display on your T-shirt from morning to night," the old man added, pointing to Snoop Dogg.

"He's a spokesman, Uncle."

"Be quiet, I don't want to hear it! And several times a week you're now spending hours at a time alone in your hut looking at shadows on a screen. What are you learning from all these so-called modern things? Isookanga, my son, those who talk of modernity want to eliminate us. Listen to me carefully. *Matoi elekaka moto te!*[8] Look at that metal tower they've put up in the forest; it will kill us all one day. And, you, what are you doing in the meantime? You enjoy it and, what's more, you even find yourself a machine to communicate with this garbage! These are bad things, believe me. It's me, your uncle telling you this. And then, too, my son, stop using that word 'fucking' all the time. Stop it! You're shocking the ancestors! Have some respect for us! And those pants you wear? Why do you wear them in such a disgraceful way? An Ekonda can walk around almost naked, but around other people he takes care to cover up his buttocks. Are you forgetting where we come from? Do you think this forest that feeds you would still exist without our customs? And what about us? Do you think we'd still be here, fearing for our future? And, Isookanga, you are that future. Remember that you'll have to start wearing chief's clothing soon."

---

8. A proverb that means "The ears are never more important than the head." Said of the young when they believe themselves to be smarter than the adults.

Words of that sort continued pouring from the old man's mouth. Isookanga remained patient and listened to the very end but without any intention of taking the laments of the antiquated elder too seriously. Before long he would get back to his game and pick up where he'd left off, ridding himself once and for all of that scheming Kannibal Dawa. The young Ekonda still needed quite a lot of points to be safe. The first-aid kit that contained the stealth weapons he'd managed to accumulate throughout his sessions with the game wouldn't suffice; his adversaries were daunting. He didn't know what they were up to—those rapacious American Diggers, Skulls and Bones, Uranium and Security, the Goldberg & Gils Atomic Project, all of them making sure he'd get his just desserts, he knew that—but Congo Bololo hadn't spoken his last yet. He was going to crush them, methodically, one by one. And then he was going to think about what he needed to put in place to get to Kinshasa; there, at least, he and his friends talked about network and no network, about USB ports, and compatible interfaces. There, at least, virtual shadows didn't scare wary, retrograde old men who could prevent a serious youth from moving ahead in life as he should.

Once back home Isookanga thought he'd come through it easily enough, but he was upset. "Right now I should be sweeping Hiroshima-Naga out of the game. Fortunately, I didn't let myself get distracted. With *Raging Trade* it's better to keep a cool head."

There weren't many compensations for Isookanga in the village, but for the past two or three months there had been one, and it was considerable: the cell tower the company China Network had installed in the area. The helicopter that had lodged the mast had made a hellish racket, but Isookanga had no complaints. The monkeys did have a few, but he was thrilled that the trees that thought they ruled over everything and everyone were finally having their tresses tousled by something stronger than they.

Obviously, since technology had made its way into the vicinity, old-fashioned minds were screaming abuses at the tower: "It's going to bring a curse upon us, the ancestors will turn their back on us!" some insisted.

"Our wives won't be able to give birth anymore," others imagined.

"We'll all become impotent," the most pessimistic among them carried on.

"What's more, the caterpillars have fled," added those who thought they were being clever.

For Isookanga it was blatant proof that those blasted little beasts had no more common sense than the members of his clan, for he had indeed been forced to walk many kilometers to find them. Such had not been the case before.

● ● ● ● ●

You should have seen the local officials, surrounded by important figures from Kinshasa, on the day the tower was inaugurated. Isookanga still remembered it with great emotion: the parade, the bearing of the delegation from the capital city, the white woman researcher and her laptop, which the young man had surreptitiously swiped. Without this device Isookanga certainly would have gone off the rails long ago. First he had to learn how to work it, then he had to find a place close to the village where he could recharge the battery on a regular basis. Fortunately, there was his friend Bwale, manager of the Ekanga Kutu Center. They had met as students at Wafania. The first day at secondary school, their *lycée*, while his classmates looked down from their full height on Isookanga with an ironic smile, Bwale had been the first to come up to greet him, and they had quite naturally forged a fast and lasting friendship.

Now he couldn't do without the computer, and the online game *Raging Trade* had become his reason for living. *Raging Trade* was the recommended game for any internationalist wanting to know how to get into the business world. It was simple. By way of armed groups and security companies, multinationals competed for a territory known as Gondavanaland. For example, the dreaded Skulls and Bones Mining Fields swallowed up any mineral they encountered on their way. Focusing on uranium and cobalt, the military-industrial multinational of the GGAP, or Goldberg & Gils Atomic Project, didn't hesitate to make off with other strategic materials if it could weaken any adversaries. Mass Graves Petroleum took care of hydrocarbon, just as Blood and Oil knew how to use firepower in the field. In the nuclear business, Hiroshima-Naga was determined to control a large part of this particularly fissionable market. Its immediate competitor was Uranium and Security, a gang of hypocrites capable of shooting you in the back a hundred times over. Kannibal Dawa was an enemy always to be reckoned with; formidable in both lobbying and negotiating, it sometimes made points without firing a single missile and was always ready for duplicity behind the scenes. In this hostile environment American Diggers had managed to become hated by quite a few players in the world: fearing neither God nor man, the team had accumulated bonuses as the days went by, and one wondered how. In this virtual universe, Isookanga represented Congo Bololo. He coveted everything: minerals, oil, water, land, anything that was good for the taking. Isookanga was voracious, a true marauder. Because that's what the game demanded: eat or be eaten.

But the critical issue continued to be the exploitation of mining resources. To this end, in real life one first had to prospect, then obtain permits from the particular governments, pay taxes, pay the workmen, build infrastructures . . . The game was contemptuous of all this. To reach its objectives, the game advocated war and all its corollaries: intensive bombing, ethnic cleansing, population displacement, slavery . . . Like any self-respecting game, it offered bonuses. Of course, one could acquire arms as well as foreign allies, points at the Stock Exchange, a "first-aid kit" that included peace treaties to lull the UN—because there, too, as in real life, one couldn't really run a war without being sheltered by resolutions from the international organization—conferences to play for time, satellite photographs, a jihadist-philosophers kit in case of need, and, to maintain the troops' morale, plenty of sex slaves. The war on Gondavanaland terrain was self-financed, but that didn't prevent penalties from being put into place. A lowering rate of raw materials was the critical risk. Another was the UN blocking the accounts because of some malicious lobbying. But the worst thing was placing an embargo on the weapons. "Vato," the rapper Snoop Dogg's hit, represented the mood in sound. What you heard was *Run nigga, run nigga / Run mothafucker, run.*

● ● ● ● ●

Isookanga didn't understand the logic his uncle persisted in.

"Why keep trotting out the customs of the past? It's because of people like Old Lomama that we, the Ekonda, are discredited in the country. That they've called us Pygmies everywhere we go since time immemorial. Don't the French speak of 'mental midgets' when they refer to someone who clearly lacks any vision? And don't the Mongo,[9] who are brothers, after all, add a note of contempt at the end of the word '*motshwa*,'[10] which everyone notices? Even the Whites, whom we criticize all the time, are careful before they utter

9. The nation or people (some say tribe) of the Équateur Province (Congo RDC).
10. Pygmy.

the word 'nigger.' Just because they're taller than the norm, all the Mongo clans—Mbole, Bokatola, Bolia, Bakutshu, Bantomba, Ngelantano—feel free to treat us this way. Lesser than anything. People who think only about eating, making cutting remarks all day long, and fornicating. Do such hooligans even have any right to speak?"

As for that last, presumably major, activity of the Bamongo, Isookanga felt especially incriminated, since, unfortunately for him, he'd never really known who his father was. All because of polyandry, an ancestral custom Isookanga found appalling. A barbaric tradition that drives a woman to consuming men at will, as she wants, as much as she wants, whenever she wants, and clearing her of any guilt in the process. If she had practiced the activity within the clan itself, it would certainly not have posed any insurmountable problems, but because of the marked fondness of the young Ekonda's mother for men over one meter seventy-five, and because of some rather tough encounters, what was bound to happen happened: she found herself pregnant by an unknown father and brought into the world Isookanga, who had to be a good ten centimeters taller than the tallest Ekonda.

This marked difference weighed on the young man like a true defect. "*Tala ye molaï lokola soki nini!*"[11] That was the sentence to which he'd been convicted throughout his childhood and even afterward. He was constantly reminded that he was only half an Ekonda, that he was, in short, nothing more than the half-Pygmy people point their finger at. All of this had a negative effect on his character, on his trust in others and in himself, and prevented him from being part of the Mongo nation in general and of the Ekonda clan in particular. That position might have bothered him more, but somehow it forced him to find his true place, all the more so since he already took up very little space politically, socially, and, above all, physically, since his importance in the human arena was almost nil.

When you use computer bits to communicate, it makes no difference whether you speak Pygmy, Lapp, or Japanese. Being a financial burden and seducing every woman? What's the point, when it's enough to pick up a transmitted connection thanks to Wi-Fi and sample the same vibrations as anyone else on exactly the same web reflections. Tall or not, who cares when the only thing that counts is the number of gigabytes? Materiality has become totally

---

11. "Look at that guy, tall as I don't know what."

Congo Inc.

obsolete. In the globalized universe of the virtual world, even the sky is no longer a limit. And from the height at which Isookanga contemplated the universe that suited him to perfection, his position assured him extra detachment.

• • • • •

Above the crown formed by the *lifaki*, *kambala*, and other precious, centuries-old trees, the sun had insisted on being impressive before going off to illuminate other worlds and, fine-tuning its spectrum, had poured purple, orange, and mauve on the jumble of clouds in front of it. Farther down, against a background of darkness, a turquoise-blue halo stretched out in the distance. Only the contours of the huts were now visible. They followed one another here and there in gloomy clustered groups along the red dirt road, making up the village of Ekanga where the Batwa lived.[12] Fires had been lit in anticipation of the night, and curls of smoke were chasing each other before they intertwined. The increased shadows loosened the movements of men and women. Once darkness was complete all around, the immense majestic mass of forest would soon appear to be encroaching and then be perceived as an unmanageable, dangerous vise by some, as a protective and loving mother by others. It just depended; it couldn't be controlled.

• • • • •

"Bolongwa, bolongwa!"[13]

Isookanga and Bwale were forced to move. Dressed in blue, a policeman had brandished his club and created something of a swell in the crowd on the main avenue of Wafania. In the center a VIP stand made of palm branches had been erected for the inauguration of the telecommunications tower. The notables had gathered on the structure: the district commissioner and his wife in the middle; Captain Nawej, the police chief, on the left; then Bosekota Ekumbo, one of the subdivision's most influential men; and finally, first- and second-rank civil servants. On the right-hand side of the first row sat the invited guests from Kinshasa: next to the district commissioner was the Congolese representative of the China Network Company, owner of the tower; then came Ikele Engulu, sent by a development foundation; next was a

---

12. The plural form of "Pygmy."
13. "Get away from there!"

white woman, whose attention was focused on a computer screen. After that came a high-ranking individual, followed at the end of the row by an Asian-looking man.

Isookanga easily recognized the people from Kinshasa by the sunglasses concealing their eyes. The young Ekonda man respected the enigmatic appearance it gave them. You might have thought they came not from the capital but from much farther away—from another planet perhaps. Everything about them was different. While Wafania's notables persisted in constantly wiping their foreheads and waving their handkerchiefs around like fly swatters, the Kinshasans remained reclined in their seats, impassive to the intense heat in spite of their suits and tightly knotted ties, and barely moving as if air conditioning had become one of the options of their organism. Isookanga was relishing the spectacle. For him it was a lesson in mastering the social graces. Besides, it wasn't every day that such an event took place. He wanted to collect every bit of information necessary for his Kinshasan future. Too bad if they'd been waiting for over an hour under a blazing sun.

Still, everything had been well-prepared. Dressed in their Sunday best, in colors that had once been vibrant, people had invaded the main street early that morning. Despite the almost total destitution, faces were radiant and gleamed with the palm oil that everyone had rubbed on their skin that day. At one point two 4 × 4s suddenly appeared at the foot of the stand where Wafania's decision-makers sat. The six local police officers, poured into their uniforms and wearing white gloves, stood impeccably at attention. Their sergeant had rushed forward to open the car door for the dignitaries. Immediately thereafter resounded the military command "On guard!" followed by a barked "Atten*shun!*" Suddenly the air had grown tense. The very trees were taking a wait-and-see approach. One by one the Kinshasans stepped out of their vehicles. Behind their smoky glasses it seemed they couldn't see a thing, as if by having different means of discernment they didn't need to. They were walking unhurriedly, sure in their body language; inertia seemed to have no hold on them.

Delightedly Isookanga took it all in, gently nodding his head. But not for very long, because suddenly another guttural command shot out from the officer's gut and everyone rose as the bugle played the national anthem. After the last note from the brass instrument, after a conciliatory "At ease!" from the sergeant, the people standing in the heat were allowed to hear a string of interminable speeches on modernity as the spearhead of development. At the

Congo Inc.

end of all this, distant drums finally announced what everybody had been waiting for: the inaugural parade.

In the lead were the six police officers, AK rifles on their shoulders, looking austere, making a show of power as they marched in goose step. Right behind them were the four members of the local Red Cross, walking proudly in their rescue uniforms. Then came the associations with their banners: the Cooperative of Coffee Planters of the Tshuapa subdivision, the Association of Market Mothers, the Association of Pedicab Drivers, the Association for the Defense of the Mpenge Dialect, and many, many more. The onlookers were unanimous in their support of the girls from the Institute of Nurses Training in their tight-fitting white coats. Then hundreds of the region's schoolchildren in blue and white marched by, preceded by the goatskin drums they had made to add a powerful rhythm to the demonstration; Isookanga couldn't recall when he had last attended anything like it. To pass the time, he let his eyes wander over the seated guests, among whom especially the white woman had attracted his attention.

"Bwale, look at that woman. She is in direct contact with the world, with the universe, even, should she want it. Look, she's listening to everything. Did you see what's coming out of her ears? It looks like catfish whiskers. See that? Thanks to the screen in front of her she knows everything there is to know. There is the future. And I, I'm here, doomed to staying here and listening to some Uncle Lomama who won't stop moaning and messing up my life. And when he isn't the problem, I have to put up with the company of old-world monkeys in the forest. Is that what life has in store for me? I'm an internationalist who aspires to becoming a globalizer, Bwale. You, you get it, don't you?"

"I'm fine right here. I'll never leave the village."

"Still, you've told me about your uncle in Kinshasa. He's invited you to come join him there and you refuse? You're totally irresponsible; you're running the risk of completely missing out on the twenty-first century."

"Somebody has to stay in the village. If only to manage the uncle's branch here. And besides, what would I be doing with someone I hardly know? We've never even seen each other, he and I. He's always lived far away from us, far away from our reality. All he's interested in is his coffee trading post. Hey, Isoo! Look, she's coming."

The white woman had gotten up and was heading straight for the two friends. They each glanced over their shoulders to make sure, but the woman's smile was actually intended for them.

"Hello, my name is Aude Martin," she said, holding out her hand to Isookanga first and then to Bwale. Directing herself to the young Ekonda, she asked, "Do you speak French?"

"Of course. I've been to school."

"I hope I'm not bothering you. I'm doing some research on indigenous people. I'm an Africanist with a specialty in social anthropology. They told me that I'd find members of the Ekonda clan around Wafania, which is why I've done everything to join this delegation to come here, and I figured you must be one of them."

"You should know, Miss, that the Ekonda are self-effacing and don't much like to mix. If I am here it's because I'm avant-garde."

"Would you be willing to give me ten minutes of your time for an interview? It won't take long. I don't want to disturb you."

"Let's go over there."

Isookanga, Bwale, and the researcher left the crowd, moving a few feet away toward the forest that stretched out on both sides of the road. Telephone in hand, the young woman asked Isookanga questions on his lifestyle, his diet, his habitat, and the customs of his tribe. She asked if they were a patriarchal or matriarchal society, what the exact place was of the women in their society, and whether life between the authorities and the population was harmonious. In short, nothing new. Isookanga replied as candidly as possible and took advantage of the opportunity to make his views of modernity known. He tried to convince his interlocutor that it was absolutely necessary to open up the forest by placing telecommunication towers everywhere so that everyone could be connected to the rest of the world. Opening up information highways, certainly, but not just that; they also had to open up highways, period, so that the consumer goods that abounded elsewhere could benefit everyone.

"What is the forest? It's nothing!" he had insisted.

Talking with Isookanga, Aude Martin had sensed an indefinable emotion from the very start. First of all, his status as a human specimen threatened by extinction in the longer or shorter term gave him an aura of fragility that had touched the researcher immediately. The young woman was rather tall. Short, dark brown hair framed a face with melancholy eyes. So he wouldn't have to keep his head raised all the time, Isookanga began his sentences by looking at her but then systematically ended up by lowering his eyes and staring out into the distance ahead of him. The young woman attributed this to an especially contemplative spirit, or at least to a form of shyness caused by an extremely sensitive heart. At the same time, the way Isookanga had of accentuating his words, of being unambiguous in his opinions, or of sometimes taking his time when uttering a syllable to better emphasize the meaning of the word instilled Aude's body with an energy she was unable to identify or locate. After the interview she went back to her seat, moved not so much by what Isookanga had revealed to her as by the encounter she knew was exceptional, worthy of a different universe, an experience one has only once in a lifetime.

In the stands people were beginning to grow impatient. The Kinshasans, as always, were trying hard to assert their presence without showing it. The villagers, on the other hand, were waving their handkerchiefs around all the more. Then a huge racket came from the sky. It was like a thousand bellowing hippos coupled with the rumble from clouds having magically turned into gigantic rocks crashing into one another. Treetops bent under an enormous gust of wind, and an oblong shape materialized that even covered the sun. It was an MI-26 helicopter, made in Russia, which couldn't be purchased without the Ukrainian pilot who came with it.

The men with dark glasses all raised their head at the same time, as if they'd noticed a signal coming from their own world. Isookanga, too, was watching the helicopter. A cable was attached to it, at the end of which hung a reproduction of what Isookanga knew to be the Eiffel Tower, only larger. The telecommunications tower the elders had been talking about for some time was balancing gently in the air.

Hovering in place very high up, the chopper flew above a square that on the order of the district commissioner had been poured with concrete a few weeks earlier. Then it began to descend with its charge like a bird of prey, letting itself drop like a stone, breaking the fall at the last minute. A cry of amazement rose from the crowd. Isookanga, who had not allowed himself to be in the least impressed by the stunt, had read somewhere that planes and helicopters from the Ukraine ran on a mixture of half kerosene, half vodka. Below, just underneath the helicopter, a Sino-Asian-looking man signaled the pilot with both arms like a great helmsman. Everyone looked up, evaluating the risks of the dangerous maneuver of the approach.

"They should go back up."

"No, they should go to the right."

"Definitely not, go left."

"Come!"

Isookanga pulled Bwale by his T-shirt. Cutting through the captivated throng, he dragged him behind the stands, where there was no one else.

"Wait here for me. Keep watch."

Isookanga brushed aside the palm tree twine of which the stand consisted and made his way through. Crawling forward he stretched out his arm and put his hand on the case containing Aude Martin's computer, resting on the ground not far from her feet. The Ekonda beat a hasty retreat the same way he had come but backward.

"Let's get out of here!"

Bwale had no time to respond as Isookanga led him farther away and deeper into the nearby forest. "Shit, how dare you!"

"Shut up, Bwale. I know what I'm doing."

The two friends sat down on the trunk of a felled tree close to a brook whose crystalline water flowed steadily from the earth. Isookanga examined the computer with his fingers.

"You think I'm a thief because I swiped that white woman's equipment? My act counts as a refund for the colonial debt! Bwale, you're getting worked up over nothing. Besides, Mongo tradition demands that a future spouse steal a chicken from his own village to prove to the *bokilo* that he will always find a way to provide for the needs of his betrothed![14] For me, my betrothed is high technology. And my test for a union with the universe goes by way of stealing the computer you see here. Accept it as such. Don't stand in the way of my plans. I am you, you are me. You are tall, I am short, so what? We are like fingers on the same hand, aren't we?"

"Shit, didn't you see how she was looking at you? Instead of trying to 'get' her, you find nothing better to do than to swipe her computer."

Isookanga didn't like to speak of anything that in some way might refer to his personal anatomy. For the young Ekonda, the verb "get" was *ekila*, taboo. And all because of his mother, who had forgotten to have him circumcised, busy as she was running around left and right. Isookanga was ashamed of his body, believing it was just rubbish.

"Bwale, forget about me. We'll go back to the ceremony now. Above all, we shouldn't be noticed. But first let me hide this machine, safe with the wild

---

14. Parents-in-law.

boars and the ants. Once they discover it's disappeared, it will cause a stir, and knowing Captain Nawej, he's capable of searching the area hut by hut to find it. I don't want to take any risks."

● ● ● ● ●

After these memorable events, Isookanga locked himself in for two days with the researcher's machine. To plug in the mouse and the headphones he connected the cables to the corresponding holes. It was easy—whoever had invented it knew what he was doing. Then Isookanga pressed a button and the screen lit up. Thereupon he had to grope around for a moment, putting his fingers all over the place. When he slid his middle finger onto a small gray square, the point of an arrow began to move on the screen, following a logic that he instantly grasped. When he moved what looked like a little rat, the point reacted the same way. He clicked on the rodent's plastic head and a window opened up. A smile lit up his face, but he quickly pulled himself together because he had to stay focused. After going through many mood swings, the young man finally succeeded in typing the letters "Congo RDC" in a long, narrow rectangle marked "Google." He pressed the button again, the arrow pointing to the word "Images." There was a click and the world opened up before him in a way he could never have imagined when his realm had consisted only of trees, trees, and more trees. That was no life. That wasn't it. Even for a worker like him, one of what they call the original people, Isookanga.

After two days, as he passed the door of the Ekanga Kutu Enterprises, the store where Bwale was in charge, Isookanga had the premonition he wouldn't be crossing this threshold many more times. At that thought he threw his shoulders back and raised his chin, the laptop hanging from one hand, a heavy jute bag from the other.

"How *moto na ngai*,[15] how're you doing, friend? Since you suggested it, I'm bringing you the computer so you can charge it for me. I'll deduct the money for the gas for the generator from my bill," Isookanga said, putting the bag down that held his friend's order: a freshly smoke-dried monkey and a pangolin, a scaly anteater, meant for Bwale's uncle in Kinshasa.

The store wasn't very large but it had everything. Remnants of wax batik, plastic kitchen utensils, packets of sugar and rice, cans of sardines and

---

15. "How are you, my friend?"

pilchards, machetes, hoes, but mostly it was a place where you could buy coffee, stored in the back of the shop in fifty-kilo sacks meant for export. A table behind the counter served as Bwale's office. On it stood a computer, without Internet, which worked only one or two hours a week when the small generator was running.

"See what life should look like!" Isookanga cried out, pointing to a calendar of the Ekanga Kutu Enterprises showing a nighttime view of the Boulevard du 30-Juin in Kinshasa. "Look at all those cars. And yet it's not even what they call a traffic jam; you should see that—it's fabulous. There would be far more red lights than what you see here, and far brighter! I can't stand the darkness or the dogmatism here anymore. Did you notice the power of that helicopter the other day? And that man with the dark hair and creased eyes, did you see how expertly he put that metal tower down? That's the sort of world I want to advance in, speaking the language of the technicians, approaching the vernaculars of tomorrow. Look, even this game I'm bringing for your uncle in Kin'.[16] By delivering that to you I'm today nothing but a common poacher. In the past they would have nicknamed me 'Isookanga the greatest of hunters.' Don't you see that going from the noun 'hunter' to the term 'poacher' is something like a disintegration? It's not for me, Bwale, this forest life. I have other ambitions; I want to have a vision of things."

After a moment of reflection Isookanga asked, "How do you call it again, with that period?"

"Dot com."

"And the other one?"

"World Wide Web," Bwale stated for the nth time.

While Isookanga's battery was being charged, Bwale gave his friend all the information he could to help him fit in perfectly with the digital world and to probe the ether thanks to waves being moved by the tip of a person's finger, from one tab to another, from satellite to satellite, throughout the vast interstellar space.

During the training Isookanga listened carefully, but, like a well-formatted integrated circuit, his brain could easily jump from one subject to another and even to both at the same time. Apart from the proliferation of headlight beams and rear lights on the calendar's photograph, the email ad-

---

16. Kin' is short for Kinshasa.—*Tr.'s note*

Congo Inc.

dress *a.isekangakutu@chinnet.cd* had prompted an idea to quietly germinate in the young man's head. Isookanga knew how hesitant Bwale was to go to Kinshasa. His uncle had invited him repeatedly to join him there, but it still didn't appeal to him. Isookanga didn't intend to let this situation go on. Family was sacred—essential, actually, for someone who wants to move up in the world. He would take Bwale's place and put an end to this separation between an uncle and his nephew.

• • • • •

After creating a fictitious address, Isookanga sent the uncle a first email, which read as follows:

Dear Uncle,

I am your nephew Bwale Iselenge. I send you greetings and beg you to forgive me for not having written you for so long, but I needed to think about your proposal to join you in Kinshasa. I have given it a lot of thought and believe that an uncle and his nephew should not remain separated. It is now my wish to be near you. I will write more soon. Your older brother, my father, sends you his regards.

Please accept my respectful greetings.

Your nephew,

Bwale Iselenge in Wafania

PS: Did you receive the wild game I sent you a while ago?

A month later he sent a second email:

Dear Uncle,

I will be in Kinshasa soon. I will entrust the management of Ekanga Kutu to a friend. I am paying for the trip myself, so please don't worry about that.

Did you receive the monkey and the pangolin?

Your nephew,

Bwale Iselenge à Wafania

And so Isookanga embarked on a whaling boat for Mbandaka-la-Douce, the administrative center of Équateur Province, on the banks of the Congo River. From there his adventure could begin—Kin' would be the next stage. The young man took a tugboat coming down from Kisangani, pulling barges with a surface of more than a hundred meters, a floating city but congested like a subway train at rush hour. There were thousands of people covering every inch of the deck. Merchandise of all kinds to supply the capital was strewn about and dangling from parts of the vessel: bunches of plantains, stocks of dried fish, live goats, various sorts of game, sacks of coal and manioc, exotic birds, palm oil in PVC barrels, and near the bow a captive monkey with a cord around his neck. People were milling about: shopkeeping mothers, rural emigrants, Mongo streetwalkers from the Mongando clan, hair stylists, aspiring law and math professors, talisman vendors, runaway minors, discharged intellectuals, two Maï-Maï who had broken with their group,[17] men and women of the cloth, war refugees, and more.

In an indescribable scramble, families were piling up, terrified of a fatal accident if the barges were to crash, invoking divine mercy to avert disease and plans by the devil, who never thinks of throwing in the towel. Under such conditions it's important to know how to flaunt your eloquence to find an opening and negotiate a space. Voices permanently raised mingled with the ruckus that resounded on this local habitat. People were holding forth in every language the river siphoned off along its course, and even beyond. One shouldn't merely use a lot of verbiage on the boat: there shouldn't be a lack of ingenuity either, among other qualities, for that will assure daily sustenance or, for some, will offer the possibility of a free beer near a steaming pot, to make one feel a little like a millionaire on a catamaran.

"Fuck, this whole fleet, it isn't for real!"

More than 80,800 cubic meters per second spreading out across 4,700 kilometers—and humanity slogging away. Night was beginning to fall. Stretched out on deck wrapped up in his blanket, rocked by the antediluvian racket of the diesel motor, Isookanga was thinking: "In 1990 individual water consumption on earth consisted of some 12,300 cubic meters. For now, the average amount of water available is no more than a little over 6,500 cubic meters. In 2025 there will be no more than 5,000 cubic meters per inhabitant. Everyone will have a problem, except Congo. Soon there won't be a single drop of water to be found on the planet. They should privatize it all. It would be entrusted to multinationals, taxes would come in like a waterfall, and the Congolese wouldn't even need to cooperate,[18] carrying on as they should like the Emirates. The demand is there and, left to its own devices, the supply steadily flows on . . . and not a soul who gives a damn."

17. Congolese resistance fighters active in the Kivu region.
18. In the Congolese sense of "doing business."

The hydraulic scandal surrounded Isookanga on every side; he could go on preparing his forecasts, but the river had a date with the ocean, and what the Pygmy internationalist was thinking was of no concern to it at all. It was already flowing when the world was created. It had quite naturally seen one or two Ramses come by, the *candace*[19] Amanishakheto, Manikongo Afonso I, Shaka Zulu, Leopold II, Hitler, Nkumu[20] Botuli In Koli, Ben Bella, Lumumba, Nasser, Che Guevara, JFK, Mao, Mobutu, as well as the valiant M'zee Laurent-Désiré Kabila, who knew that he was only passing through. In the distance a sinking floating island, set off against the dusk's orange and dark red light, outstripped the line of barges and vanished around a bend like a ghost: the same one that the steamer of Captain Teodor Korzeniowski, who later took the name Joseph Conrad, had rounded as he plunged into the heart of darkness.

19. Title of the queens of Meroe, an ancient kingdom in Nubia in what is now Sudan, slightly north of Congo.
20. Customary chief.

2

WHO ARE YOU?
你是谁?

Isookanga was holding a young smoke-dried python, rolled up in a circle. He turned to a mother dressed in a *pagne* that said, "My husband is capable."[1] He needed to be done with it: "Give me thirty dollars."

"Twenty."

"All right, I'll take it."

After weeks on the water, the boat finally moored in Kingabwa, Kinshasa's commercial port. Dockworkers were busy unloading and there was a general crush because, all at once, part of the crowd had come from the city to do their shopping while others, loaded down with their countless packages, wanted to disembark. For his part, Isookanga had no interest in lingering. He pocketed the money from the game he had just sold, stuffed some smoked antelope and a porcupine in the canvas bag he was carrying, then laboriously made his way to the gangway that would take him to solid ground.

---

1. A *pagne* is a piece of fabric usually around two yards long, wrapped around the waist as a skirt.—*Tr.s' note.* Every *pagne* pattern is given a title or saying.

Stepping out of a taxi-bus in front of the central train station, Isookanga couldn't get over it. In the village, when he'd typed "Kinshasa" in Google's long rectangle, he had seen many marvels, but what was displayed before him surpassed everything. Seeing the Boulevard du 30-Juin stretching out in front of his eyes, Isookanga was sure it could incorporate all of Wafania, Monkoto, and Basankusu combined, and perhaps even Boende. The buildings lining it were even more stately than the trees of the forest. A huge throng was scurrying along, and the young Ekonda fell in with them, checking the uncle's address: Avenue Boyota in the Lingwala district. Someone told him it was near the Fine Arts Academy and showed him which public transportation to take.

"Avenue de la Libération! Libération!" A taxi-bus came charging down. Hanging on to the open door and thumping it with his fist, the conductor shouted, "Avenue de la Libération! Libération!"

Isookanga rushed forward to find a spot, but that wasn't easy for someone with no experience in the sport. Faced with the swarm of passengers that pounced on the vehicle, he didn't get very far because of his small stature; still he managed to squeeze between a muscular soldier and the impressive décolleté of a mother who, judging by the dust that covered her from head to toe, was probably selling manioc flour at the market.

● ● ● ● ●

"And who are you?"

"Bwale Iselenge. The oldest son of your husband's big brother."

"Oldest? Why are you so short then?"

Isookanga didn't know what to say.

Ten minutes earlier, he had knocked on the gate of the uncle's house. At first the guard turned him away, taking him for a peddler with his canvas bag. When he introduced himself as Bwale Iselenge, the boss's nephew, the guard had to let him in. He showed him a bench under a mango tree and asked him to wait as he announced his presence to the lady of the house.

Now she stood there before him, towering over him at her full height, a barely concealed disdainful pout on her face. Her unrelenting gaze traveled from Isookanga's eyes to the T-shirt printed with Snoop Dogg's smirk. "Go back over there and sit down. Anyway, Ambroise isn't here yet."

A long time later the guard opened the gate for a Mercedes, its motor rumbling. The uncle came out of the car and after a quick glance toward the bench went into the house. Immediately thereafter, Isookanga clearly heard the woman screaming. Among the words he could make out were "parasite," "take advantage," "what will my family say," "he's too short." The tone gave him to understand that his pseudo-relative was trying to vindicate himself for something that wasn't his responsibility, but in the shrew's eyes he was certainly at fault. The woman flung another two or three commands at him and then it was silent.

Instantly the uncle appeared on the terrace. "Come here."

Isookanga moved forward.

"My wife says that you are my brother's son. Are you actually Bwale Iselenge?"

"Absolutely."

"And how old are you?" he asked, a bit alarmed by his interlocutor's stature.

"Twenty-five, almost twenty-six, Uncle. I'm the one who wrote you not long ago and who sent you the anteater. You suggested that I come to Kinshasa, and here I am," Isookanga added with the most radiant smile he could muster.

"I know, I know, but I didn't expect that my big brother's son would be so . . . that he wouldn't have the family's build."

Isookanga continued to watch Ambroise Iselenge without saying another word, his smile now bigger than ever.

"Well, then, so be it," the uncle said, resigned. "Do you have any plans?"

"I have to register somewhere. At an academic department."

"It's a little late, but what is it exactly that you want to do?"

"Globalization, computer technology, Uncle." Nothing could temper the joy on Isookanga's face. He leaned down to his canvas bag. "I couldn't come here without bringing you some game." He stuck one arm into the bag. "I've brought you smoked antelope feet and a porcupine. And a little *bieya*.[2] You're crazy about that, it seems, and it's in season now."

"Oh, thank you."

The uncle was looking Isookanga over. His wishes notwithstanding, he couldn't bring himself to trust the individual before him more than halfway, in view of his height. The little guy claimed to be his nephew, no one could assert the contrary yet, one had to stay open to the possibility. For now, at least,

2. A plant heart that tastes like heart of palm and looks vaguely like macaroni.

the most important thing was to reassure his wife, in the hope she would understand that he couldn't just send this guy away who allegedly was his relative. No matter how small this Ekonda was, he would have to check things out before making any kind of decision. For most of the people from the village who promised to come to the city, the plan often remained only a pipedream to be trotted out year after year. Meeting no resistance, this one had actually come to Kinshasa in just a few months. Ambroise Iselenge sensed the level of the young man's motivation. But how could so much impetus be contained in such a minuscule body? Besides, as far as he knew, in his family they were all tall. They even called him Engambe Ambroise.[3] Why was this nephew's build so paltry? Ambroise Iselenge's gaze went down a notch.

"Fine, we'll get you settled. My wife will take care of you . . . Darling?"

And the man disappeared. Disdain imparted through each of her gestures, Madame put him up in one of the bedrooms. She showed him the bathroom, showed him the toilet bowl, asked whether he was familiar with its purpose, and, looking as if she weren't touching it, handed him the only towel he was allowed to use.

After having dinner with the family in desolate silence—across from the two kids who wouldn't stop laughing whenever they looked at him—Isookanga excused himself and went to his room. That night the young man couldn't fall asleep right away, not because of the euphoria he felt being in the city surrounded by a loving family but because hearing Mr. and Mrs. Iselenge arguing at length, he vaguely sensed that somehow he was at the heart of the issue. He told himself that a session of video games would take his mind off it. Half lying on the bed, he switched on the laptop.

When the lands of Gondavanaland appeared on the screen, Isookanga forgot everything else, focusing on carefully moving surface-to-surface missile launch pads around. To clear the terrain where he expected to make progress, he began by engaging his Katyusha batteries. It looked like fireworks. The troops of Mass Graves Petroleum, cells of Skulls and Bones Mining Fields, and members of the security services recruited by American Diggers were falling, brought down by the storms of shrapnel Congo Bololo was hurling.

Congo Bololo was a raider of the worst kind. By seizing all the raw materials of the lands he'd managed to capture, thanks to his talent for dividing

---

3. Ambroise the giant.

the forces, he'd succeeded in weakening other rivals as cunning as Uranium and Security, which could no longer procure supplies of either munitions or fuel, its supply lines stretching out progressively from east to west on Gondavanaland's terrain. Because once he'd helped himself not only to the minerals but also to lands where there was nothing, Congo Bololo was able to ban all flights over his aerial space by putting up surface-to-air missile launch pads. According to the blogosphere, he was also one of the few to own stealth weapons, but obviously no one had seen them yet, since the planes only went out at night to strike and then disappear.

The Goldberg & Gils Atomic Project was still holding on, for its cobalt and depleted uranium shells were causing damage, notably on Hiroshima-Naga's armored vehicles, which to the intrepid Isookanga suddenly seemed even more timorous. After conquering lands through the use of white phosphorous bombs, Congo Bololo could exploit gold. More sought after than ever in these times of rapidly depreciating currencies at the Stock Exchange, the precious metal additionally earned a significant number of points.

After adding up his gains, Isookanga turned off the computer and tried to sleep, but still overheated from the battle he'd just waged, his mind kept drifting to the music playing outside. At one point he couldn't help but think of the village he'd left behind and the safety it ensured. The afternoon of his departure he had gone to say good-bye to Uncle Lomama, but, sitting in front of his hut, the old man hadn't even turned around. Glasses on his nose, pen in hand, he was pretending to be studying a notebook. He was sullen with his nephew, but what did he blame Isookanga's mother for, who for years had been spending her time running up and down river to ply her trade, worrying as much about her son as she had about the first *safou* she'd ever picked?[4] Abandoned and forsaken, Isookanga preferred to follow his destiny alone. From a nearby bar he could hear "Orgasy," Fally Ipupa's song:

> *Mongongo na ngai eyokani ti na libanda ééé*
> *Soki ba ko yoka, ba yoka na bango*
> *Est-ce que vie na ngai mpe eza na maboko na bango?*
> *Bango bakoka kosala ngai nini?*
> *Po ngai mowei ya bolingo oyo*

---

4. Non-sweet fruit that is plunged in boiling water for two minutes before it can be eaten. Very good at breakfast with *chikwangue*—manioc—or bread.

Congo Inc.

Nazalaka na problèmes na ba vivants te, non,
assurer ngai, WW Bob Masua.[5]

For a moment Isookanga felt a little sorry for himself. Would his love of high technology condemn him to a night of uncertainty? In order not to sink into counterproductive homesickness, he closed his eyes, invoked the mysterious Bob Masua to reassure him, and then wisely forced himself to put the charming singer's words into perspective, thereby shaking off a feeling of abandonment.

● ● ● ● ●

As the Mercedes was leaving the property in the morning, its roaring motor awakened Isookanga with a start. He went into the hall, took a quick shower, put on his Superdry JPN jeans, pulled on his T-shirt and his chain with the rhinestone pendant, and slipped on his blue flip-flops. Taking a dim view of the day to come, the young man warily went out into the courtyard.

The guard was sitting on the bench, dunking a thick slice of bread in the tea he was drinking. After soaking it thoroughly, he noisily stuffed it down. Fully focused on his chewing, he would occasionally pick up a peanut from a sheet of newspaper next to his cup and flip the nut straight into his open mouth. Staring off into space, he said, "*Vanda!*"[6]

Isookanga sat down. The guard came back to earth. "Do you drink tea?"

He picked up a teapot from behind the bench, served Isookanga, and handed him a slice of bread.

When Isookanga had swallowed half of it, Lady Iselenge showed up. "Your uncle has gone to work but asked me to tell you this, in case you really are the son of his big brother: he never gave my husband the responsibility of taking you in here with us in Kinshasa. And you look like a Pygmy! A normal Mongo isn't small like you. Who can prove to us that you actually are Bwale Iselenge? You village people—as everyone knows—only come to the capital city to cash in on our money. A Pygmy can claim not to be one, just to line his pockets."

---

5. "My voice has been heard all the way outside / May those who want to hear, hear it / My life, is it in their hands? / What can they possibly do to me? / Because I am a martyr to this love? / I have no problem with the living, no, reassure me, WW Bob Masua."

6. "Sit down."

Mother Iselenge leaned forward and said, "Look me in the eye and tell me you're not a Motshwa."

Isookanga didn't answer.

"You see? I'm sure you're an impostor. Bwale Iselenge couldn't possibly be your size!" She stretched her arm out in a horizontal line. "There's the door, I'm not keeping you here. I've already put your things on the veranda; all you have to do is get them."

When Isookanga left the place, he let his instinct guide him. Without knowing it, he was heading for Camp Lufungula. Wandering off, the canvas bag with the computer on his shoulder, he followed the flow of people and came to Avenue Kato. Near the Great Market, he turned in to overcrowded streets with stores displaying items imported directly from Dubai and China. Especially textiles. Famous-label clothes were abundantly represented among these—Gucci, Vuitton, Adidas, Emporio Armani, they were all there. Isookanga understood better now why they were called luxury labels: everyone was scrambling for them. The Chinese had gotten the point: overpopulated as they were, they had to find something to keep them busy. On the other hand, people on every continent wanted name brands so they could show off. Why not cater to them? Two billion arms could supply whomever they wanted, within whatever time they wanted, at the lowest possible cost. Nobody on earth could do better than that. This way everyone could get out while the going was good, and social stability was preserved with universal elegance.

Isookanga made his way through the crowd, which grew steadily denser as the day went on. When he felt a little hungry he bought some manioc bread, sat down on a step, took a piece of smoked *bowayo* out of his bag,[7] and calmly started to have his snack. Then he bought some cold water in a small plastic packet sold by some young peddlers: "*Maï yango, oyo! Eau pire! Eau pire!*"[8] Guided by enticing smells when the sun was well past its peak, he came to a fence concealing a *malewa*, a clandestine restaurant, where he ordered chicken with rice and beans. After quenching his thirst with a Fanta, sipping it one drop at a time, as it had been very long since the last one, he paid and

7. Electric eel.
8. "We have water! Pure water! Pure water!" *Tr.'s note*: In French it is also a play on words, as "pure," here mispronounced as *pire*, means "worse."

continued to drift through the market, wondering where he might be able to sleep that night.

Toward the end of the afternoon the market women started to pack up their goods and return to the outlying districts where they lived. The needy were gathering abandoned products that were unfit for sale. Isookanga noticed many children among them, undoubtedly street urchins. The sun began to set and then it was night. The Great Market consisted of a dozen or so pavilions whose hexagonal roofs were shaped like gigantic flowers on cement stems. Isookanga walked through a labyrinth of deserted tables and, a little to the side, found a corner where he could sleep. He took out the blanket he'd brought, wrapped himself up, and tried to fall asleep as shadows glided through the night and cries rang out in the darkness. A moment later Isookanga was dozing off.

"*Yo, ozosala nini awa?*"[9]

A violent blow to his ribs woke him up. He sat back up with a blank look. About ten kids, between the ages of six to fourteen or fifteen, were glaring at him belligerently. When Isookanga got to his feet, their eyes opened wide. The Ekonda was smaller than some of them but had the face of an adult. Judging by their expressions, it was obvious that there weren't many Pygmies in Kin'.

"*Yo nani?*[10] Where do you come from?"

Isookanga told them his name, but that wasn't enough; the youngsters grew more and more threatening. Then all at the same time they began to talk.

"You, what are you doing here?"

"Excuse me but . . ."

"Be quiet!"

Isookanga got hold of himself. He came from the forest, that was a fact. He wasn't very big, but before anything else, he was Ekonda and would show these little guttersnipes what he was made of. To start with he put on a phony smile. "*Ba masta, likambo nini, ko?*[11] We're not going to fight."

When the first blow rang out, Isookanga was ready, bent his knees dodging it, and got into the *libanda* wrestling position.[12]

9. "Hey, you, what the hell are you doing here?"
10. "Who are you?"
11. "Friends, what's the problem?"
12. A form of wrestling practiced by the Mongo.

"*Ba masta, to luka* compromise."[13]

"What's going on here?"

A girl of about sixteen made her way through, authoritatively, shoving the assembled boys aside with her elbows. "You, who are you?" she asked Isookanga.

"Auntie, I was just passing by, I wasn't hurting anyone, I was sleeping and then they came. I see that you understand the situation, Auntie; explain it to my brothers here."

It had been a long time since anyone had addressed Shasha with words like these. She sized him up and told herself he was a strange fellow. He looked like an adult but had the body of a child. That pleased her. He shouldn't be like all the other men she knew. She could tell his smile was phony, but it was far less ugly than many of the ones she'd seen in her life.

"Leave him alone. I'll deal with it. You there, take your things and follow me."

Isookanga didn't need to be told twice. He picked up his bundle, the blanket, and followed the girl to a corner outside the buildings that served as the market's management office.

Shasha occupied a niche of two-by-two meters. Bodies lay around on cardboard, wrapped in *pagnes* and blankets.

"What's your name?"

"Isookanga."

"I'm Shasha. They call me La Jactance, the Haughty One. You should never have come here. The Great Market at night is Okinawa world, the Arab world.[14] I have the feeling you're from the village. You don't know the city, do you? You don't know where to go? If you're looking for security or to steal money, my man, you didn't really come to the right place. We're just *shégués* here.[15] *Tozanga mama, tozanga papa. On a rien à perdre.*[16] Can you understand that?"

"I just arrived in Kin', that's true. I went to stay with relatives but we didn't get along. I had to leave. I was sleeping at their place, just temporarily."

"What did you come here for?"

---

13. "Friends, let's compromise."
14. An expression that means a world of kamikazes.
15. Street children.
16. "We have no mama, no papa. We have nothing to lose."

"I came to experience the world of high technology and globalization, Auntie."

"And that's it?"

Shasha didn't really understand, but everyone has his own reasons. "Go over there, at the end."

She unrolled a foam mattress for herself that was at best two centimeters thick and, wrapping herself in a *pagne*, vanished without any further ado.

"Sleep well," she added as she twisted around to find the right position.

Isookanga slept with one eye open at first, for shadows kept drifting by. Something fishy was going on in the alleyways, intermittently bathed in the headlights of the infrequent cars still on the road. This whole section of the city had had its electricity cut off.[17] Exchanges were being made in the secrecy of darkness. Murmurs and sighs had a sexual undertone. Unscrupulously, some offered their body for money, others did the same but paid for it instead. At night the marketplace became the stage for sordid haggling around a single, very coveted commodity, but negotiable solely in shrouded terms.

Slowly exhaustion engulfed Isookanga. After a while he no longer tried to decode the movements of the silhouettes he could distinguish in the distance. This night he would be able to sleep. In any case, he knew nothing about the particular wildlife wandering around here, and it certainly wasn't—he could smell its scent—the same kind he had only recently rubbed shoulders with in the forests of the lower Tshuapa region. He would take time later to find out more about it. Would the now established globalization drive people to veiled behavior even in everyday life, to a ghostlike secrecy? Like in dummy companies? Like accounts in the Cayman Islands? Isookanga wasn't sure of it yet, but what mattered for now was that he was finally in downtown Kinshasa, the capital.

● ● ● ● ●

"*Sala noki!*"[18]

With a touch of hysteria in her voice, the adolescent girl—not yet known as La Jactance—had uttered the words as she kept walking at a high speed. The little boy behind her got up from his fall, not worrying about the tears

17. Interrupting the power supply to relieve the pressure on certain parts of the electric network.
18. "Hurry up!"

that blurred his sight, and started running after his sister so he could catch up with her. She was carrying a younger child in her arms. They had to keep moving.

She had gone to the fields earlier with her little brothers to gather peanuts for the manioc their mother was getting ready to cook. It was past noon and the deep blue sky seemed to be suspended from the heavens. The air was quivering with the scorching heat. Besides the murmur of a warm breeze through the leaves there wasn't a sound. Green shades of fields and tree groves flocked toward the valley, then up the crest of the next hill again, and on toward infinity.

After an hour of gleaning, laughing, and chasing birds of many colors, the children had gone home. As they arrived at the edge of the small group of clay and straw-walled dwellings surrounded by banana trees, they realized the scenery had radically changed while they were gone. The ground was littered with bodies lying hither and yon. One might have thought they were piles of rags, were it not for the shreds of blood-oozing viscera poking out. Here and there sticky pools had turned the soil brown, marked by deep jabs in certain spots where someone had left traces of resistance to the slaughter. Kitchen utensils, stools, hearths were strewn everywhere as if a storm had passed through. The entire village had been massacred. The girl had heard nothing. The killers had used bladed or blunt weapons so as not to be heard, or quite simply to vary their method. They had slit throats and used clubs and bludgeons to crush skulls from which a grayish jelly mixed with blood escaped; fecal matter trailed the area as well. The girl rushed forward. The two boys stood back, clutching each other.

In front of their house the pot with manioc leaves had been spilled on the ground amid the still smoking embers. The father lay curled up, his hands covering his face. His forearms were slashed and his head hacked open by a machete. A scarlet stain appeared between clumps of his hair, as when you open a pomegranate with your fingers. A little farther down she recognized her mother by the *pagne* they'd thrown across her chest. From the center of her wide-spread thighs something emerged obscenely, something the girl recognized as a thick piece of wood. Unrelentingly staring at the sky with now glassy eyes, her mother seemed to be waiting for a sign.

The adolescent chose not to keep looking. Besides, all the bodies had become formless piles already merging with the earth. Walking backward, she rejoined her brothers, her hands covering her mouth to keep from howling the unspeakable that had suddenly immobilized the land.

"Come."

Leading her brothers on a blind trail, she chose a path that disappeared into the shrubbery. Those who had committed what she'd just seen were certainly not far away. She, who would soon be called Shasha, figured she'd need to put some distance between herself, her brothers, and the area that had witnessed such a paroxysm of savagery. That's how they left their region near Butembo that day, with bare hands and their heads burning.

Since their birth, North and South Kivu were the theater of the most horrendous atrocities on a large scale. The Whites called it a low-intensity war. On several occasions, they'd been forced to leave the village with their parents because of clashes that were accompanied by the persistent echo of machine gun and mortar fire. This time there had been no sign of what had happened, but the armed groups that performed ethnic cleansing were roaming through the region and forcing families to leave their land or to submit to the worst abominations: they destroyed women's vaginas, they sliced off men's genitalia and stuffed them into their victims' mouths before finishing them off.

That is how the children started off on their journey toward the west, toward Kisangani, toward the river, looking for a kinder haven. They walked all day without stopping, the older of the boys almost running to keep up with his sister while she carried the smaller one in her arms like a precious possession. To rest every now and then the girl put the boy down and, without complaining, he would toddle along as best he could. They avoided the roads, hoping to escape the horror that hung permanently over this part of the Democratic Republic of Congo.

In the evening, when the sun draped the horizon in a purple veil, they collapsed in a thicket and, like logs, didn't move again until the next morning. They were still numb with fatigue when they woke up, but they had to keep going.

"I'm hungry."

The littlest one had just uttered the very words the girl didn't want to hear. She gave him the peanuts they had gathered the evening before.

"We'll eat more later. We've got a long way to go. Come on!"

And they continued their trek. Often the girl would raise her head to the trees in the hope of spying some fruit or anything else appetizing, but it seemed that nature herself had disowned them. Later, their throats dry, they came upon a spring where they could quench their thirst, but since they had no container, they couldn't bring any of it with them. They nibbled on the remaining peanuts and filled their bellies with some more water.

The road kept going. The unevenness of the terrain almost twisted their ankles with every step. The branches they didn't manage to avoid ripped their clothes as effortlessly as a knife blade. From time to time, they found old hunters' tracks they would follow in the hope they would come to a village or find some people. They wandered on until the evening, then began to drag their feet because their empty stomachs made them dizzy. The girl and the older boy did their best to control the lightheadedness that overpowered them more and more frequently, tried not to think about their thigh muscles, now hard as stone.

Then the sky opened up and sent waterfalls crashing down. The rain fell in buckets, diluting the dust that covered them. They found shelter in the hollow of an enormous tree trunk and snuggled close together. The rain continued to come down violently. Its racket covered up everything around until dawn.

"Wake up, we're leaving."

The older of the two boys opened his eyes. He was shivering.

"What's wrong with you?"

His teeth were chattering so much that he could barely speak.

His sister touched his forehead. "My God, you're burning up!" Malaria? This really wasn't the moment.

"Come here." And she covered Trésor's shoulders with one of the *pagnes* she was wearing.[19]

The third day their trek was even more unbearable. The boy tried to hide how weak he felt, but there was nothing he could do—he really wasn't well. His steps were so unsure that his big sister had to carry him. The little one followed, trying desperately to stay in step.

"*Ya' Charlene!*"[20]

---

19. The first name "Trésor" appeared in Congo in honor of Bleu Marius Trésor after July 8, 1982, the day that he scored the first goal against Mannschaft in the semi-final of the Soccer World Cup. Thousands of children were also named Giresse and Platini. Not one child was named Rocheteau, Six, or Amoros and certainly not Rummenigge, Kaltz, or Hrubesch.

20. "Big sister, Charlene!"

Congo Inc.

The little one had fallen and chafed his knee. The girl tried to quiet his crying, telling him that it was all gone, everything was fine, but it seemed she would have to carry him as well. She lifted him up into her arms while she tied the older one to her back with a *pagne*. She was walking much more slowly now with her two burdens, yet still managed to cover a few kilometers, taking a short break every now and then. She quickly ran out of steam from the effort, but still she held her own. The older boy was shivering with fever, violent spasms contracting his muscles. He was hurting all over and couldn't keep from moaning. They had to stop before dusk, because he had started to vomit a transparent, gooey liquid speckled with green particles from the raw leaves they'd eaten the night before.

Watching the fever's progression, the girl didn't really sleep that night. To check his temperature, she put the palm of her hand or her lips against the sick child's skin. Finally, she dozed off, after a long series of retching the boy had to grapple with that left him weaker than ever.

The next day they walked as they had the day before, the sister carrying her two brothers. She was completely drained. They were going through an area with fewer trees; the sun had started heating the air hours ago, and the girl's clothes were drenched with sweat. She was more and more worried because, tied to her back with the *pagne*, Trésor was mumbling incomprehensible words with ever greater regularity. She was hoping the illness hadn't affected his brain, one of the risks with malaria. They had to make frequent stops. The boy's eyes suddenly rolled back so that only the whites were visible. Toward the end of the afternoon neither she nor the two little ones were in any shape to continue. The girl piled up some branches and they sank down into them.

In the evening the rain came down in sheets; lightning tore across the sky and made the dark outlines of the trees a terrifying sight. The children had taken refuge beneath the undergrowth, but thick drops came through the leaves and soaked them anyway. This is how they passed the night, waterlogged, shivering, but fortunately with calmer stomachs thanks to the rather tasty tubers they'd eaten during the day. They had even drunk some rainwater, which they caught in a large leaf they folded into the shape of a shell. But the older boy was just not doing well at all.

"Wake up, please."

He wasn't moving anymore. Other than some intermittent lurches, he was completely motionless. His breathing was arduous. Out of desperation the girl decided to abandon him. She couldn't carry both children indefinitely, and the older one's health had now deteriorated so much that he was undoubtedly going to die. She was familiar enough with the signs. She had to make the choice to leave only with the little one, so at least one of them would live. She could no longer feel her legs and thought her arms were going to fall off.

"We'll be back. Wait for us here. I'll bring you medicine and food. Sleep a little more if you want."

The child still didn't move. It was as if he'd fallen into some sort of a coma. His eyes were closed, and at that moment he couldn't see the tears flowing down his sister's cheeks. The little brother was watching, wondering what had happened to the world they'd left only a few days before.

The girl was on her way again, clasping the little one against her chest. She tried not to think about the one she'd left behind. From time to time, the little one asked her when they were going back to get Trésor.

"Be quiet!" is all she would answer.

They walked until evening. Was it the exhaustion weighing her down or the child sinking fully into her arms? It seemed to her he was heavier now. Too quiet as well. They found shelter, hoped that the rain would spare them. As she put the little one down, the girl thought his forehead felt very hot. Sleep knocked her out before she knew it. There was no storm that night.

● ● ● ● ●

The girl knew something was wrong with the child by the grayish color of his skin. It was ice cold. His limbs already stiff. The boy had died during the night, gently slipping toward oblivion. Gripping the child's body, the girl let out a long scream. After digging up the soil with the help of a branch, Kolo Eyoma, the one they would name La Jactance, buried her brother under a thin layer of earth, then hurried off in the opposite direction. The little one was dead, and now it was a matter of getting to her other brother, who was perhaps still alive.

"Forgive me for abandoning you, Trésor. Don't die. Wait for me, I beg of you."

All day long the girl muttered this litany like a prayer. She walked, windswept, indifferent to the roots and stones obstructing her path. At times she even began to run like a crazy woman. Red from tears, her eyes recognized the way she'd come the day before as best they could. She had to get to him, the one she had abandoned, before it was too late.

She walked on relentlessly until nightfall. At dawn the next morning, looking like a madwoman, a mantra on her lips, she pressed on with long steps through the mist that covered the landscape.

"Forgive me," she kept repeating relentlessly. "Don't die."

The child appeared so suddenly before her eyes that the girl's chest contracted in a spasm. Trésor was lying in the same place, but now he was staring at her with a lucid, glistening gaze. He was smiling. She approached him with uncertain steps, her hands out, not believing her eyes.

"I knew you'd come back," he said to her.

3

PAPER TIGER
纸老虎

Not far from the Great Market, the night, a witness to the depravities of the squalid shadows ceaselessly moving about within, had slipped away—in utter disgust—and left space for the day, which was tentatively beginning to break through. Zhang Xia, a Chinese national, had just opened his eyes. Next to him, lying on a piece of cardboard and wrapped in an olive-green blanket in front of a fabric store on the Avenue du Commerce, Old Tshikunku was fast asleep. He had pulled the blanket completely over his head, and only a fist tightly gripping the shaft of a spear stuck out from what otherwise might have looked like a suspicious package.

Zhang Xia was stretched out on a wooden lounge chair facing the street. He inhaled deeply as he stretched his upper limbs straight out in front of him. Without any further ado he got up. He poured some water from a jar into a bowl and rinsed his face. He went on to light the fire in a small iron brazier, then took a teabag and some sugar from behind the chair. After fanning the fire with a bit of cardboard he put the water on to boil.

"Old Tshitshi!"

"What's the matter?" the olive-green shape on the ground responded. "What do you have to tell me? That the sun's up? What's so special about that?"

Grumbling, the man they called Old Tshitshi sat up and yawned expansively. With the spear in his lap he stretched his aged joints to loosen them up, then grimaced. "Sleep well, Zhang Xia?"

"Very well," the Chinese man said. "Thank you, sir."

"Thank you, sir. Sir? You're not going to keep that formality up, are you?"

"The tea is ready," Zhang Xia said in response.

The old man shook his head and studied the younger one. Old Tshitshi had tried everything but couldn't get him to relax, even though it had been several weeks since they had been living together—or rather that they had shared the same space, the cement slab of a store not far from the Great Market where Old Tshikunku, known as Old Tshitshi, was the night guard.

Their meeting, in which the planetary situation had played a big role to the extent that it favored the movement of goods, had been almost fortuitous. Zhang Xia didn't realize it perhaps, but some people thought of him as a simple asset. Not as consumer goods, obviously, but he could easily pass for capital equipment.

Zhang Xia had arrived in the DRC as baggage of Mr. Liu Kaï, both a civil and private engineering contractor. First he'd learned some bits of French, then landed in Lubumbashi in Katanga, paradise of strategic minerals. After laying out large amounts of money to acquire a concession for himself, Liu Kaï had ordered an enormous mechanical digger from China. He put Zhang Xia in charge of the machine, and together they had moved tons and tons of soil by truck through Zambia and Tanzania to Dar es Salaam, from where it was shipped by freighter across the Indian Ocean to Singapore to end up in Guangdong on the South China Sea. His boss maintained it was rare soil, but Zhang Xia didn't understand this designation, considering there was nothing else to see for miles and miles and they could take as much of it as they wanted at modest cost. Zhang Xia knew that in order not to incur taxes too exorbitant for his liking, Mr. Liu Kaï, a smile frozen on his lips, maintained to the local authorities that he was looking for copper but hadn't yet found any, that the signs weren't exactly positive, and that the tons of soil hauled away consisted merely of samples to be analyzed.

Business had been rather good for Mr. Liu Kaï and Zhang Xia until the moment it was discovered that the banks, with crooked publicity men as their accomplices, had managed to exacerbate Western greed and exploited it as part of an enormous trap intended to divert their cash. The money was suddenly gone, nobody knew where, but was probably hidden between two algorithms contained in the operating systems of the computers of the NYSE, Nasdaq, Dow Jones, DAX, CAC 40, FTSE 100, or Nikkei 225. They were still searching for the exact ones. Credit having been cut off, Liu Kaï had to put the key of his enterprise under the door, pack up his bags, and go to Kinshasa, where he would wait and see what would happen next. He had brought Zhang Xia along, endlessly repeating to him that they weren't merely partners but were also essential to the smooth running of society and a guarantee of its security. To convince him, Liu Kaï occasionally had him sign a document. No one had told him yet but Zhang Xia was a straw man. Straw comes in handy. It's isolating, ecological, biodegradable—in the trend of the early twenty-first century, in short—and it burns fast and well.

One day, when Zhang Xia came back from an errand his associate had asked him to run, the receptionist at the shabby hotel in Barumbu where they were staying told him that Mr. Liu Kaï had just paid and left.

"Did he leave a note for me?" Zhang Xia asked shyly.

"No, nothing."

Without money or shelter, Zhang Xia roamed around distraught for days on end. At night he would doze off wherever sleep overpowered him, until the day when he sat down on a concrete slab to rest from his long walk and began a conversation with Old Tshikunku. The latter knew everything there was to know about life and its vagaries. The evening seemed endless. Between long periods of silence, the Chinese tried to tie some conversations together, one attempt more useless than the next; it was late.

"Well, I'm going to get some rest," Old Tshitshi said. "Here, take my chair. I'll lie down on the ground over there, near you."

Spear in hand, the old man bundled himself up in the olive-green blanket and dropped off to sleep. Zhang Xia stayed in the chair until dawn. Every now and then his head would sink down on his chest because he was exhausted, but through pure willpower he managed to raise it again each time. All night long he forced himself to keep it straight up.

Very early in the morning, having thanked him for the seat, he went back to wandering through the city, but came back that night and once again Old Tshitshi let him have his chair. Considering the situation he was in, Standard

& Poor's would have readily awarded Zhang Xia a triple A: one A for "Abne-gated from his home," another for "Abandoned like a dog," and one for "Ah, life!" It had been going on for more than three weeks now, and it didn't look as if the end were in sight anytime soon.

After drinking their tea and sharing some bread from the woman who had just settled on the sidewalk two stores down, Zhang Xia wiped his mouth with the back of his hand and said to Tshitshi, "I'm going to buy ice." He took a step, turned around, bent down, and added, "You're like a father to me, sir."

The old man stood on the slab, blanket around his shoulders, spear in hand pointing toward the sky. He nodded and said, "Little One, that's what I've been telling you. A son doesn't constantly say 'sir' to his father. Where do you think you are?"

● ● ● ● ●

"Trésor, *lamuka!*"[1]

Isookanga opened his eyes and stretched. It took him a few seconds to realize where he was. Would waking up outdoors in the heart of a city be one of the elements of a globalized model? Isookanga told himself this wasn't the time to have any qualms about his future; there were more pressing things. Shasha was up, shaking *pagne*-swathed bodies. The head of a ten-year-old surfaced.

"Ah, *Yaya!* Be gentle."

"Isookanga, let me introduce my brother, Trésor."

Pointing to another child of about the same age, she said, "This is Mo-dogo. Don't take him too seriously; he tends to say just about anything that comes into his head. Isn't that so, Modogo?"

"*Yo waa nnex!*"[2]

"I've never seen anyone as foolish as you!" Shasha cried out angrily. "Those diabolical words of yours again? Don't you realize where that's gotten you?"

Turning to Isookanga she added more kindly, "Modogo was a child sor-cerer before. He frightened everyone in his village. His parents took him to

---

1. "Trésor, wake up!"
2. "You are next!"

the priest, who made him repeat some of his favorite phrases. He uttered them quite trustingly with everyone present. The guy and his deacons decided Modogo was possessed to the max. They did everything to him: laying on of hands, fasting for three days, beatings at home when they assumed the devil wasn't far off. Isn't that right, Modogo? Show Isookanga how the priest was trying to chase the devil out of your body."

"Leave me alone," the boy said defensively but without conviction.

"They forced him to leave home," the girl went on. "That's when he came here, strengthening our ranks."

Turning to Trésor, who was dragging his feet to slip into a pair of old Nikes, she called out, "You haven't gone to get bread yet?"

"But you haven't given me any money yet, Ya' Charlene."

After breakfast they all left to attend to their own business. Considering the crowd that had been milling about since dawn, it was clear there would be plenty of action. Isookanga decided to visit the city, where the Boulevard du 30-Juin peaked his interest. He had to take another look at those grandiose buildings, those stores filled with high-tech products, those cars that seemed to be in a race, competing in the Grand Prix of Doha. He wanted to watch the people of Kinshasa, some of whose specimens he'd studied in the village when the antenna was inaugurated. He wanted to be like them: a calm attitude, focused on keeping his spine and head straight, self-assured, with the stability of a watertight Lloyd's of London. Before getting to that point he had to immerse himself in the city air.

Isookanga went down the avenue, making the most of the least little scene. Near the Presidential Galleries he changed ten dollars. They gave him back wads of Congolese francs. First he bought a backpack, more practical than his jute one, to cart his meager possessions around. From a *shayeur*[3] he then purchased a black T-shirt with a skull on it, which he stuffed into his bag, as well as a pair of Dolce & Gabbana sunglasses. He felt different the minute he put those on his nose. Imperceptibly his gait changed, gravity already releasing some of its hold over him. With the bag on his back, he turned onto a street on the right and was back in the Gombe district, where clusters of vegetation shared their space with beautiful buildings erected on well-maintained avenues. At times the vertical structures looked like tracks in the bush, but the

---

3. An illicit street vendor who sells a variety of things: cigarettes, tissues, ties, condoms, etc.

affluence was tangible everywhere, even for a Pygmy who until now hadn't given it any thought. Through his scratched sunglasses, Isookanga sensed that the neighborhood suited him quite well; in fact, it really fit him like a glove: the designer monogram on his frames matched the surrounding setting perfectly. Isookanga noticed the trees around him and fully understood the people who lived here. There was shrubbery around their homes, but not too much, just enough to provide some shade, not as in Équateur Province, where it occupied every inch of space and swallowed up the horizon.

He went back to the boulevard, crossed, and returned to the center of town, where, like a human tide, the horde of passersby pulled him along toward the Great Market. Looking for a bit of coolness, he sat down on the steps of a gallery in front of a store that sold electrical appliances made in the Middle East and in Asia. He took a piece of electric eel from his bag, broke off a piece, and started to chew. His saliva softened the flesh, which, since it was smoked, had become as hard as wood but now regained its flavor. Smoke and heat removed the moisture and the polyunsaturated fatty acids without eliminating any of its protein benefits. Isookanga chewed carefully, appreciating every molecule that touched his taste buds. The *bowayo* was the most tantalizing item around. The young Ekonda knew its delicacy had been appreciated since time immemorial. The almost mythical animal was an integral part of the collective imagination of the Mongo nation.

The *bowayo* is not just any animal. Stouter than a thigh, it can grow longer than a meter. It's very dangerous, it's a monster. You have to approach it cunningly, for at the smallest of threats it's capable of discharging electricity of up to six hundred volts from quite a distance. A power station all by itself. That's not all: it can come out of the water and climb up palm trees to pick the nuts of which it's very fond. Consequently, the *bowayo* is officially taboo for women. When this dish is served, the husband fears that if his wife eats the eel's head, she will no longer be docile in the conjugal home. Should the taboo be broken, she will magically be wearing the pants and her spouse will have to be forever submissive to her. As soon as it's served, a prudent husband will check the dish to make sure that every bone and all of the skull's flesh is there, to guarantee no part of it has landed in his beloved wife's stomach while she was preparing it. At least he is forewarned. The *bowayo* is a strange fish.

Upon reflection, Isookanga thought such a drastic law was commendable, given that Mongo women practice polyandry, the most harmful of all customs. They even dare to sing that "the male organ is merely a tenant in that of the female." If, on top of having to hear that, the man were also to lose his marital supremacy, what would be left for the unfortunate ones born between Ikela, Mbandaka, and Monkoto? Except for the flavor of the animal, however, the young Pygmy wasn't concerned with this part of the story, since he didn't anticipate being married anytime soon. For now, he would rather become integrated into a wider environment, whatever that might be.

● ● ● ● ●

"Excuse me."

Isookanga stopped looking at the animated show in the street to focus his attention on his left. A guy who resembled Deng Xiaoping—only younger and thinner—had just put down a large polystyrene box beside him. Standing there was Zhang Xia, who greeted him and bowed. "May I sit?"

"Go ahead," Isookanga answered.

After getting settled, the man opened the box and took out a small packet filled with ice-cold water. He bit off one of the corners, then stopped and took out a second bag, which he handed to Isookanga, who thanked him. In a few gulps Zhang Xia greedily inhaled the water.

Isookanga broke off a piece of fish and gave it to the young man, who took it and put it in his mouth. For a moment he held it between his tongue and his palate; what was at first similar to dry wood regained all of its original quality. The young Chinese had just discovered the succulent taste of *bowayo* meat. "It's delicious. I'm Zhang Xia. I'm from Chongqing."

"My name is Isookanga. From the Tshuapa, *mwan'Ekanga pire*."[4]

Sometimes it's good to take your time, put things into perspective, and try to have a more poetic view of things as you clear your mind. It allows you to whisper. The noise surrounding the two young men raised a monstrous racket—cars moving around were creating a bullfighter's dance; cops giving tickets a little farther down made swindling a lifestyle—but they were just taking a quiet break. Steps went up to the store on their left, and the flows of customers going in and out were paying no attention to the two.

Isookanga studied the man beside him who'd said his name was Zhang Xia. The polystyrene box apparently contained nothing but small bags filled

4. "Pure child of Ekanga (Mongo land)." Here, the mythical village of the Batwa.

Congo Inc.

with water. True, it was fresher than what he had been drinking before. The man certainly had to be making less profit, since he bought more ice than his competitors; they were fighting over the market of a product that with every passing year was growing scarcer on the planet.

Isookanga put the corner of the little bag in his mouth and took a gulp of the delicious liquid. "What do you do to your water? It's not bad at all."

"Lots of ice. I get it very early; during the night I cool what I sell in the morning, and I cool it longer than anyone else."

"Oh, yeah?"

From the first sip Isookanga understood that the man was particularly shrewd in selling a highly appropriate product. Without a digital code, however, you don't get anywhere. Isookanga mused as he chewed his piece of fish.

"Are you in globalization, too?"

"Unfortunately, yes. For me globalization is crap. I was doing just fine in China. I'm from Szechuan. Do you know Szechuan?"

Isookanga admitted he did not.

"I left my wife there. Gong Xiyan. She's very beautiful. And left my son, too. I should've stayed, but trusting someone made me leave. I was working with Mr. Liu Kaï in Chongqing, where we did a lot of construction. A large city. Mr. Liu Kaï told me to come with him to build whole cities in Congo. I thought he was fair with me and so I went along. We were in Lubumbashi. You know Lubumbashi? Then the trouble began. We left and came to Kinshasa, and Liu forgot about me. I work a little, I sell water—the best water in Kinshasa, or at least I hope so. Pure water. You want some more?"

"You should go after that guy. He's a crook. He should pay you damages."

"You need a lot of money to take someone to court; it isn't worth the trouble. I'm boycotting him. I'll work it out and it won't ever happen again. Experience is a lantern that only sheds light on the path you've already walked. I can't do anything else; this is all I have," he said, indicating the polystyrene tub. "How will I get back to China now? My wife is waiting for me. I told her that I wouldn't be gone for long. She has a lot of problems being alone with our son."

While Zhang Xia was pouring out his heart, Isookanga examined him carefully. This man—you'd say a reincarnation of Comrade Deng—had taken a flight with China Airlines from Dubai. From there, after a stopover in Addis Ababa, another with Ethiopian Airlines straight to Lubumbashi, and now he was stuck somewhere in Kinshasa. It just wasn't right!

"I also felt stuck in the village for a while," Isookanga thought, "and I managed to get away. The canopy, the trees, they tried to hold me back in every possible way. Uncle Lomama tried what he could, but no luck. Thanks to the computer and the Enter key, I was strong enough to leave that trap of forest and village life. Becoming a chief . . . without any raw materials? Without any service industry? There has to be a way out for this guy." Zhang Xia's was a Far Eastern story and he was, after all, at the heart of the globalized system. Weren't they the ones to whom the Whites referred as tigers?

"Do you have a computer?"

"No, all I have is this," Zhang Xia confessed, pointing to the box.

"With a dual processor you could straighten out your problems in no time. You've got to try. I'll come back before long with my machine. I hope to pick up something where you are. Where I am now it's hard. Where do you live?"

"Not far. Avenue du Commerce, with Mr. Tshitshi, at the fabric store."

"Listen, I'm an internationalist like you. I've tasted your water. I don't know any other that's as cold as yours; it's like water from the forest spring at home. But something's missing from yours. It could have an extra flavor of the land. Like what we have at home. I'll make you a proposition: you and I, we'll join forces to think things through. Together we'll be a veritable dual-core, you'll see. We'll maximize the sales curve. This evening we'll get together, we'll check the computer, we'll study the situation according to the principles of volume retailing."

Zhang Xia had listened to Isookanga without any real conviction but told himself that, after all, it would change the rut he was in. And besides, after being so gutlessly abandoned by Liu Kaï, this was the first person other than Old Tshitshi in whom the young man had confided.

"All right."

Zhang Xia stood up, picked up his tub, balanced it on his head, smiled at Isookanga, and said, "Come see me."

"No problem."

"Pure water! *Maï yango oyo!*[5] Pure water!"

With a rolling gait, caused by balancing the box of water on his head, Zhang Xia went off to continue his trade, broadcasting the slogan most fre-

---

5. "I have water here!"

quently heard in the city. The young Chinese offered an essential, sought-after product, especially at this time of day, when the rays of the sun, with the dust as their prism, burned skin and neurons in a jumble that encompassed a concert of car horns, an unrelenting crush, and the stale smell of station wagon diesel, which was worth twelve hundred dollars a barrel on the Shanghai stock exchange just then.

4

INAUDIBLE SCREAMS
听不到的呼喊

The insistent horn of a 4 × 4 seemed to make no impression whatsoever on the throng that indiscriminately crowded the sidewalks and the road and, furthermore, had to be begged to move away from the bulky hood.

"Bloody people, they don't hear a thing! And then they're surprised that we have to use force, always more force," the passenger sitting in the back on the right was thinking.

After a few unctuous words from the driver, the car finally managed to get parked. The doors opened, bodyguards in combat fatigue and armed to the teeth stepped out. Kiro Bizimungu fell in behind them and entered a building on Avenue Tombalbaye. An imposing figure with a shaved head and dark skin, he took the elevator to the fifth floor accompanied by two body-guards.

His office was sparsely furnished; there were no huge piles of documents to be seen. Bizimungu shut the door, sat down, loosened his tie, and wondered how he was going to spend the day. Kiro couldn't stand inactivity anymore. Peace accords had been signed in Windhoek, Namibia, and he had been given to understand that he was needed in Kinshasa: the country required new administrators and Commander Bizimungu had to be one of them. Somewhat grudgingly he had left the Kivu maquis and traded fatigues for a suit and tie. But he still couldn't see what he'd gained by the exchange. He had acquired a position, so what? Despite the prestigious plate attached to the wall in the lobby of the building, "Office of Conservation of the Salonga National Park," Kiro Bizimungu realized on a daily basis that a natural park would never compensate him in any way whatsoever. He and his armed group were fighting for power.

Since he had arrived in Kinshasa, he'd come to the conclusion that true power was found in wealth, obtained thanks to infallible pragmatism and firepower that needed to be kept going. Only with these key elements was it possible to conquer vast territories overflowing with minerals buried just below the surface of the earth: all the gold one could wish for, Kisangani diamonds, cassiterite aplenty, but, above all, columbite-tantalite, also known as the metallic ore coltan. Controlling a region also meant helping oneself to taxes, to exploiting the labor force, to the women his men would need, and to blood, a commodity one could let flow as a pledge of total submission.

Cargo was transported without a break from the other side of the border in Rwanda, having instantly become the authorized crossroads of strategic minerals. Everything turned into a deal down there. Business was running smoothly, an exchange in raw materials working at full capacity. The war in Congo had started in 1996 in Kivu, and Kiro had participated in it, as had many Tutsis living in the region, ensuing from the recurrence of pogroms at home in Rwanda. The ties to their country of origin remained strong, and when the Tutsi genocide by the Hutu erupted in April 1994, their services were quite naturally called upon. They fought in the ranks of the Rwandan Patriotic Front (RPF) to stop the holocaust taking place just on the other side of the border.

Two years later, calls had come in from former RPF comrades-in-arms who in the meantime had taken power in Kigali. They asked Kiro, as well as other men, to help make the land and riches of Kivu accessible in order to ease the lack of resources and the demographic pressure that had come down on Rwanda to some extent. Rapid development was perceived as the only way out of the latent barbarism. Under supervision of the APR—the new Rwandan Patriotic Army—an alliance of rebels was created from a vague assortment of nationalities, calling itself the AFDL,[1] and started off on a war footing to accomplish the grand work of regional development. The pretext for starting the horror was the threat that the members of the former Rwandan army and other genocidal folks present on Congolese soil had been posing for two years. For a pretext was certainly needed to bring such a project to an end. One needs an alibi when preparing a great crime, and this was nothing less than a crime: the systematic and methodical eradication of a population based on criteria that, with a little patience, would certainly be revealed one day.

Since then, under names that could change at any moment, Kiro—now Commander Kobra Zulu—and his men had spread terror and woe among the Ituri in Maniema for years. That part of Congo had become a zone of lawlessness, where human flesh was churned out like meat in a slaughterhouse and where only firearms still had any say in the matter. Those who were born there had to understand that their fields, their homes, their wives were at the disposal of the new conquerors and of the multinationals working in the sectors of high technology and the mines.

Kiro Bizimungu sorely missed that time. He and his faction had turned themselves into globalization's zealous auxiliaries, and the international community had compensated them accordingly. Some of his comrades-in-arms—a combination of Rwandans and Congolese—named by the United Nations, had become vice presidents, ministers, chiefs of staff, or brigade commanders. He, however, was appointed as CEO of the Office of Conservation of the Salonga National Park. It was a joke, because the man couldn't have cared less about flora and fauna, just as he hadn't given a damn about his first bullet in an enemy's head. What was above the soil—whether that be men, women, children, old people—barely mattered to him; what counted for him was what lay beneath it.

His phone rang, interrupting his thoughts. It was one of the bodyguards in charge of his wife's security. "Yes."

"Commander, Madame wishes to go out; she has a day of deliverance at the church."

"Again!" A pause. "All right, then. Take her there."

---

1. Alliance of Democratic Forces for the Liberation of Congo-Zaire.

Kiro despised these services and prayers to which people devoted themselves on a daily basis. His wife attended the church of the Reverend Jonas Monkaya, the Church of Divine Multiplication, in Ndjili. As had so many others, she had caught faith like a virus, and all she lived for were evenings of prayer, days of fasting, acts of mercy, retreats, and offerings without end. The pastor said this, the pastor said that. The activity was starting to seriously exasperate Kiro Bizimungu; it was turning into a compulsion. Yet, at the same time he couldn't prevent it. You don't forbid someone to pray, and she really did need to get out.

Still, he would have liked to stop her. It had been almost two years since he'd brought her from the East. A change he didn't understand had started to take place in him recently. For several months now he was no longer able to take Adeïto the way he wanted to. Even when his head was burning with the desire to force open her thighs, pounding them as he heaved himself up and down, his body wouldn't follow suit. He didn't get hard where it was needed. The problem had sneaked up on him. Precisely because of all that praying. Adeïto was in the habit of reciting a long invocation just before going to bed. Uttered with her extraordinary fervor, promises of divine absolution, convictions worthy of the International Court of Justice, the seed of the seductive serpent, the blood that Jesus shed when he was executed—every one of these words had begun to echo in Kiro's mind in spite of himself. And while he was listening to them as he lay on the bed—waiting for Madame to finish—it disrupted the steps needed to produce his hormones without his realizing it. When at last her luscious, warm body pressed itself against him, his mind, unsettled by the strong words she'd delivered on her knees, seemed incapable of connecting with the lower part of his body. The more Kiro Bizimungu thrashed around to get inside her, the more he felt his power abate only to vanish completely until he tried again the following night.

The situation persisted. Adeïto pretended not to notice anything. After he struggled with himself for a while, she would grab a *pagne*, wrap herself up in it tightly, turn her back, and switch off the bedside light without a word. Surely he could blame it on a lack of action, Kiro Bizimungu consoled himself. He was in a rut, no longer reaping his ten or twenty thousand dollars a week. Now he had to wait for a salary at the end of the month like everyone else. And the suit and tie didn't flatter his ego either. In his beast-of-war gear he had sensed that he was being noticed. When he was the rebel commander Kobra Zulu, when he would appear with his men, he was the devil himself.

When he wore the perfume of gunshot fragrance and swooned at the scent of blood, his sex would swell and harden until it hurt.

Depressed, Kiro Bizimungu told himself he was going out to get a drink somewhere. But where? The looks he got in this damned city these days had nothing to do with what he'd previously known; they were rarely welcoming looks, and he much preferred to see eyes full of fear, which was far more in keeping with his inner soul—his service record could attest to that.

For a moment Kiro Bizimungu, dismissed warlord, observed the graphics, maps, and posters pinned to the wall. Salonga National Park stretched out mainly over Équateur Province. On the photographs in front of him there was nothing to be seen but a tangled dark green cover over the entire center of the country. They called it one of the lungs of the earth. But what good did that do if he, Commander Kobra Zulu, was no longer able to breathe properly? It strangled him with rage. The man despised a great many things, and the only one he deemed worthy of his esteem was the United States of America. To take hold of Vietnam they had turned to Agent Orange! Who had complained? If at least he could manage to get hold of that, even if just a small amount, all of these trees would be done for. Ultimately, he was the boss of that space. With oil proliferating below, what was one supposed to do with all that green stuff? Not to mention the diamonds and other invaluable products. Kiro dreamed of a Congo made peaceful by napalm, where all that needed to be done was to exploit the riches of the subsoil. The labor was there, all that was missing was the political will.

Having scrutinized what looked like a display of broccoli, Kiro felt sick and then decided he would down two or three beers—even if admittedly it was a bit early—which would do him a world of good. He abandoned the views of the damned park, got up, and called out, "Déo!"

"Commander?"

"*To ende!*"[2]

• • • • •

It wasn't by accident but by necessity that the street children had made the Great Market their stronghold. First of all, they had to eat and the place was the city's granary. Then, too, they could earn a little money by helping

---

2. "We're leaving!" in Swahili (the language spoken in the east and south of the DRC).

Congo Inc.

regular customers carry their shopping on their heads in cardboard boxes. Other activities consisted of black-market sales, watching cars, petty theft, or even pickpocketing. Sometimes they also managed to work for an intelligence service, monitoring and tailing subversive individuals. They could report on citizens.

During the day, the kids ran around the market, alone or in groups. They were recognizable by their looks, the kind you don't mess with. Frailty was inconceivable, to the point where the little ones created an ironclad arrogance in an attempt to build a wall around themselves. Or else they had the look of infinite sadness because—as the Kinshasans said—they were living *na kati ya système ya lifelo*.[3] They had remarkable physiques. Their lives of insecurity had dried up their muscles, making them as hard and gnarled as rope. There were no chubby children among them. They lived from day to day, clinging by tooth and nail to life and the asphalt.

Isookanga had been impressed by the determination of a girl like Shasha la Jactance. On the first day, she introduced him to everyone and demanded that no one bother him again.

"But Shasha," Modogo said, "that guy is fully grown already. If he stays with us, we'll lose our credibility as street kids."

"That's true, Yaya, adults will think we need them to survive."

"Look at him," Omari Double-Blade intervened. "Who would take him for a child?"

"Trésor, you're talking nonsense. And you, Modogo, be quiet!" Shasha cut them short.

"Jesus fucks me! Jesus fucks me!"[4] the little upstart ventured, annoyed.

Like many of his pals, Modogo distrusted adults and knew the reason why. They were a totally conventional breed; they had no imagination. They lived in a narrow-minded world without any horizon, Modogo thought. To redirect his life, he himself had, once and for all, opted for the movies and DVDs. When he was younger, Modogo had thought life was monotonous and singularly lacking in excitement. School every day, homework, was a drag; the only thing that could rouse any thrills in him were horror movies. When he had still lived at home, he could spend whole afternoons on end having a great

3. "In the system of hell": you burn but you are not consumed; suffering is interminable.
4. In William Friedkin's *The Exorcist*.

time watching *Scream 1, 2,* and *3* in a continuous loop. Friedkin's *The Exorcist* was one of his favorites, because he felt just as misunderstood as the little girl in the story. Everyone had joined forces against her for no reason. While other kids played, he made himself nice and scared. To further enhance the sensation, he would view the films in their original English-language version so that he understood nothing, making the scenes even more perplexing. He loved listening to the American actors run their dialogues with a probing or cruelly hateful look.

It had taken the boy some time to memorize the most important diatribes. His pronunciation left something to be desired, but he packed them with all the meaning as he interpreted it and managed to toss off the phrases in a funereal voice that seemed to come directly from beyond the grave. In doing so, he had especially succeeded in terrifying his family, beginning with his mother. One day when she sent him to run an errand, as he took the money his face suddenly turned sullen, although not really on purpose, and he spat like a cat, "*Ou waaïï you?*"[5]

He was the first one to be taken aback by it. His poor mother stared at him wide-eyed but said nothing. On another occasion, it was his father who witnessed the phenomenon. "*Yo waa nnexx!*"[6] he threatened when they asked him a question on the future imperfect that he found too difficult to answer.

After a while his parents began to wonder what to do, and for the zealous Christians they were, each slightly thorny matter was bound to find its solution in the church. That's where they took Modogo. One Wednesday night the pastor received them after the evening service, preceding Thursday and Friday services. The deacons and deaconesses all wanted to be present to observe this child who was probably an unadulterated product of the satanic world. What came out of his mouth was neither Latin nor the speech of any Pentecostal language, nor did it sound like any idiom a simple Christian could understand.

They placed Modogo in the center of the room where everyone had gathered. Prayers rang out on all sides and hands were stretched out above the child's head. The pastor ordered every demon to depart and, above all, not to return again. He conjured up the wall of Jericho, which would come crashing down on them and break their bones if they so much as appeared to be

---

5. "Who are you?" in *Scream* by Wes Craven.
6. "You're next!"

staying in the neighborhood. He concluded with the affirmation that his victory was as sure as the crossing of the Red Sea, which, he reminded them all, had not been accomplished by swimming across. Modogo found it all very entertaining. He was in seventh heaven. Hands clasped, eyes closed, he was savoring the moment. But right after the pastor's "Amen" they heard a hollow "*Oo mag hhöd!*"[7] come out of the boy's mouth.

It was an outrage. People tried for weeks to break the spell of the young incubus. No result. At home, destitution and insecurity had chosen to take refuge and—the pastor avowed—Modogo's activities were primarily responsible for that. The little boy's life had become untenable. One day he got on a bus in Selembao, where he lived, and didn't get off until the final stop: the Great Market.

That was several months ago. When he was still living at home with his parents, he had thought he was the only kid like that. Arriving where he was now, he came to understand that he was sorely mistaken: countless child witches were haunting the Kinshasans. Becoming a street kid was never a choice. Many had lost their parents, one after the other, and left to their own devices had ended up in the center of the city, where part of the progeny of the millions of victims of the Congo war could also be found.

Among these young drifters was Omari Double-Blade, the former child soldier. He had come to Kinshasa as baggage of a warlord and, following a vague political compromise, was integrated in the national army. One day he'd had enough of the military and left his group of men. La Jactance found him sitting on a low wall and picked him up. The child still represented danger, but Shasha understood that he simply needed to be constantly reassured, and would be as long as he was told that everything was all right.

There were girls living in this microcosm, too, like Shasha la Jactance. And for them there was no other choice but to offer their bodies for a few dollars, or for nothing at all when several went at it in full force. The end of the day was when the girls got ready, made themselves look beautiful—braiding hair, straightening it with some ammonia potion, soap, and a bit of sulfuric acid, no doubt. They'd lend each other clothes, they'd wear something new, they'd rail at each other over nothing at all.

---

7. "Oh, my God!" in no matter which blockbuster American film.

When night came, the market was empty of merchants. Darkness fell like a curtain. The tables had been emptied, and another scene from a different play was in the offing while they waited for adequate lighting. Here and there abandoned bulbs diffused a little self-conscious light. The set comprised some dilapidated furniture, closed shutters, the shadows of piles of refuse sprawling beneath their putrefied smell. The actors were mature men, the actresses were barely pubescent children who, beyond the footlights, played the leading roles, unfortunately.

"Shasha, *mobali na yo, ayei!*"[8] It was Marie Liboma who spoke those words.

A 4 × 4 with the UN logo approached in the half-light. The car stopped, its motor running. Inside sat a white man in a beige uniform and a blue beret on his head, observing the group of kids with a metallic, impassive look. Shasha crossed the street, balancing two small dishes on her head, as when you go to visit a particularly pampered lover. Twisting her skinny hips, the girl did her best to walk like Kate Moss. At sixteen she was lucky to have the body of a fourteen-year-old little girl. She got into the car and it left.

Isookanga began to notice what was going on around him and grew worried. The principle of more liberal relationships escaped the young Pygmy.

Beside him Marie Liboma, chewing gum in her mouth, burst out laughing: "Don't make that face, Old Isoo. You really think La Jactance is afraid of that white man? It's nothing to her. Okay! Me, I'm off, going to wander around," she added, smoothing out her hair in which she'd attached Day-Glo blue locks.

Isookanga picked up his bag, put it on his back, and announced he had some business to take care of nearby.

"Old Isoo," Omari Double-Blade said, "you're not kidding, I'd say. Business already?"

"Just because I'm from the village you think I worry about distance? I make deals, my boy. I'm meeting up with a Chinese businessman," Isookanga answered as he headed toward the Avenue du Commerce.

• • • • •

---

8. "Shasha, your guy is here!"

Isookanga didn't have to look long for Zhang Xia, for everyone in the neighborhood knew Old Tshitshi, who was enthroned on his wooden chair, the younger Chinese sitting next to him on a small stool.

"Hello," Zhang Xia greeted him.

"Hello."

"Old Tshitshi, let me introduce my friend Isookanga. Where from again?"

"From Tshuapa, pal, pure *mwan'Ekanga.*"

Old Tshikunku studied Isookanga from top to toe. "You're from Équateur?"

"Yes, Old One, I arrived not long ago."

"Where do you live?"

"Close by, Old One, at the Great Market."

"The Great Market? Don't tell me you're living with those young devils!"

"Yes, but don't worry, I'm not young. I'm almost twenty-six."

Old Tshitshi sized Isookanga up again, but this time he looked him in the eyes. "All right. Sit down," he told him as he gave up his seat.

Zhang Xia intervened: "Would you like some tea?"

Isookanga didn't need to answer. Zhang Xia put a teapot with water on the small brazier with some still smoldering embers. The old man, spear in hand, sat down on the steps and proceeded to become immersed in the night that had spread out in front of him.

"You have the computer?"

Isookanga took it out of his backpack and sat down in Old Tshitshi's chair. He raised the lid and pressed a button. He clicked on windows, tabs, and finally found what he was looking for. "Look."

Advertisements for various brands of mineral water paraded by on the screen. Isookanga asked, "What do you see that all of these waters have in common?"

"It's water," Zhang Xia responded.

"It's better than that! Most of these brands belong to one, and only one, multinational. What's the difference between them?"

"The level of mineral salts?"

"Maybe," Isookanga answered. "But nobody's sure of that. The major difference is the taste."

Zhang Xia didn't speak.

"I have something for you." Isookanga placed the laptop on the ground and took a plastic bottle labeled "Fanta" out of the bag, with a dark brown

Coca-Cola-like liquid. "With that you'll get rich and you'll be able to get back to China."

Zhang was still totally silent.

"Wait," Isookanga went on.

He took out two small bags with frosty water and a disposable syringe with a needle. He unfolded a sheet of brown paper and put his gear on it. He uncorked the bottle, poured a little brownish liquid in the cap on the ground, then grabbed the syringe. "Don't worry, I boiled it."

Isookanga took a sample of the syrupy substance in the cap, pressing the plunger of the syringe, watching his motion carefully like a first-class doctor. Satisfied, he smoothly shot the syringe just below the knot of one of the plastic bags of water and injected a few cubic millimeters of his product. Then he gave the other packet to Zhang Xia: "Taste it!"

The Chinese bit off one of the corners of the little bag and sucked it up.

"What do you think?"

"Not bad." Zhang Xia made a little grimace; the water was not as fresh as his own.

"All right. Now taste this one."

Under Isookanga's scrutinizing gaze Zhang Xia took the treated bag. "I don't know," Zhang Xia said, a little gleam in his eyes.

"You see?" Isookanga exclaimed. "What do you notice?"

"I don't know, but this water tastes like . . ."

"Rivers, trees, earth, clouds."

"Yes, exactly, there's that . . ."

Isookanga went on: "It's a sweetener I came up with. I call it E26 because I'm almost twenty-six years old. Isn't it good? It's the flavor of local soil, which is the trend nowadays, the return to nature."

"Yes," Zhang Xia answered without coming much closer.

"But that's not all."

Isookanga went back to the computer. "Take a look." Graphics appeared. "See this here. I've researched household costs by country, including detergents, deodorants, toothbrushes, squeegees, brooms. I also looked at budgets for shampoos, antiseptics, pesticides, and rubber gloves across the world. Did you know, for example, that the number of washcloths bought in Austria in a single year could cover the surface of Germany twice? Here's a question for you: of these countries which ones do you think are most frequently at the top of the list of national cleanliness?"

Zhang Xia checked the screen: "Singapore, South Korea, Monaco . . ."

"Don't look any further," Isookanga interrupted and stood up.

He stuck his hand in his pocket and pulled out a piece of paper folded like a diamond cutter's parcel. He unfolded it, took out a small, bright red sticker with a white cross in the center, and showed it to Zhang Xia. "The Swiss Confederation! Now tell me what it is that people in Congo need to fear most? Microbes! Statistically, and in the collective unconscious, Switzerland is the world's number one in cleanliness."

The Pygmy then promptly stuck the little emblem on the packet of flavored water. "That's all there's to it! When they see this red and white sign people will come running because, since it's made in Switzerland, they'll be convinced it's the cleanest water around. Have some more! Look at me."

Isookanga grabbed the packet, took a sip, and then, his mouth forming the shape of a heart like the great wine tasters, sucked it up and swallowed. Zhang tried to do the same.

"When they drink your E26 flavored water, they'll think of the shade of trees, the scent of humus, the sound of thunder. And with your extraordinary chill added, believe me, they'll quench their thirst in no time and still want more. And because you have an enhanced product, you'll see your business grow very quickly."

"You think so?" Zhang asked.

"It's not hard to check. We'll test it tomorrow if you want. You give me half of your water packets, I'll treat them, stick the Swiss flag on them, and we'll soon see whose stock is sold out first. I'll be done before you, I'm sure of it. And if that's the case, I suggest we become partners. You bring the Alpine cold, I bring the Forests and Rivers E26 sweetener. We'll call it 'Eau Pire Suisse,'[9] and you'll see, we'll become the leaders in the market."

Zhang Xia told himself he had nothing to lose; on the contrary, he would gain a partner, and with this win-win formula he would stay faithful to the ideal of equity developed at one point during the congress of the Chinese Communist Party.

To perfect his E26 sweetener, Isookanga had put some water and a large piece of *bowayo* in a previously sterilized, old bottle of Nido powdered milk.

---

9. A play on words. It is meant to be *Eau Pure Suisse*—Pure Swiss Water—but Isookanga's mispronunciation makes it sound like *pire*, i.e., the "worst."—*Tr.'s note*

He placed the container on the embers of the grill of a guy who sold turkey thighs and drumsticks next to where Shasha lived. The electric eel had been simmering on a moderate fire for more than an hour while Isookanga repeatedly took it off the grill to keep it from cooking too fast. The juices had to turn into a concentrate of *bowayo* with its delicate, fragrant flavor, only ten times stronger. Once it was mixed with the water, Isookanga imagined, it would make the people who drank it feel they were hearing a river sing in the Équateur's shaded forests, purified of its amoeba, its Ebola virus, its typhoid fever, because it was made at the foot of the Swiss Alps, a few minutes away by Learjet from the financial institutions on Zurich's Banhofstrasse.

After putting the finishing touches on his commercial strategy and displaying a few rudimentary principles of globalization, Isookanga double-clicked on an icon and *Raging Trade*'s main window appeared. Zhang Xia knew of the game but had never played it before. For a moment they worked together, Isookanga at the keyboard, the young Chinese counting points. Congo Bololo was a pragmatist. With not enough troops at its disposal, it had based its strategy on perfecting its military tactics and on its choice of weaponry. Thus, it favored rapid reaction forces and the use of helicopters, but, above all, Congo Bololo banked massively on intelligence, which was crucial when expecting to carry out actual surgical attacks. The multinational Congo Bololo was a past master in this area. Its infiltrating agents could place GPS markers wherever they wanted: at the core of radar stations, in underground firing sites, inside the arsenals that were concealed in residential districts.

So, by the virtual light of a pale moon, the walls of a mountain split open under Zhang Xia's startled eyes; platforms emerged from the waters; camouflage nets were pulled out of the fuselage of planes comprising Congo Bololo's stealth squadron. Twelve formations of six B-2 bombers took flight at close to the speed of sound, followed by a geometrically complicated formation of F-117s that were meant to complete the destruction the first had wrought. Mostly, the planes, each loaded with eighteen tons of bombs, were sent to the north and west of Gondavanaland. They achieved their destructive task, spreading death on the positions of American Diggers, Mass Graves Petroleum, Kannibal Dawa, and Goldberg & Gils Atomic Projects, largely concentrated in the north.

Isookanga was going strong; he thrust a few GBU-31s, each of them close to a ton. Then with unstoppable forcefulness he sent off some JDAM guided bombs. From the positions he was holding on some small islands, he sent a few Wave Riders to burn the control centers that Blood and Oil and the bunglers from Hiroshima-Naga had scattered around on floes in the continent's extreme south. He ended with an abundance of A-Gs and G-Gs,[10] fired off from every side at once. Zhang Xia watched the balls of fire explode with incredible speed on idyllic landscapes composed of grassy hills with crystalline rivers running through them, craggy gorges in thousand-year-old mountains or, conversely, on the sites of a mine under the open sky, of an oil complex, or on a stricken village, where man would have become wolf to his fellowman.

After the aerial attacks, ground troops obviously needed to be sent. Isookanga took great pleasure zooming in, for it was on firm ground that Congo Bololo's assorted platoons had the best opportunity to prove their effectiveness in battle. As a commercial body, it enjoyed a special feature that destabilized the rival troops psychologically: not only were its units made up of all the sons of bitches that Gondavanaland could bring together, but they also included an impressive number of amazons recruited among the women of the Mongo, Bashi, Amazigh, and Ashanti nations. Their sections might be positioned anywhere and they were always there to clean up as needed. Each one of Congo Bololo's elements performed like a titan. They were merciless, veritable masters of pillage. Hidden inside a Toyota pickup truck, the cannon of a .50-caliber machine gun appeared on the screen and began to launch projectiles that smashed the chests of those men whom Congo Bololo's furies and boors were slaughtering on the battlefield.

Every now and then Isookanga had to change weapons and fire small rockets of enriched cobalt to stop the Merkava tanks of the Goldberg & Gils Atomic Project, which were attempting incursions from the bluffs on the left and right. The two young men were holding their breath. They recognized the muted soundscape but could much more clearly hear Isookanga's fingers clicking away as he strove to annihilate anyone who came between the raw materials and his dreadful weaponry. That was *Raging Trade*, all right; it showed no mercy. *Run nigga run / Run nigga run / Run mothafucka, run*, they could hear as they played.

• • • • •

10. Air-to-surface and ground-to-ground missiles.

While on a slab on the Avenue du Commerce the consortiums were waging an excessive war, at Waldemar Mirnas's villa Shasha la Jactance was standing with knees slightly bent, her hands gripping the table, moving her buttocks up and down on the stiff sex organ of the MONUSCO officer,[11] who sat on a chair with his pants undone and his head thrown back. The girl sped up her movements, and the man gave an almost desperate cry that didn't stop until she had made him pour out his last drop of sperm. She was the child whore, dressed merely in a soubrette's minuscule white apron, beneath which her small, vulnerable breasts pointed up. The leftovers of a meal were still on the table—with a place set for just one. The adolescent tore herself off the still pulsing penis, the man quivering as if an electric shock had hit him. Without a word she began to clear the table. She stacked the two dishes, the plate, the silverware, and disappeared into the kitchen. On the chair the still dazed Waldemar Mirnas was breathing heavily, trying to collect his wits in the muted light of the dining room of a villa in the Gombe district of Kinshasa, the capital of the Democratic Republic of Congo.

11. United Nations Organization Stabilization Mission in the Democratic Republic of the Congo

Congo Inc.

5

PERSISTENT TURMOIL
持续的喧闹

Corporal Zembla and Omari Double-Blade might never have met, but one never knows what destiny has in store, especially when it comes to collecting fines in cash. Around the marketplace that particular day, the citizen-victims of Officer Zembla's harassment were lucky they hadn't argued as much as usual, so that his collected profits increased. Consequently, before noon the corporal and his colleagues had already downed quite a few beers at the neighboring *nganda*.[1] In the afternoon, coming from a *malewa*[2] where he'd knocked back two more ¾-liter bottles after eating a grilled tilapia with *chikwangue*—manioc—he felt an urgent need. The beer was pressing down on his bladder. Strutting about, he headed for an alleyway between two buildings, where he knew he could relieve himself.

Omari had been strolling not far from the same spot two minutes earlier. It was about four o'clock and some of the merchants had already begun to pack up. Omari worked as a *shayeur*—selling neckties and pirated DVDs as

---

1. Clandestine bars.
2. A dance originating in Congo; here the bar where it is danced.—*Tr.'s note*

he roamed the streets. He would cross over to the boulevard and go back up to the Bon Marché, trying to sell his items to passersby and patrons of open-air bars. The boy had done well and decided he was finished for the day.

He was going back to his spot near the administrative buildings when his blood froze as someone screamed, "Soldier Mushizi Omari!"

The boy turned and ran. Soldiers from his former unit were hot on his heels. He zigged and zagged, avoiding crowds and tables collapsing under the weight of merchandise as best he could. As he darted away he lost his DVDs, which came crashing to the asphalt. In the increasing brouhaha, one could plainly hear the word *moyibi*—thief! It made Omari run ten times faster, crossing the street and propelling himself between two tall buildings to escape from his pursuers.

Belching, Corporal Zembla buttoned up. What a hell of a great life he had! Easy money, job satisfaction from scribbling tickets, extorting cash from offenders, overpowering lawbreakers. Living off adrenaline and able to quiet his frenzy with the help of a few beers at certain hours of the day. It was ideal!

He was taking his time, making the most of the coolness offered by the shade between the high walls, when he suddenly heard, *"Moyibi!"* Almost immediately, framed by the two buildings, a running silhouette stood out against the sun. Zembla was well trained, his musculature well oiled, his willpower unfailing. He drew his weapon, aimed, and fired. The bullet hit Omari in the left side of his chest. The boy stopped short, lost his balance, and crumbled to the ground like a rag doll. He stayed that way for a few seconds, then quietly slumped to his side, legs quivering with spasms.

Even before a circle could form around the body, a cry was heard: *"Babomi* Omari,[3] *eeeh!"*

Chaos followed throughout the Great Market as street kids came running from every direction. A few seconds later the only ones around Omari's corpse were the *shégués*, the four soldiers, and Corporal Zembla, the weapon still in his hand. One of the adolescents snatched it from him, and that's when everything went awry. The boy fired a shot in the air as a signal for the crowd of regular customers to stampede and for the street kids to attack. As one man they jumped the five law officers. Assaulted from all sides by the kids, one of the officers had the terrible idea of pressing the trigger in the A-position,[4] fir-

---

3. "They killed Omari!"
4. Automatic firing position, while position S refers to the semi-automatic position.

Congo Inc.

ing a shot. The explosion got lost in the air but multiplied the rage of the youth tenfold. In a split second the officer was trampled like a snake.

What had begun with a rush of just a few dozen from every direction had turned into hundreds now crowding the Great Market, because the *shé-gués* were everywhere—inside the city and in the surrounding districts. From Lingwala to Masina, from Bandalungwa to Binza-Delvaux, from Kalamu to Righini, by way of Ozone and the Kintambo Department Store. No need even to ask at Camp Kauka, at the central prison of Makala, or among the *kuluna*,[5] the Barumbu daredevils. They were in the tunnels, on the sidewalks, in every nook and cranny, on garbage dumps, sitting on the low walls, at the foot of the steps to administrative buildings, at the Limete money exchange, near the Yamaka forest. There were swarms of them, like rats in the sewers of New York, Paris, or Mumbai, the result of various plague epidemics generated by the state, poverty, marginalization, bad governance, and war. They drifted around the city, invisible like microbes on long-festering human tissue.

After overpowering Zembla and two of the soldiers—the two others had managed to get away—the hundreds of rampaging kids demolished everything in the market: tables were flying around, metal shutters were ripped from storefronts, windows shattered by stones hurled from all sides. Some of them took refuge under Pavilion 4 with the hostages and the confiscated weapons while the rest continued the wreckage. The destruction was complete in no time. More and more kids seemed to be arriving, soon numbering more than two thousand. The entire perimeter of the square the market formed had been invaded. Stores, *ligablos*,[6] cold storage rooms, warehouses, an illegal diamond dealer, the Greek undertaker—everything was ransacked, and then they salvaged a coffin for Omari. The children were crying with anger, the girls covering their faces with ashes to express their grief. Wearing nothing but *pagnes* wrapped high up on their calves so they could fight more effectively, they were rowdy, some rolling their eyes to vent their anger and deep despair, while others were tearing their hair out. Between defacing private property and uprooting signposts, the boys assumed warrior postures, their skinny torsos rounded, howling erupting from their throats, their tendons about to rip.

---

5. Urban gangs of Kinshasa.
6. Small kiosks that sell everything.

"Aleka, aleka! Botika ye, aleka, ko!"[7]

Isookanga had just heard the news. Accompanied by Zhang Xia, he turned up in the mayhem. He froze before the body of poor Omari, around whom hundreds of children stood clustered as a gigantic clamor soared under the huge canopy of Pavilion 4. Lamentations fused with sobs, since every child was weeping for Omari. His past had certainly made him the fiercest of the lot, but he also had the biggest heart and, at fifteen, was among the oldest ones; each of them could attest to Omari Double-Blade's kindness.

The *kadogo*, the former child soldier, was laid out in an open coffin, one of the AK rifles by his side. With bands of white fabric tied around their foreheads like shrouds, some girls surrounded him, weeping their eyes out as they caressed his face, voicing their sorrow.

"Omari, you left without having any time to really grow up," they said.

"Our Omari, you're breaking our hearts. How could you leave us like that, without even a warning, Omari?"

And, "Omari, is it true then? Does this country really eat its own children, not giving them any chance for survival, all alone, without any papa or mama?"

"Ah, Omari! What are we going to do? How can we go on without you, Omari?"

And the outcry grew into a monstrous drone that ran through the entire city, going far beyond the Great Market, spreading beyond the various districts as far as Jamaïka, Masina, Ndjili, Kimbanseke, and all the remote areas to the north, south, and east of Kinshasa. Standing close to the body, their jaws clamped shut, the boys were shedding tears. Desperate, Isookanga contemplated the coffin in silence. As for Zhang Xia, he had no clue. Why was this boy dead? What about the anguish flooding every heart, so wrenching and intensely cruel?

"Robocops!"

After hours of vandalizing and cursing the enforcers of the law, the latter arrived in two trucks and were now lying in wait, parked a stone's throw away. The PIR—the Rapid Intervention Police—had decided to do its duty. The officers wore helmets and harnesses as if they were at war, their weapons out in the open. They kept their distance, waiting to see what would happen.

---

7. "Let him through, let him through! Let him go through!"

"Old Isoo, what are we going to do?" a boy calling himself Gianni Versace inquired nervously.

Not knowing how to respond, Isookanga turned to Zhang Xia. Jacula la Safrane, a sassy fourteen-year-old girl, insisted, "You're the only grown-up among us, so tell us what to do."

Tied up and sitting on the ground, the two soldiers and Corporal Zembla were nervous and afraid. Their faces swollen, their bodies bleeding from the blows they'd taken and, like most hostages, their expressions pathetic. Shasha la Jactance broke away from the coffin, wiped her tears with the back of her hand, and stated resolutely, "Old One, *na ngai*,[8] we're holding hostages; they'll be forced to negotiate. We're not going to let any of these three go, no matter what."

"But, Shasha, we have to make demands. What can we ask for? After all, we can't stipulate they bring Omari back to life."

"No, but we can require that these adults take their responsibilities toward us seriously. That's the least they owe us, Old Isoo."

"All right, let's see what we can do."

He turned to Zhang Xia. "Zhang Xia, you come from a country that has achieved its revolution; what's your advice?"

Briefly the young Chinese felt flustered, but not for long. He deliberated. "Everyone must die one day," he said to the Pygmy, "but not every death is equally significant. A writer in ancient China, Sema Tsien, said this: 'Humans are mortal, to be sure, but some deaths weigh more heavily than Mount Taishan while others are lighter than a feather.' Comrade Omari's death weighs more heavily than Mount Taishan because he was hunted and slaughtered by reactionary fascist forces. We can't let that go. Listen!" he added, his voice stronger as he addressed the audience, his arms raised like an orator.

The chatter beneath the awning of Pavilion 4 faded; the crowd was all ears.

"*Shégué* people, let us unite to bring down the American aggressors and their lackeys! Let the *shégués* listen only to their courage, let them dare do battle, let them brave trouble, and the whole world will be theirs. The brutes will all be annihilated!"

8. "My Old Man."

A collective cry rang out. The children seemed to agree with Zhang Xia's comments.

Isookanga thought it was time to intervene and whispered in his friend's ear, "But Zhang Xia, it's got nothing to do with the Americans."

"They behave in the same imperialist fashion!" Zhang Xia countered in a new tone.

He continued to address the kids: "What is the truly indestructible great wall? The masses, the millions of street kids who support the revolution with all their hearts and all their dreams. There, that's the real great wall, and no force will ever be able to destroy it. The counter-revolution cannot break us; it is we who will break it. Once we have assembled millions and millions of *shégués* around a revolutionary government and developed our revolutionary war, we'll be in a position to crush any counter-revolution. That's how we'll control the Great Market and all the rest!"

An indescribable ruckus of angry shouts, fists pounding on tables, and blunt objects banging on metal could be heard: the revolution seemed to arouse the support of the youthful public.

"Colonel coming!" Mukulutu, who was the lookout, warned.

Indeed, escorted by two men, a field officer had come out of one of the vehicles and was casually approaching Pavilion 4. They seemed to want to negotiate.

Civilians—women and men—with cameras and microphones materialized near the police cars. From the distance one could see the logos of the RTNC—the national television—and of another dozen private channels among the fifty or so that broadcasted from Kinshasa, but also of the foreign press on their way to Brazza to cover a relocated literary festival. France Inter was there, TV5 Monde, Reuters, Al Jazeera, the BBC, *La Dépêche* from Brazzaville, CNN, a Chinese blogger, the RTBF—the Belgian TV and radio—and many more. Empathic and standing a little farther back were Elizabeth Tchoungi and Laure Adler of France Television, Marianne Payot from *l'Express*, Yvan Amar from RFI—Radio Française Internationale—with an ultrasensitive directional mike to pick up the words in French should an insurrection take place.

The kids were holding a staff meeting beneath the awning of Pavilion 4. They were moving and gesticulating wildly, each of them wanting to speak. Shasha had to intercede. "All right! Listen to me! Old Isoo here is our leader. He's the only adult in all of Kinshasa—with his Chinese friend—who cares about us at all. The proof is here: he's with us to mourn Omari. He could have done anything else while we were fighting. He could've been in China today if he wanted. You know he gets around, don't you?"

Sounds of approval. Shasha went on: "So I, Shasha la Jactance, I say that he's the one to speak for us. He's an adult with an education; he'll stand up for our cause and for Omari's memory as it should be. What do you want? Tell us!"

Then came the upsurge of the greatest cacophony ever heard since Babel, with the one exception, perhaps, of UN assembly meetings just before a vote on a resolution on Palestine. In the sweeping uproar, Shasha nevertheless made the following demands: expenses for Omari's funeral to be paid, financial compensation for his loss, the opening of reception centers and the establishment of professional training for street children, a general amnesty, as well as other requests of lesser importance. Everyone seemed to agree. They even took the time to congratulate one another.

The ball was now in Isookanga's court, and he had to make a decision. "Listen," he said to Zhang Xia, "I'm going to see what I can get from the colonel there. You stay here, be unobtrusive. We'll stay in touch. I'll check in with you when the time comes. I'm trying to gain some time; be prepared for any eventuality. You and I are going to globalize the revolution, friend. Shasha! Watch the prisoners closely and, above all else, be on your guard. These people outside wish us nothing but harm; they're worse than crocodiles in the marshes."

Pulling at it, Isookanga readjusted his T-shirt with the skull and said, "Little Modogo, Marie Liboma, *tokei mission!*"[9]

"Right away, Old One, *na ngai!*"[10] Marie Liboma retorted, chewing her gum more fiercely than ever.

● ● ● ● ●

When Isookanga came within a meter of Colonel Mosisa, the latter involuntarily drew back. He thought it was just some little fellow approaching, but what was this in front of him? A guy with the face of an adult who must have been at least about twenty-five years old. Was this devilry?

---

9. "We're going on a mission!"
10. "Totally, Old Man!"

"What d'you want?" he barked.

"Didn't you want to see me? I'm the spokesman for the *shégués*. I've been officially mandated to speak on their behalf."

"Who are you, first of all?"

"I won't tell you anything. Before we set anyone free, here are our demands."

Isookanga handed the officer a piece of cardboard with some writing on it. Colonel Mosisa was expecting anything but the situation now presenting itself. Logically, it should have been a child coming to negotiate, not some guy from heaven knows where, taunting him with a filthy piece of cardboard, and in the city where he was a full colonel, to boot. It was an insult! Weren't they afraid of the National Police anymore, or what?

Frowning, Modogo stared the officer down, hoping thereby to bring a curse upon him mentally. Marie Liboma kept abusing the rubbery sweet in her mouth.

"Colonel!"

"What is it?"

One of the two police escorts spoke to him as if he were trying not to be overheard. "Colonel, they have a Chinese advisor."

"What are you talking about?"

Screwing up his eyes, the law officer carefully surveyed the distance, looking for something in the area of Pavilion 4. "I think I saw a Chinese man, Colonel."

"What do you have to say?" the Pygmy asked.

"Huh? Yes, I read it. But really, aren't your demands a bit exaggerated?"

"Not at all; these demands are totally legitimate and normal."

"Legitimate, legitimate. That remains to be seen." And the officer scanned the pseudo-document once again. "All right. Suppose they are. In any case, it's not up to me to decide on a reception center and funeral expenses. Where the ransom is concerned . . . you wrecked everything and on top of that you now want to be paid, too? As for any professional training and amnesty, I might be able to do something. I could grant each one of you amnesty and then cart you off to the police station to be trained for the National Police. How does that sound?"

"I gather you don't understand us."

"You're the one who doesn't understand anything, you little hoodlum!" The colonel was losing patience. "You will release those men immediately and give back the weapons you have, or else—" He stopped in mid-sentence, for a 4 × 4 with impressive grillwork had just parked next to the trucks transporting the troops.

"You, wait for me here!" the officer said, pointing a threatening finger at the Pygmy. He went over to the vehicles.

Isookanga didn't wait: he gave a sign to his companions; all three turned their backs on the authorities and headed toward their own group. Flashes crackled and cameras immortalized their notorious lack of respect forever.

"If that guy thought he was going to make me surrender to some aggressive takeover bid, he's sorely mistaken," Isookanga thought. "We're going to exact the highest possible price for the hostages; we'll force that condescending character to make us a really good offer."

As soon as the emissaries reached the entrance to the pavilion, cries rose up and words like "There you go!" and "Old Isoo, the great *shégué*," and "Little Modogo, Marie Liboma, the *shégué* elite!" They resembled those who might have the courage to defy a boa constrictor by entering its mouth and coming out without a scratch, without a bite, without even feeling strangled, nothing.

"What did he say?"

"Nothing much; he thought he could just make fun of us."

"*Yo mothas ining in heïl!*"[11] Modogo interjected with a fearsome look.

• • • • •

"So, Colonel, what's going on here?"

"The hostages are still in the hands of the terrorists, Governor."

"What exactly do they want?"

The officer handed him the piece of cardboard.

"Who's their representative?"

"Some short little man who . . ."

Colonel Mosisa turned around only to notice the absence from this no-man's land of Isookanga, Modogo, along with Marie Liboma, who had also gone back, still doggedly chewing her poor piece of gum.

"All right, I see."

---

11. "Your mother is burning in hell!" in *The Exorcist* of William Friedkin.

He glanced absentmindedly at the demands scribbled on the bit of card-board but maintained a sententious, serene look on his face to impress the horde of journalists, who were growing restless:

"Are you going to satisfy the kidnappers' demands, Governor?"

"For how long have the twenty thousand *shégués* in Kinshasa been a problem, and what measures are you planning to take now that the situation has gotten out of hand?"

"One *shégué* has been killed; do you plan to diligently carry out an investigation to identify the offender or offenders?"

"Governor, aren't you afraid that certain Islamist affiliations may have been able to infiltrate these youth networks as we've seen in other African countries like Somalia, Kenya, Niger, or Mali? In their new strategies we're noticing similar ways of operating. Do you believe there's an escalation in power in these small *shégué* groups, Governor?"

"Does the *shégué* problem originate from the government's Department of Security or social action? Can you answer me, Governor? And what about the *kuluna*?[12] Can one draw a parallel between them and the *shégués*?"

"I won't answer any questions for now. We must avoid unnecessarily risk-ing the lives of the hostages by talking a lot of nonsense."

Liwa éé, liwa éé, mama abota ngai po na liwa.[13]

"Colonel."

Standing right behind Colonel Mosisa, the same escort as before un-obtrusively and halfheartedly uttered, "Colonel, they're singing a war song, Colonel."

Beneath the awning, a chorus of voices started to sing a battle song in homage to the former soldier Mushizi Omari Double-Blade, who'd fallen far from his native Kivu. The young ones were galvanized to confront the dra-matic context that had so brutally ensued.

> *Liwa éé, liwa éé, mama abota ngai po na liwa*
> *Liwa éé, liwa éé, mama abota ngai po na liwa*
> *Elumbe, elumbe. Elumbe, elumbe*
> *Ebembe, ya moto, ngoya éé, ngoya éé, Ebembe, ya moto, ngoya o.*[14]

---

12. Urban gangs.
13. "Death, death, my mother brought me into the world to die."
14. "Death, death, my mother brought me into the world to die.
    The corpse is still warm, the corpse is still warm."

Congo Inc.

The children gestured and danced with jumbled movements, waving their arms and legs in every direction, their faces belligerent or else hilarious, mouths wide-open, to put the spotlight on this world's disparagement. In accompaniment they beat on tables and on every other surface that could make noise, at a muted, persistent cadence like the war drums of today.

Isookanga, Zhang Xia, Shasha la Jactance, Marie Liboma, Little Modogo, Gianni Versace, Armored Mukulutu, Jacula la Safrane, the other *shégués*—including Trésor—were gathering around to decide on a response to the governor. They were racking their brains, but it was Zhang Xia who spoke up first, because he was the only one thoroughly familiar with the principles of revolutionary combat. Looking them in the eye one by one, he said, "The *shégué* army does not wage war for the sake of war, but only to disseminate propaganda among the masses, to organize them, arm them, help them create the revolutionary power. Without those objectives war wouldn't make sense anymore, the *shégué* army, like our struggle, would have no reason to exist any longer, and we'd be doomed to submission. Let's not be conned by them, armed as they may be. Reactionaries are paper tigers. On the face of it they're terrible, but in reality they're not all that powerful. Just look at how lamentably our prisoners have lost face. Comrade Isookanga, you go back there and state our demands with the utmost resolve. We must get the maximum. This is the way to go, for what's contradictory is useful, and it's from struggle that the most beautiful harmony is born; everything is achieved through discord, and we won't let the enemy catch its breath."

"Fine. I'm off. Modogo, Marie Liboma, *to tambola!*"[15]

On the front line facing them, the governor, one hand on his back and in control of the situation, was walking up and down broodingly, as he had seen in images of Napoleon and François Mitterrand.

"Colonel, come look."

The same escort was holding a camera with a lens as long as an arm pointed at the urban terrorists. The soldier handed the camera to the officer.

"Look, over there, at the central pillar."

"I don't see anything."

"Wait."

15. "Let's go!"

Indeed, Colonel Mosisa finally detected a Chinese hidden by the pillar that supported the roof of the pavilion. He'd appear, he'd disappear; all you could see was his shadow.

"Shit!" the colonel thought, "he looks like Deng Xiao Ping, but younger and thinner." He handed the camera back to the escort, who returned it to its owner, a young curly-haired man, a correspondent for the *Herald Tribune* in Brazza, who also worked for *Libération* and Fox News.

"Governor, we have a problem. My men have just discovered a Chinese advisor among the insurgents, probably an instructor."

For a moment the governor lost his composure. "A Chinese, you say?"

The authority was rattled, brooding. A Chinese agent with that vermin obviously meant they shouldn't get them too upset under any circumstances. The governor was a man with very single-minded ideas, and to him the sign was clear. A Chinese advisor, here, present at the riots with hostages taken, signified the direct intervention of the Exterior Security Department of the Chinese Minister of Foreign Affairs. They wanted to do a Tiananmen Square on him. Very bad for his public image. As far as what he knew of the regime in place over there, his position as governor provided him with no protection at all. One couldn't fight that. There were still plenty of avenues to redo in Kinshasa, tons of asphalt to spread, miles of gutters to cement, and how could that be done without China? And the press was milling about. All of it had to be played down, and as quickly as possible.

The *shégué* delegation had just reappeared. The children and Isookanga were looking grim; their approach was calm, the skull on Isookanga's T-shirt flaunted like a warning. The governor glued a smile onto his face and took a step forward as a conciliatory sign. Isookanga recalled one of Zhang Xia's maxims: if you want to know what a mango tastes like, you must taste it, and if you want to understand the theory of revolutionary methods, you must participate in the revolution. Isookanga felt quite comfortable with this, very comfortable in fact. While Yvan Amar did everything possible to get a clear sound and not lose a single syllable of what was being said, the journalists were already positioning themselves like a horde of hornets in heat, kilowatts overheating, to get the most dramatic picture of the confrontation that, in no less than a five-hundredth of a second, might bring them a World Press Award or a Pulitzer Prize.

The governor knew how to play his part. For starters, he received Isookanga with a stern look. Flashes went off full-force. The city boss took the folded bit of cardboard from the inside pocket of his jacket and pretended to reread it carefully. Only then did he speak, his gaze lowered to the Pygmy. The reporters made sure that the red On lights of their microphones were lit.

"I understand your pain and I commiserate with the tragic loss of your colleague. However, your demands are way out of proportion. We will, obviously, take care of the funeral; we are aware of the young deceased's family situation. As for the training and community centers you're demanding, I can make you the solemn promise, here and now, to do everything within my power to make that sincere wish for reintegration a reality. Colonel Mosisa and I myself will grant you general amnesty on the condition that there be no second offense, or else we'll be forced to come down on you with the most extreme ruthlessness. As for the various damages, I've brought some money; it's in my car. You'll sign a receipt and it will be yours."

"Mr. Governor," Isookanga countered, "the press is here, they've heard you. We only hope that you will keep your promises."

The official held out his hand to the young man and smiled from ear to ear at the cameras. Once more he reaped a maximum dose of flashes going off. He wanted to add something about working in the field and the sacrifices the government was willing to make to improve the social climate, but he didn't have a chance, for Isookanga cut him off, calling out to the bouquet of mikes: "Drink Pure Swiss Water! Very clean water from the Swiss mountains!"

Then the members of the press surrounded them. Before Isookanga could go on, a hurricane with a smile and a strand of hair covering one eye appeared before him: Aude Martin, the researcher he'd met when the telecommunications tower was inaugurated and, parenthetically, the previous owner of the computer now in the Pygmy Isookanga's possession.

• • • • •

After a brief interview with the writer Elizabeth Tchoungui and the journalist Laure Adler, Isookanga and Aude Martin sat down on some beer crates in a bar near the Avenue du Commerce. When his conversation—on the whole quite friendly—with the city's governor came to an end, Isookanga was entrusted with the money for the funeral and other compensations. The police officers, the press, and everyone else were now gone, although they did leave a few elements of the Rapid Intervention Police force behind, who wandered around with Kalashnikovs slung over their shoulders. The researcher insisted on having a conversation with the young Pygmy. The computer on his mind, this embarrassed him somewhat at first, but he didn't show it. After all, the only thing he was hanging on to was nothing but an infinitesimal bit of the colonial debt, so he was at peace with himself. With his bottle of beer in front of him, he felt no guilt whatsoever.

The place was tiny and filled with brash young guys and unspeakably shameless girls. The customers were mostly drinking straight from the bottle, gulping down their beverages so they could get drunk faster. With powerful basses and guitars that sounded like piercing claws, with his hip gyrations and lecherous body language, Werrason,[16] the King of the Forest, incited them all to plunge deeper into their own depravity. As the young woman watched Isookanga, she was trying to understand what was going on inside her. Without a doubt, something irresistibly powerful drew her to him. He was the shortest one in the room, but she sensed he was the one with the greatest energy. He had such determination, something he had just proven again in his resolute negotiations with the city's highest authorities.

Aude Martin was sensitive to that wild, free spirit. The first time she had come from Belgium, her country, to Congo it was to start her research, but she had stayed for barely a week. Admittedly, she'd spent a few hours in Wafania but had allocated most of her time to expatriate colleagues who were as boring as the theses they were writing. This time around she had lingered; alone and left to her own devices, she was completely free. Discovering Kinshasa and its people had been a shock to her. There was the extreme poverty of which she was aware, but there was something else that only her intuition and senses recognized. Confronted incessantly since her childhood with the mysteries, the violence, the subjugation of the African continent—especially of the former Belgian Congo—she was hoping that by coming here she could share and even, however slightly, relieve the pain of a people that for so long had been the prey of her race, and it didn't seem there was any end to it.

Aude was moved in Isookanga's presence. He could ask her for anything he wanted; she was ready to grant him every request he'd make. She was ready to give it all so he could at last have access to a relative peace. With everything this country was going through! Struggling to dance to the music of Wenge Musica Maison Mère, one of the guys took a wrong step and almost fell on both the beer and the young woman. As if triggered by a spring, Isookanga

16. Werrason is the stage name of Noël Ngiama Makanda, a musician from the DRC.
—*Tr.'s note*

instantly planted himself in front of the giant. The young Pygmy reached only halfway up the torso of the man, but his hard, intransigent glare drove the guy to apologize unreservedly.

"*Skizé*,[17] Old One."

Without a word Isookanga sat back down, a majestic look on his face. Aude Martin—knowing nothing of the practice of birthright—was aware only of an extraordinary, mysterious authoritarian power that had passed between the two men. And suddenly it seemed as if a ball of fire exploded at the level of her chest, whose white heat then spread through her, descending and intensifying somewhere around that sensitive area between the hips, consuming her to her innermost depths. A kind of elusive ache settled in her throat, leaving her weak, without any resistance, moist between her legs.

"You know," she said, her eyes damp, "I'd like to have more time with you. My article on your people needs to be more in-depth and only you can help me. Would you like to? Please," she added gently.

Isookanga took a sip of his beer, taking his time to respond. "I'll see. I'm thinking. You know, I'm not that interested anymore in what goes on in the forest or with my people. I'm a man of the future who goes along with his time. Me, I'm globalizing."

Listening to the woman talk, paying very close attention to the tone she was using, a note of alarm had sounded in Isookanga's unconscious. He didn't like it. He sensed a trap that he should absolutely avoid. The funeral wake was waiting; he had to bring this to an end. "Let's make an appointment; we can get together again one of these days. How much longer will you be in Kinshasa?"

"I'm leaving soon. Will you make time for me?"

"Of course. But I really have to go now."

Isookanga paid for their drinks and they went out into the night that had just fallen. He brought her to a taxi stand.

As they walked along, despite all kinds of threats lurking in the darkness—the ¾-liter bottle of beer Aude Martin had downed contributed a lot to this perception—she felt perfectly safe with the young Pygmy. It had been a long time since she had felt this way, since she'd experienced this sort of bounty. The last time was in her family home in the opulent suburbs of

17. "Excuse me."

Brussels when she was still just an anxious child, a little helpless in the face of life, when only the presence of her father was able to reassure her. Next to Isookanga the young woman knew that she would be able to express the depths of her soul, that this encounter would let her be herself at last, again become the wild child she'd once been, without fearing society's unfair reprimands. In his hands she would be protected, as if in a cocoon, shielded from any danger despite the uncontrollable upheavals of her soul.

"Here are the taxis. Take the first one in line. Where do you live?"

"I'm staying near the Academy of Fine Arts."

"*Moto, tika ye na Libération.*"[18]

She wanted to kiss Isookanga as they do in her country, but from a bit of a distance he held out a robust hand—which added to troubling her hormonal system even more, particularly around the soft flesh between her legs.

• • • • •

Isookanga went back to the wake for Omari Mushizi under the roof of Pavilion 4. The crowd had not diminished. The lamentations had subsided, but every now and then a cry from the heart would burst forth to evoke Omari, former child soldier, and the sobbing would start all over again.

"Hey, Omari, *eeeh!*" Shasha la Jactance exclaimed, clapping her hands once only. She was sitting on one of the tables close to Isookanga. "You should've seen him when I first met him, Old Isoo. Right here at the market. He had just escaped from the army, was sitting somewhere."

"Why do they call him Double-Blade?"

"You don't know why, Old Isoo? Because when he was in the war he once caught a prisoner in the tall grass. He took away the man's rifle and they returned to the camp. Omari kept him moving with his hands up, threatening him only with daggers, one in each hand. His own in his right hand, his enemy's in his left, not even needing the Kalashnikov. That's why the child soldiers called him Double-Blade."

She turned pensive. "Omari was weird at first. Always in his own little corner, got angry over nothing. I was the only one who understood him. He was like my brother. We had our own little secret. One evening the two of us went off to throw the AK into the Gombe River. He wanted to forget every-

18. "Man, drop her off at the Avenue de la Libération."

thing. You know, Old Isoo, this war has done a lot of damage. He was eleven or twelve at the time, just a little older than Trésor is now. It was already late in the day by then."

• • • • •

Actually, there was no need for a Rolex that day to know that it was well past noon. Empty stomachs and a merciless sun reminded the frenzied crowd going about its business at the Great Market that the daily race for survival had long been started. Focused on their mission, people didn't seem to notice the boy on the low wall, holding his AK-47 in the crook of his left arm the way you rock a doll. His much too large uniform led some folks to carefully give him a wide berth. His shoulders shook from his heavy sobbing, and every now and then he'd raise his head toward the sun as if he were trying to dry the tears that were burning his face. The little guy seemed not to hear the cries from the women vendors heatedly bragging about the quality of their wares. Men carting heavy boxes made their way through, ranting and raving, and yet the child's ears didn't pick up on it. Omari, the young *kadogo*, couldn't stop weeping. Perhaps his spirit was trying to forget the heroic journey he'd made under the most awful suffering for the conquest of Congo, the forest-lined roads so valuable for ambushes, the training in terror that paralyzes or that you inhale, the iron discipline.

After the rebels of the AFDL had taken his town in the eastern part of the country, after the gunshots and the cries in the night, everyone left home. Children like him were the first to approach these liberators whom they'd been waiting for in both fear and hope. Then the wind of freedom had intoxicated him, and one day of great ecstasy made him leave his home and family. They immediately thrust a rifle in his hand, an AK. They advised him to treat it with the utmost respect, to care for it as if it were the apple of his eye. He learned to take it apart and put it back together again. He came to handle it so well that in the end, he and the gun were one. Firing off many rounds, he told himself that the smell of the powder spreading around surely made for stronger warriors. During one operation, the first time he'd ever pointed his weapon at a man and felt the machine jump in his hands three times, he measured the range of its power. From then on Omari never laughed again.

The *kadogo* stopped sobbing for a moment and glanced at the crowd in astonishment as if he were waking up from a nap in public. He stuck his hand in the folds of his faded uniform and took out a transparent aqua-blue plastic gun, flashy, magnificent. The boy contemplated it for an instant as it lay in the palm of his hand like an offering. He picked it up by its butt and aimed at the sky. Slowly he turned the toy at different angles to watch the sun's rays creating iridescent streams of light. He let the rivulets of water playing inside the transparent mechanism subdue him. He aimed carefully and gently pulled the trigger. As the pin went down, his heart swelled with a feeling he was unable to identify. A thin stream of water squirted up to the sky with force, then fell back down on the child's face like rain. Omari lowered his arms, then his head, as new tears gave expression to all his sorrow.

That morning he'd left Camp Kokolo with his unit. They carried out some routine missions on the riverbank. When he saw the water pistol at the Great Market he stopped. He fell behind the squad as he made an about-turn to look at the toy again and maybe buy it. The vendor accepted a small price. Coercing a man who was selling fresh water, Omari immediately filled the little weapon. When he pulled the trigger, an irresistible urge to laugh came over him, which he quickly repressed. He pulled it again and then couldn't stop laughing anymore. Afterward he could no longer find his unit. He had seriously broken the rules and the military code. This was desertion and would be severely punished: whippings, jail time, maltreatment. Distraught, Omari circled the market over and over again. It seemed the crowd had swallowed up his comrades. Now he was sitting on a low wall, the Kalashnikov in the crook of his arm, his young soldier's heart raw; while some ignored him like a stone on the roadside, others carefully avoided him like the skin of a snake drying in the sun.

6

THE WOMEN THEY KILL
被杀的女人们

Kiro Bizimungu's 4 × 4 was parked on a street next to the Great Market. The doors on the passenger side were open to let some air in. In the front seat, a soldier in fatigues had one boot on the ground as he absentmindedly grabbed a cigarette. Another was standing outside, his back against the car, the barrel of his weapon pointing down. In the backseat, Kiro Bizimungu was forcing himself to read a newspaper, looking up frequently to check the crowded street. He hated coming here, but his wife's car was at the service station and he certainly needed to accompany her. An unspeakable multitude, as always in this part of the city, made one doubt some of the convictions about this city one might otherwise hold. All the slightly intelligent polls describing it were at their lowest point. They all confirmed that this group of people was done for, that the country's poverty was deep-rooted even though the stores and the stalls at the Great Market were collapsing under nothing but stuff and merchandise bought, paid for mostly in currency that didn't show up on any World Bank listing. It even seemed as if there was a shortage of everything, but at first sight it went unnoticed.

At the same time, the population that permanently compared itself to Job at his worst moments, arrived each day with its Congolese francs, its dollars, its "wounded soldiers";[1] in cash, in wads, held together with rubber bands hidden in the folds of a *pagne*, slipped inside bras, stuffed in socks, carried in traveling bags; to buy, to sell, depending on the supply and demand, always going up. The people formed something like a herd of wildebeests having nothing to do with one another, each moving in its own direction in utter disarray.

Near every self-respecting herd there were prowlers known as the inevitable scavengers, such as hyenas, jackals, vultures, embodied by delinquents and the otherwise uncivil who, at their own risk, were in the business of pickpocketing; snatching small gold chains and earrings, that would leave a mutilated earlobe or a neck lacerated by the precious metal. Above this food pyramid were the great predators, the policemen and military men in civilian clothes attempting to get out while the going was good. They attacked as a group while isolating the quarry, showing their teeth, only to finally leave the victim undone from part of his nest egg and frustrated because there was nothing he could do about it. It was the law of the jungle of the Great Market, where everyone inevitably had to pass through sooner or later. The enormous racket, the car horns, and the noise of the motors conveniently covered up the complaints of those who in broad daylight were held ransom this way.

Kiro Bizimungu was busy reading an article on *shégués* who had fomented a riot. It mentioned a Pygmy; you could see him shaking the governor's hand. Because the photo of a shadow standing next to a pillar wasn't very clear, they claimed he had the support of China. Kiro had seen the guy on television two days earlier. A member of the police had accidentally killed a *shégué* and the street children had run amok. They'd taken one police officer and two soldiers hostage. They did have guts, those kids, the former rebel concluded. Then a Pygmy had come to negotiate with the authorities and apparently had handled it very well, because Kiro remembered seeing him smiling broadly on the screen and the hostages being released without a fight.

Kiro began to cogitate. After all, this was the first time that one of his citizens had appeared in the media since he'd been named the director of the

---

1. Extremely crumpled old bills.

Conservation Service of Salonga National Park. And what an appearance! This guy was good. He and the man certainly had a few things in common. First of all, they each belonged to a minority misunderstood by other people. Granted, Kiro thought, in a country of more than four hundred ethnicities everyone was ultimately a minority, but some more so than others. He was a Tutsi and the other was a Pygmy, which somehow established a parallel between them. The other common point was the position of the rebellion they had successfully managed to adopt. Neither of them tolerated anyone else having control over their life. The guy hadn't said anything of consequence in front of the camera except for a phrase about fresh water from Switzerland; perhaps he wanted to mention his ethnic neutrality—Kiro wasn't sure. But everyone was set free, and the Pygmy had accomplished it without any bloodshed while almost all the demands they'd made were satisfied, and all of it within an hour or two. It was an extraordinary feat not everyone could have pulled off.

"Pure Swiss Water!"

The first thing Kiro Bizimungu saw was a large polystyrene container with red measles-like spots, strolling around by itself and, underneath, a diminutive creature who at the top of his voice was shouting himself hoarse: "Pure Swiss Water! *Mayi yango oyo!*"

It was him, all right, Kiro realized—no doubt about it. "Hey, you!"

Isookanga stopped in front of the 4 × 4.

"Give me a packet of water."

The young Ekonda glanced at the bodyguard leaning against the vehicle, who grabbed the container and put it on the sidewalk. Isookanga opened the box, took out a plastic bag filled with water, and through the window handed it to the former commander, who accepted it, bit off one of the corners, sucked, stopped, nodded his head, and said, "Not bad, that water of yours. Does it really come from Switzerland?"

Isookanga smiled. "Why shouldn't it? We live in a globalized world, Old One. Today we shouldn't ask where things come from anymore. If Louis Vuitton has its bags made in Guangzhou, what do they say? Paris, right? That's all. Free circulation of goods. Is it good? You like my water?"

"It's great! Give some to my men."

Isookanga was only too happy to oblige. The guy leaning against the car grabbed a packet, bit into it, and then, with his large hand right in front of the

AK slung across his shoulder, he squeezed it the way you squeeze an orange. The contents vanished into his mouth in no time. He flattened out the plastic to catch the last drops and threw it in the gutter as if it were an old banana.

"Where are you from, Little Man?"

"From Tshuapa, *mwan'Ekanga pire.*"

"You know who I am?"

"No, Old One."

"I'm your boss."

Seeing the surprised look on Isookanga's face, he added, "I am the new director of the Conservation Service of Salonga National Park. I'm in charge of that area now. You know it?"

"I do, but now I'm a Kinshasan, and what goes on down there is no longer of concern to me. What is a forest, after all?"

Kiro listened to the guy carry on about globalization—whose cornerstone didn't consist of trees but of stock options—and was thinking it over. He needed to find out more about the region he now managed, and the odd fellow in front of him was the perfect person to help him out. And, in view of the turn his conversations were taking, the young man would distract him, that much was certain.

"Listen," he said, handing him his business card, "my office is nearby. Stop in, I'm there every day. God willing! Bosco, you see this man? If he stops by the office, send him up."

"Here, for your water." Without counting, the guard handed the Pygmy a wad of bills.

"OK!" Isookanga said. "I'll come by. Take a packet, it's a gift." He gave him three. "See you soon."

And the Pygmy moved on, chanting, "Pure water! *Mayi yang'oyo!*" He continued his trade, evading the crowd, the container balanced on top of his head, his mind and pockets filled with dreams.

A moment later Kiro's long-awaited spouse appeared, accompanied by a bodyguard in fatigues carrying a large cardboard box filled with staples, which he put in the back of the 4 × 4. When Madame had settled down, the guard closed the car doors, glanced around at the human bustle, and then jumped into the back of the departing vehicle, its horn unrelenting to force its way through.

● ● ● ● ●

Congo Inc.

The relationship between Adeïto Kalisayi and Kiro Bizimungu was a peculiar one. They had met, if that's the term, in the territory of Mwenga in South Kivu, where someone—surely a great sorcerer of globalization—had decided that the soil was more fertile than elsewhere because it was packed with stones and rare metals. Scratching it just a little was enough to increase the options on any one of the new generation's telephones. The diviner had claimed that all they needed to do was bleed the surface soil of Kivu in order to own telecommunication satellites that would provide the most mind-boggling performances and possibilities. By creating permanent devastation down there—which wasn't very difficult—they would acquire the means to develop a buildup for the highly sophisticated technology and thus be forever invincible. And by driving the effort a little further, if they managed to eradicate its population as quietly as possible, they would be able to attain the stage of master among the world's masters.

And so the men of Kiro Bizimungu, known as Commander Kobra Zulu, had turned up in trucks to contribute to fulfilling the utopia of former statesmen and billionaires who had gathered in Urugwiro Village.[2] It was a matter of radicalizing the exploitation project to which Kiro and his cronies had decided to devote themselves. As for those inhabitants of Kivu who were neither willing to go into hiding nor disappear, Kiro and his men would need to terrify them sufficiently so they would end up leaving of their own free will. Being awarded the Nobel Peace Prize is one thing; capturing the Global Citizen Award granted by the Clinton Global Initiative is another: there's no beating around the bush.[3]

Kobra Zulu's battalion had originally been deployed to take the village by stranglehold, and then shots had rung out, spreading total confusion. Men, women, and children were killed on the spot. They dragged people from their huts and homes and brought them together at a crossroads with a little market, a few vending stalls, and a *toleka* service station.[4] A few knocks with their rifle butts were enough for the soldiers to destroy the last panels of a billboard. They hauled a man from the largest house and tied him up with

2. The seat of the presidency of Rwanda.
3. A prize awarded by Bill Clinton and his foundation, which His Excellency Paul Kagame, president of Rwanda, received in 2009 for public service for the effort his country accomplished in the area of export.
4. A wooden motorized bike used as taxi, made by craftsmen.

electric wire to the now exposed iron bars of the ruined billboard. They tore off his shirt and his pants and he stood there, naked. His feet apart, his arms stretched out wide, he gazed at the crowd before him.

Normally the place was animated with villagers coming to buy needed staples that the little commercial center along the road had to offer. Today it was a very different scene. The population present was made to attend the demonstration of the new order that had been established in Kivu and throughout the east of Congo. A few days earlier, not far from there, a convoy of Rwandan soldiers and rebels had been attacked by Maï-Maï,[5] which resulted in enormous losses. It was a matter of reminding the largest possible number of people that subversion belonged to the past, that any resistance would be mercilessly repressed. To instill this idea, they had to resort to acts that would be branded in the villagers' minds forever. To set the example, a traditional village chief would be sacrificed. Extreme terror was the most efficient short-term and long-term way to deter any revolt.

Held at bay by weapons of all calibers, the gathered population was silent. The soldiers looked grim. Everything seemed rooted to the spot. The leaves on the trees barely stirred in a warmish breeze. Only the agitated eyes of the torture victim were still moving. They turned from left to right, occasionally pausing at one person, calling each one to witness. The crowd had been ordered to keep silent, to watch carefully, and, above all, to not dare shed any tears.

The session about to take place would take a little time but not much. One simple rule had been established. Simple but delicate in its application, it was known as the "rule of steadily accelerated subtraction" and consisted of cutting up a man into pieces in such a way that, before he bled out, he could be present, cognizant of the dismemberment of his own body, his reproductive organ in his mouth.

After a swift speech by Commander Kiro Bizimungu, the large knife went to work, snipping, cutting flesh and fat around the testicles and penis of the hostage. The man was tightly bound, but extra arms proved necessary to hold him down. Despite the chief's ghastly howling, the soldier in charge worked deftly, with steady, almost elegant gestures.

5. Combatants fighting the Rwandan occupation.

Congo Inc.

Then one of the soldiers began a song in Kinyarwanda. Right away other voices responded, accompanied by clapping hands. One man leapt up, brandishing his assault weapon above his head like a lance. It spun around and around with the sky as backdrop. Another began to mimic the courtship display of the crane, arms wide like wings. A third warrior hurled himself vertically up to an incredible height and fell back down, one knee bent and the other leg behind him. He rolled his head several times, imitating a lion threatening his prey. Smiles appeared on the soldiers' faces. Voices mingled to chant an ancestral song invoking past glories. Boots drummed the rhythm, shaping powerful bass tones. Dancers beat the time by pounding their hands on their battle dress, shaking the Kalashnikovs and RPG launchers. Counter chants moved through the atmosphere while the brown and green spots of the men's fatigues whirled around in a furious dance.

To bring the application of the torture rule to a perfect end, they cut the victim loose and laid him out on a cement slab that functioned as a butcher's block. They had to resort to a machete to break the bones and slice the ligaments that were not yet giving way. The people tried not to hear the appalling death rattle coming from the man's chest as he was dismembered. Then there was nothing but the unbearable sound of blade against stone, cutting small sections of meat. One of the soldiers emptied a large basin full of manioc hulls and brought it to the soldier in charge, who placed the pieces of the chief's body into it, the grimacing head on top of the pile of meat as at the booth of a particularly perverse butcher. They set the whole thing in front of the crowd so that each person could analyze and contemplate the "rule of steadily accelerated subtraction" implemented in Kivu in the coercive context of an all-out liberalization.

When the hacking was done, horror followed upon horror and all the automatic weapons began to crackle at the same time, causing clouds of cordite to rise into the air. Bodies fell one on top of the other in the narrow trap the confusion produced. Several soldiers set upon a woman to hold her to the ground, one grabbing an arm as in a vise, the other dislocating one of her legs, while a penis penetrated her. Men and children were forced to witness the violation. Most of them were shot with 7.62-caliber guns; others had their heads crushed with clubs or hammers as soon as they had stared the desecrator in the face. One soldier on his knees before the wide-spread legs of a woman brutally drove his dagger into her anus, then raised it in one sharp move to slice through the flexible, hard membrane separating her rectum from her vagina. They needed to cause irreparable, permanent damage, make the blood flow in profusion, and reach a paroxysm of pain. Husbands who saw the rapes and the carnage became impotent for all time. It seemed useful to keep some of them alive so they could bear witness.

Each rebel group had its own technique to mutilate a woman's genitalia: some pushed a piece of rough wood through the vagina into the belly, which they turned like a key that refuses to obey; others took a close-range shot at it; still others, using barber's scissors, snipped off all the fleshy protuberances of the sex organ so that the large and small labia and the clitoris were all sliced away. These procedures didn't always kill, but they did leave the victim physically and psychologically destroyed, doomed to become the prey of swarms of flies, for they were now incontinent for life. Kiro Bizimungu himself preferred the dagger. The resistance of flesh and cartilage led to a greater awareness of the act, which contributed to hardening the hearts of his men. This method rendered them even more impervious, if that were possible, a point they had to reach so as to achieve any job of ethnic cleansing.

In the immense chaos one of the women attracted his attention. Kiro would never know why. Was it her way of fighting back without a single cry, of not giving up until the bitter end? Or maybe it was the effect of the light on her thigh, which his men had laid bare, where one long, extremely taut muscle had taken possession of him like a spell? Impossible to know for sure.

"Bring her to me," he heard himself say.

After the military operation, he had taken her with him to the scrubland, the sector under his control. Locked into a bedroom, she received him every night. She was there to keep his metabolism stable, to help him lower the level of endorphins that he copiously secreted throughout the day in battle— pushing against each other—until one of them surrendered. Generally, it was Commander Kiro who begged for mercy in a groan coming from the side of his loin as the sperm escaped from his penis in uncontrollable spasms.

Eventually he began to grow attached to her. Didn't want any other women, hoped to help the woman, Adeïto, emerge from her silence. No matter how much he lambasted her, it got him nowhere. She would cover her face with her forearm and would emit nothing but a stifled breath and a regular rolling of her hips that made him tip over. He wanted to hear her moan, but each time he was brought down by the slippery warm trap where he found relative appeasement. That is how they lived for a while until the peace accords were signed, and some months later his armed group was transferred to the political party and he was assigned to a post in Kinshasa. Kiro Bizimungu had weighed both sides but couldn't resign himself to be separated from the flesh of the curvaceous Adeïto, and so he brought her with him.

He certainly didn't want to lose her in Kinshasa, so he assigned permanent bodyguards to her. She was forbidden to go out and could only move when she was carefully escorted. The only place she was allowed to visit was the church. Since her entire family had been decimated, she saw no one, she had no one. Apparently, coming to Kinshasa had not made a dent in her docility. Over time she passed from sexual slave to the status of just slave. Through this baleful connection Kiro had grown more than attached to her. Running after women in this city of lunatics didn't appeal to him; he mistrusted everything and everyone. His battlefield instinct intact, he still behaved like a quasi-wild animal.

• • • • •

As if to alert the listener, the cello's bow brushed the strings twice in a row, but then the notes soared like birds set free to mingle with each other, the better to enrapture the audience, the better to snare them in their airborne web. Deep basso sounds that grabbed the belly, strident high notes as disconcerting as the screams of an intensely hysterical woman. Overrunning the concert hall, the sounds blended into a riotous fresco that insidiously succeeded in touching every nerve in Chiara Argento's body. They were now raw. For over an hour she had been completely submerged in Bach's music and only came around when the applause broke loose and the bravos burst forth.

As she opened her eyes, Chiara realized there were teardrops on her lashes. She rose, troubled and trembling. Holding her little evening purse, she left her seat. She moved away from the crowd, excusing herself, went down a crowded massive staircase, got her coat from the cloakroom, and found herself back in the coolness of the street. A light drizzle was still falling on New York, but the young woman wasn't bothered by it. She needed air. Tiny droplets of rain created minuscule patterns on her thick black hair. She pulled the light-colored coat around her slender figure and tried to prolong the headiness of the music as she compared the city's lights to shimmering tinsel at parties.

Chiara Argento tried not to think about anything. Other than the view she so wanted to be fairylike, she noticed only the gentle hiss of tires on the wet asphalt every time a car passed by and the tapping of her high heels on the sidewalk. Despite the familiar atmosphere, she clearly perceived muffled, distant explosions, which were obviously in her head. Yet, she had treated herself to the evening's recital to stop them. She needed the disruptive song of the cello. Sounds that intertwined, able to bring a soothing sweetness. *Some things cannot go unpunished!* she would repeat to herself. She had been working for a few years for the United Nations at the Department of Peacekeeping Operations, and since the Kivu file was hers to handle, impunity was beginning to nauseate her. She simply couldn't take it any longer. It made her flesh crawl and there was nothing she could do about it. She had chosen the cello and Bach this evening to mitigate her inner torment.

An empty cab passed and she raised her arm. "Park Avenue," she told the driver.

The car took off and the scenery began to stream past in pastel-colored tracks, punctuated by soft reds, lemon yellows, mellow blues. Through the window the hues caressed Chiara's aquiline profile, the glow of her gaze occasionally piercing the shadow of the passenger compartment. The cell phone in her bag began to vibrate. She took it out somewhat clumsily.

"Yes," she said. She listened for a moment without saying anything. "No, not tonight, Celio. All right. Good night to you, too."

She sank deeper into the soft seat. The streetlamps directed an intermittent, regular lighting into the car. Gradually Chiara found the rhythm again of the music she had just experienced. When she managed to relax, Suite No. 1 of the Prelude gently reentered her mind like drops of rain would to form a brook, a river, the cloudbursts hurtling down the streets and squares of San Giorgio Ionico, her native village in Puglia. Finally she closed her eyes and let herself be carried away by the whirlwinds of the unrestrained Mstislav Rostropovich. Not to think anymore. Not about Kamituga, not about Kivu, not about Congo, if only for the space of a single evening.

7

THE WORLD IS YOURS
世界属于你

The faithful had come to the Church of Divine Multiplication of Ndjili in large numbers. They came from all over the city, common folk as well as members of the upper middle class as the dark glasses and large cars parked throughout the neighborhood proved. It was Sunday and everyone was in their best finery. Women wore their most elegant outfits, were draped in their prettiest *pagnes*, and showed off fashionable hairdos. Men displayed their finest neckties, and the children looked like models in an online sales catalog. As people waited for the service to begin, songs and devotions had already started. With eyes raised, some were chanting out loud, and in the murmur floating over the congregation, brighter voices were heard when the message directed to God was especially important and ran the risk of not reaching him.

Her eyes closed, Adeïto Kalisayi was wrapped up in herself, her lips begging for a peace she would never again find. She was seated in the first row, as usual. The place was huge. The church occupied a former nightclub building, could hold a thousand people, and it was packed. Families were seeking redemption or other, less respectable things, such as piles of money, a new wife, a new husband when the previous one would no longer do. They also asked for remuneration for work done, for the shunting of a professional or sentimental rival, or, more basically, for the president of the republic to be defeated in the next elections.

The Church of Divine Multiplication, legally recognized by its own statutes, was always full. Because of his title, and in a country stricken by shortages of all kinds, the Reverend Jonas Monkaya's promise of the multiplication of what one might obtain—a thousand Congolese francs, a wife, a cassava mill—represented a most important stake, and he was the demiurge who would know how to attract such blessings through his sermons and his sensational invocations. The Reverend Monkaya held a major trump card: he had once been close to the world of show business. He'd been a wrestler under the name Monk, which he owed to an American musician called Thelonious Monk, whose spitting image he was. They also called him Reverend Monk, because at the time he patronized the ring, decked out in miter and clerical cross, he had been seen blessing his opponents with the sign of the cross before knocking them out.

One fine day the Monk presented himself at a well-known church, where he displayed his gris-gris and fetishes. Before the dumbfounded faithful he publicly confessed that he was dropping wrestling and sorcery to devote himself to God. He had instantly been incorporated into the church and thrust into the deacon's seat. After spending a year studying the market and learning the ropes, he told himself, "If I can manage to convince women to sleep with me in no time at all, I should certainly be able to sell a bit of artificial heaven to clients who are less jolly than my conquests." After secretly organizing gala events in Katanga, Zambia, and Zimbabwe, he received an impressive grant. In the very heart of Ndjili, Jonas Monkaya then purchased a closed-down nightclub, which he fixed up and opened under its new name, the Church of Divine Multiplication.

But if the man had an indisputable sense of marketing, he had the gift of gab above all, and knew how to give his sales pitch to God. More than one of his faithful followers had profited by his intercession. The guy also knew how to draw the Lord's attention to himself—by his wardrobe, in the first place. He wore the finest-cut suits with the most celebrated designer labels: Armani, Hugo Boss, and Corneliani were his favorites. To shine before the cheers of his people, he sometimes showed up dressed entirely in Yoshi Yamamoto or in something baroque labeled "Gianni Versace." His jewelry confirmed it: the thousand lights of his chain bracelet, of his tiepin and the pens attached to the breast pocket of his suit were a direct reflection of God's glory. Outside, the chrome of a big-engine BMW bought in Dubai and parked next to Mama Reverend's Porsche Cayenne served the same purpose. But the reverend was closely followed by the divine gaze primarily because he knew how to preach. He had the imagination and the theatrical sense necessary to exalt the hearts of his sheep, who, thirsting for salvation, drank in his words as if from an inexhaustible spring.

Dressed in white and gold satin robes, the choir appeared on the podium. After lining up, they began with *Vers toi, Seigneur*—Unto You Lord—with musical accompaniment. Instantly the ambiance moved up a notch; part of the hall rose and began to dance and sing, clapping their hands enthusiastically. Many others continued to pray, eyes closed and frowning, focused on whatever need they wanted to be granted. The prayers and praises went on for a long time, interspersed with loud exhortations, and then the pastor appeared the moment the choir began a song even more poignant than an Alicia Keyes love song. Some wept—men and women alike—their palms upward in a sign of relinquishment. Microphone in hand, the Reverend Jonas Monkaya prayed as he strode across the stage like Otis Redding brought to life. Every now and then his voice soared over those of the faithful, imparting a tempo, uniting the multitude under the divine unction. After a while he headed for a lectern placed in the center of the podium. Immediately the volume of the voices dropped. The reverend had just attached the microphone to his stand; the word of God was about to be delivered.

"Halleluiah," he said.

"Amen!" the hall responded.

"Halleluiah," he repeated.

"Amen," the assembly said again.

"My very dear brothers and sisters. God spoke to me last night. He said, 'Jonas Monkaya!' and I answered, 'Here I am, Lord!' Then he confided this to me: 'Jonas, my son, I am not pleased. I sent my archangels Gabriel and Michael on an inspection tour. What they reported to me when they came back has me deeply saddened.' What, then, brothers and sisters, do you think the archangels might have seen when they came here to earth? They realized that some among us had left the Church of Divine Multiplication to head toward ruin."

The pastor continued more emphatically: "They left the Church of Divine Multiplication to head toward ruin, dear brothers and sisters! That is what the

Lord revealed to me last night. 'Those people left to go where?' you will ask. They have left to move to that new—how shall I phrase it?—church, known as the Church of Heavenly Abundance, in Masina, that's where!"

There was a cry of bewilderment.

"Yes, brothers and sisters, some people have deliberately chosen the path to ruin. Where? In Masina. Why? Because they thought they were clever, although they're nothing but Tintins, inconsistent beings who have no soul.[1] This can't go on!"

The pastor hit the lectern with his fist. An anxious buzz floated above the assembly as Jonas Monkaya took control of the situation. Satisfied, he continued: "After I answered, 'Here I am, Lord!' God in his great mercy also advised me not to be angry with them but rather to alert those whom the devil will try to persuade to do the same. As the Gospel says, the prodigal son can go back to the fold—insofar as the devil will let him go—the door will always remain open to him. Halleluiah?"

"Amen!" the congregation agreed.

"That is why the Lord has charged me to deliver to you a message of faithfulness. He has commanded, 'Jonas, zealous servant, teach them the terrible story of Abraham and his nephew Lot.' Open your Bibles to Genesis chapter 13, verses 8 to 11."

When the pages stopped rustling, the herder of sheep read, "'And Abraham said unto Lot, *Let there be no strife, I pray thee, between me and thee, and between my herdmen and thy herdmen; for we be brethren. Is not the whole land before thee? Separate thyself, I pray thee, from me: if thou wilt take the left hand, then I will go to the right; or if thou depart to the right hand, then I will go to the left.* And Lot lifted up his eyes and beheld all the plain of Jordan, that it was well watered everywhere . . . Then Lot chose him all the plain of Jordan, and Lot journeyed east.' Amen!"

"Amen!" the congregation agreed.

"By starting and building colonies in the Jordan Valley, Lot thought he had made the right choice; the deal of the century, brothers and sisters. Why? Because he thought he'd seen great abundance. The river freely flowing, the mirage of green pastures, the prospect of crooning days to come. Ibrahim, on the other hand, preferred to have the Lord decide for him. And he left, in the

---

1. Tintin is a well-known cartoon character created by the Belgian cartoonist Hergé. —*Tr.'s note*

Congo Inc.

opposite direction from Lot, toward the land of Canaan, Ramallah, Gaza, all of that. The poor nephew, settled in Sodom—air-conditioned villa, artificial swimming pool, marble everywhere—foolishly thought that Ibrahim, moving farther toward the Egyptian border, was going to find only desert, insecurity, and would be forced to dig tunnels to get supplies. He was sorely misguided, my dear friends. Because you all know how the story ended. It ended shamefully, as you know. Sodomites, high on hashish and ecstasy, turned up at Lot's house by night to take serious care of the two archangels whom the nephew had taken in. I don't need to tell you that Gabriel and Michael, already doing inspection tours even then and sleeping on the sofa, were not at all amused.

"God is not the pope, my dear friends. He doesn't wait for instructions. He moves when it concerns his children. After all the fondling, after the hearings and the trials, Lot and his family were forced to leave Sodom, which was to be destroyed very shortly thereafter by the nuclear strikes of almighty Yahweh. On the road to exile and emigration, his wife, his gentle better half, the mother of his children, suddenly disobeys, turns around, and is instantly transformed into a pillar of salt. Right there! In front of her offspring and her husband, brothers and sisters! Not long thereafter, even before they finished mourning and were settled some other place, his own daughters goaded Lot into the most abject alcoholism. He ended up by sleeping with them, one after the other, and both at the same time, repeatedly, night and day."

A sense of horror came over the congregation. Prayers were rapidly said to ward off ill fortune and beg for divine forgiveness.

"Dearly beloved," the Reverend Monk continued his harangue, "God does not change. He continued to bless his son Ibrahim because he had selected the road the Father had chosen for him. Lot wanted abundance. Ibrahim was seeking multiplication. God continued working in Lot's life because he remained faithful, brothers and sisters. Never once did he waver. He didn't believe in the smoke and mirrors of the Jordan, in occupied territories and Operation Cast Lead.[2]

"Believe me, God gives everything to children who are faithful. If Moses had lived today, do you think that Jehovah would have let him come down the mountain barefoot? No, the Lord would have given him an air-conditioned

---

2. Operation Cast Lead is also known as the Gaza Massacre, an armed conflict between Palestinians and Israel from late December 2008 to mid-January 2009.—*Tr.'s note*

V8 4 × 4 so he could have transported the tablets of stone on which the commandments for his people were inscribed. Do you actually believe that in our time Mary Magdalen could have washed the feet of Christ with those discount perfumes they sell on the Avenue Kato? No. With the elegance that is his, the Lord would have provided her with Guerlain, Dior, Chanel, or Nina Ricci.

"For the multiplication of loaves and fishes, Jesus would have *always* invited everyone to the swankiest three-star restaurant in Tel Aviv, where they would have served them water that he would have instantly changed into Château Margaux and Montrachet. Because God is marvelous. He is a multiplying God. Mere abundance is for those who lack faith, for those who suffer from a decline in their love of Jesus, for those—men and women—who no longer have a true desire to reach eternal life in heaven. Yes, indeed!

"Dearly beloved, God will certainly forgive those people, but let them remain in Masina. What are they thinking? That we'll cry over them? Too bad. We shall not feel sorry for them if they don't want to slip on the golden parachute of divine multiplication, as we do, contractually guaranteed, signed with a Montblanc pen by the invisible hand of the Lord himself."

Ululations and cries rang out, as when Vita Club scores against T. P. Mazembe at the Stadium of the Martyrs in Kinshasa. Frenzy overran the hall. The people, standing, chanted prayers that rose directly up to heaven without any layover, without any decompression stage, smoothly, like an Ariane rocket several stories high.

"He lives!" the reverend shouted.

"He lives!" the faithful responded in unison.

The song entered their hearts and souls, flowed beyond the plot of land, resounded in every sector. The orchestra went wild, the keyboard player striking the chords at a furious rhythm. The guitarist made his instrument mew like Avedila Nkiambi, known as Little Fish, or Flamme Kapaya in their better days.[3] The percussionist, vigorously beating every drum, scattered the demons as in a cataclysmic bowling game. With just three fingers the bassist managed to shake the spiritual foundations of the children of God. As for the members of the choir, they were bouncing up and down in place, in a

---

3. Both are well-known Congolese musicians.—*Tr.'s note*

complete and total trance, their spirits no longer in Ndjili but in a kind of sub-Saharan, not especially Catholic, nirvana.

The Reverend Jonas Monkaya, alias the Monk, swept away by the music, had now left the lectern with the microphone glued to his mouth, swaying from left to right as he moved forward, hopping along, perspiring, his body shaking with spasms, no longer himself. While the baritones, tenors, altos, and sopranos sang, "Please don't go / Jesus loves you so," to the music of James Brown's "Please, Please, Please," Brother Kasongo, the deacon, placed a gold and white cape over the shoulders of the man of God, which the pastor tossed off with a brusque and sweeping motion, as if he scorned the things of this world, forcing the acolyte to replace it only for him to throw it off again—and so on and so forth—until the moment came when he left in a renewed faith of indescribable fervor.

It was clear to see that Jonas Monkaya was a master of footwork and verve, far more than the pontiff himself. Had he been chief rabbi, the Wailing Wall would have disintegrated under the force of his sermon as if a drone had struck it. Had the Monk been dressed in the robe of the Russian Orthodox prelate, the women of Pussy Riot themselves would have been prostrate before him; faced with his authority they would have dropped their balaclavas. The Five Pillars?[4] His converts claimed that he alone devoted himself to at least three of them. Truth be told, very few people were as good as he in the city of Kinshasa, where the competition certainly wasn't lacking, but where he brought all of his intelligence to bear to make a buoyant market profitable.

● ● ● ● ●

"Are you done?"

"Almost, Reverend."

A machine made to count banknotes was finishing up rustling hundred-dollar bills.

"How much?"

"A little less than last Sunday, Reverend."

"God Almighty!"

The Reverend Jonas Monkaya had just returned to his office after shaking hands, giving lots of advice and blessings to the faithful who had approached

4. The Five Pillars of Islam: Faith, Prayer, Charity, Fasting, and Pilgrimage to Mecca. —*Tr.'s note*

him at the end of the service. He was standing in front of a large table behind which sat Brother Kasongo, half hidden by a pile of tens of thousands of Congolese francs and dollars. The pastor was wearing a dark gray Armani suit and a pair of black J. M. Weston shoes with a buckle on the side. He took a pair of Cartier glasses from his breast pocket and scrutinized the Congolese francs, careful not to touch them, since many of them were in deplorable state. Then he grabbed a wad of hundred-dollar bills, smelled them with closed eyes, and delicately put them down again.

"Brother Kas, this won't work anymore. That Church of Heavenly Abundance won't stop taking shares of the market from us. I had a premonition that the launching of that congregation would cause me harm. If it keeps going this way, you'll soon see them listed on the stock market."

"But, Reverend," the deacon intervened, "we can't complain; we did take in enough money to cover our expenses, and quite comfortably at that."

"Let's talk about that, shall we? Everything is going up: electricity, water, maintenance, food donations for the poor, my entertainment allowance, trips to every corner of the world to spread the gospel. It's no easy task, Deacon."

"I agree, Reverend. We should pray more, call upon the Lord."

"Brother Kas, you really think I was waiting for you to suggest I do so? I have prayed, the Lord heard me, and I had a vision. Listen carefully. I was dozing; it was late. Suddenly I heard sobbing and I sat up. I saw a people in chains, captive, a luckless situation. Just like our financial one, which hasn't been increasing for a long time now. Where were these people held prisoner? You'll never guess. In Egypt, Brother Kas! How do I know?"

"Because you saw Moses as a baby in a basket?"

"No, Brother Kas. What I did see, under a blinding sun, was a gigantic golden pyramid that towered high up into the sky. And Moses? That was me, in a night-blue shantung suit by Hugo Boss. I was delivering God's people by erecting the highest pyramid ever—not one of those built by clambering slaves, but one created for the bold: the financial pyramid that will yield more than we can hope for. Deacon, what would you say if I were to give you a quarter of what's on this table, in one fell swoop?"

"Halleluiah!"

"Exactly. Imagine that in order to receive this money it would be enough for you to wager one-hundredth of the sum this quarter represents. What would you do?"

"I'd bring that one-hundredth to the offering plate, dancing and singing, carried along by the joyful prospect of receiving a lot of money."

"Brother Kas, God has inspired you. That is the opportunity we are going to give to the faithful of the Church of Divine Multiplication: the multiplication by one hundred of a first outlay. We'll become the only church in Congo where God renders a hundredfold in hard cash."

"Really, Reverend? That means that if I contribute a hundred dollars, I can get ten thousand back?"

"Precisely. But, careful! God gives when he wants to, as he wants to. He is all-powerful, he doesn't act like the rest, he doesn't set any fixed dates. Therefore, every now and then, when someone has repeatedly given us a hundred dollars, he'll one day receive ten thousand dollars, by chance."

"But, Reverend, what if someone pays five thousand dollars? Could he see five hundred thousand dollars come back to him? That's enormous; that's a guaranteed windfall."

"You don't get it. In order to touch such an amount, and before the Lord manifests himself, you must have paid those five thousand dollars at least a hundred and one times, believe me. The almighty God is a good manager. And besides, Brother Kas, people don't often have that much money to give. Wasn't there a great politician once who said, 'You must tax the poor; they don't have much money but there are many of them'? From now on, each person will write his name on the envelope that is meant for the offering. God must be able to recognize his people."

"Reverend, I feel that we are going to be blessed. When the first beneficiaries receive their money, everyone will want to subscribe. But how will they receive theirs? The money surely won't be wired from an account in heaven, after all?"

"Yes, it will. The chosen ones will receive a check issued by Paradizo Limited. Tomorrow it will be your responsibility to take the necessary steps to create a company by that name. You will open an account and order checkbooks."

"All right, Reverend. I can see it all now: the Church of Divine Multiplication, the place where the tithe is returned a hundredfold. The whole city will be talking about it. They'll come from all over, they'll knock each other down to deposit their money in front of the podium. We'll be forced to buy the lot next door to expand the building."

"Halleluiah, Brother Kas?"

"Halleluiah," he approved.

"God is a multiplying God," the pastor continued. "When he gives us, his servants, a hundredfold, he will multiply that. Brother Kas, I just had a vision, just now, right here," he added, standing motionless with his eyes closed, index finger on his temple. "We must give the faithful a way to transfer the money via text messaging. Do you know the WAP portal?"[5]

"No, Reverend."

"Find out about it. Money is volatile. One must be able to pay it at any time, no matter where one is. The growth rate will increase. From this moment on, prepare yourself psychologically for a new table. Soon this one won't be large enough anymore, and you'll need different machines to count the banknotes. A new car, too. We'll have to see about the rank of pastor. Fine! Let's close up shop. Enough work for today. Tomorrow you'll do what needs to be done to open a dummy company. Paradizo Limited: the only one capable of bringing heaven to earth, on the condition of putting in some of your own, of course."

● ● ● ● ●

Isookanga sat in Kiro Bizimungu's office at the Conservation Service of Salonga National Park. He was looking at wall posters that showed mostly aerial views of the virgin forest. There was a map of the Central Basin and charts of growth and decline,[6] levels of rainfall, zoning map percentages, and, right above Kiro Bizimungu's head, a head-and-shoulders portrait of the president of the republic, looking self-assured, almost placid.

"Little One. May I call you that?"

"My name is Isookanga, Old One."

"I'm glad you came by. I don't get many visitors here. Like you, I'm new in Kinshasa. True, I'm becoming integrated, but I know very well that many regard me with suspicion, primarily because of the position I have. Nevertheless, I really deserve this post. I fought for it. Many of my men have fallen so that I could occupy this seat. And you, what are you? Are you Mongo?"

"Pure Ekonda, Old One."

---

5. WAP stands for Wireless Application Protocol.—*Tr.'s note.*
6. The region between the Congo River and the Kasai River.

"They don't like us. They find us suspect. You, because your customs are weird and you are small; me, because I'm Mututsi. It seems that at the height of colonization you stole a boat without leaving any traces. Is that really true? You're really something.[7] On TV I saw how you led the rebellion at the Great Market, and I liked it. I like people like you—determined, calm, intelligent. But what are you looking to do in Kinshasa?"

"Globalize, Old One."

"Globalize?"

"Yes. Be in the mainstream, get involved in high technology, communicate with the world, be in trading, stuff like that."

"And what about the forest?"

"That, Old One, is so square. I was there not long ago, but I left as fast as I could! They really should stop that retrograde romanticizing, which consists of having people believe the forest should be extended. Can you imagine? Where would they put the highways, superstores, parking lots, production centers . . . at the top of the trees? One has to be realistic and go with the time."

Bizimungu contemplated the surfaces bloated with green on the posters and told himself he had done well to invite the young Pygmy to come and see him. They were thinking completely alike.

"Little One, you are perfectly right. You see, they gave me this office to protect all that," he said, pointing at the posters. "They refer to that as lungs. How can you breathe in such an environment? There are too many trees; they smother everything! Just think that underneath all that there are priceless riches. And I'm the boss of it all, but what good does it do me? And because of all the green you see there, we can't touch anything."

"What kind of riches, Old One?"

"What kind? Oil, Little One, and lots of it! Diamonds, gold, and other very, very valuable things. If I could put my hand on some of the products I'm familiar with, I would erase all that in much less time than that damned desertification they've been talking about for decades and that we're still waiting for."

"It's not easy, Old One. At home there are elders like my uncle Lomama who absolutely insist on preserving everything as it stands. Outside of their harmful propaganda for the preservation of the virgin forest, they use all

7. Allusion to a persistent legend concerning the Mongo people.

kinds of techniques to maintain the canopy above their heads. Demagogues, Old One, megalomaniacs."

"Techniques?" the former commander Kobra Zulu inquired.

"Yes, some sort of ancestral techniques, or whatever. Down there, as soon as a tree is a little under the weather, they huddle by its side, talk to it, invoke the ancestors, concoct mysterious medications, and the wounded tree straightens out right away. They're really diabolical, Old One."

"Is your uncle able to do that?"

"Of course! With drugs."

"And do you know what he does?"

"Some."

Kiro Bizimungu took a few moments to reflect, his eyes upon the young man. "If that guy knows how to cure a tree," he thought, "he must know—with a little searching, or maybe not even—how to destroy it unobtrusively, without leaving any trace of some sort of poison."

"Déo!" Kiro Bizimungu thundered.

The soldier on duty outside opened the door and entered, not in any great rush.

"At your orders, Commander."

"What will you drink?" he asked Isookanga.

"A Fanta, Old One."

Kiro Bizimungu ordered the soldier: "Go downstairs, get one beer and two Fantas, and hurry up!"

When the door closed again, he turned back to Isookanga.

"Little One, I want to see you in my office more frequently. You and I, we need to talk. I'm the administrator of the entire forest, and that makes us almost like brothers. We have the same nationality. We have to see each other, we have similar ideas, we need to stick together. I'm like you—all that green in front of me is depressing. You were lucky coming to Kinshasa to catch some air, or else what would have become of you, can you tell me that? What are those people thinking? That powerful computers, iPhones, or missiles are manufactured with a tree trunk? We need copper, tin, cobalt, coltan. To really develop, we need petroleum, and a lot of it—barrels and barrels. For the people to eat their fill, we need packaging factories, intensive scientifically transgenic agriculture. We can't allow all of *that* to proliferate," he added, sweeping away the vegetation represented on the walls with a wide gesture.

"Old One, those are wise words you're speaking. When a political decision-maker speaks like you, Old One, it's as if the wind of progress blows in your face. I'm going to get some information to help you. We should be able to do something."

At that moment Déo came in with the drinks. The soldier took the caps off the bottles with his teeth and put them on the desk. Kiro Bizimungu stood up to get glasses. He put them down and filled them as he sat down again.

"Here's to you, Little One!"

"Here's to you, Old One."

And they both finished their drinks in almost one gulp, because the power supply was off again and the air-conditioning wasn't working. As a result, the heat in the office was unbearable. To create a little breeze, the French windows were open wide onto a balcony, and you could hear the ruckus of the traffic below in counterpoint, the insistent chant of car horns, the polyphonic sound of the voices of Kin's people floating over the vast metropolis at all times.

8

ETERNAL DRAGON
永存的龙

Isookanga had finished his rounds. He deposited the cooler at the Great Market and went to see Old Tshitshi on the Avenue du Commerce.

"Hello, Old One. Zhang Xia not here?"

"He's coming, he went to the cybercafé."

"To the cybercafé? But he was supposed to wait for me. I have what we need right here."

"He went to get some emails. He's been thinking about his wife and son a lot these days. Have a seat."

The day was ending, and the hustle and bustle in the streets and stores was beginning to slow down. The night guards had taken over on the steps of the businesses that were already closed or about to be. At night the center of town became quiet while the more remote areas grew livelier, the sector reserved for the affluent and those who didn't worry about rules. The common people, those on the fringes like the neglected of the *shégué* community, didn't live there.

Zhang Xia appeared.

"How's it going?" Isookanga asked.

"Don't know." The young Chinese looked even more morose than usual. He handed his friend a sheet of paper. "Read that."

"I'm not a sinologist yet, brother, but I'll get there."

"It's an email from Gong Xiyan, my wife. *'Dear husband,'* she writes, *'the days are going by, I'm thinking of you. I try to live on with little Zhang Yu, who resembles you more and more. Despite his laughter, nothing can comfort me about your absence. My work brings me satisfaction and everything could be fine. The days are long, they go by slowly, the way the Chang Jiang River winds, which I see from the window of our house. A gentleman stopped by. Come back, my love, come back to us soon. Gong Xiyan.'"*

"And . . . ?"

"Don't you hear something troublesome in this message?"

"Listen, Zhang Xia, I know you think about your wife and your child all the time, but you're here to work, my friend. If you want to get back to China someday, you'd do better not to fret so much. Everything's fine with your family, there's no need to worry."

• • • • •

At first sight there was, indeed, no reason to worry about Gong Xiyan and her little boy. The landscape in front of their apartment window varied very little from one day to the next. Despite the dust clouds the bulldozers stirred up, from the top of the hill on which they lived one could see in the distance the building site of a gigantic bridge covered with cranes, evenly spaced, like robots—arms outstretched—as far as the curve in the Chang Jiang River, which showed through the mist thanks to the shimmering reflections on its surface. And farther still, beneath a heavy sepia sky, the massive buildings of the city of Chongqing, slashed by the setting sun, were outlined in a gold-colored copper halo. The metropolis rose imposing and glorious— an autonomous structure like a plinth—in the steep, inaccessible province of Szechuan.

The man spoke calmly, almost in a whisper. His glasses concealed the gaze behind them, but his smile seemed friendly. The hair parted on the side made him look like a serious student. Gong Xiyan was sitting in her modest living room on the sofa; he was on the edge of an armchair leaning slightly toward her so that their knees could have touched. His plain gray suit, its sleeves a bit too long, tried to reduce his stocky mountain peasant's corpulence, but it was in vain. Having shown her his business card, the chief of police, Wang Lideng, declined the offer of some tea, but his tone remained courteous.

"You said that your husband is in Congo?"

"For more than a year now."

"Fine. But we think we know he was in China not long ago. Are you familiar with the company Eternal Dragon?"

Gong Xiyan turned her face to the police officer and answered, "No, sir."

The man shook his head, seemed to think a few moments, and then informed her: "Madame, you say you don't know Eternal Dragon and yet your husband was at the head of this company. We found the trace of several stays in China not long ago."

"I can't tell you anything more. He isn't here any longer and I haven't seen him for a long time."

"What do you know about a certain Liu Kaï?"

Again Gong Xiyan looked at Chief Wang. The young woman's eyes were on him, but her mind was miles away, far from everything else.

Faced with her distraction, the chief no longer knew what to latch on to and suddenly found his thoughts were elsewhere—with Gong Xiyan. He kept staring at her for a moment, then snorted like a bull in the sudden dazzling brightness of the arena. He stood up and picked up a framed photo from the low television table. It showed Gong Xiyan and Zhang Xia on their wedding day.

"How long have you been married?"

"Almost four years."

He picked up another photo, a portrait of Gong Xiyan this time. He looked at it for a long time before asking, "Do you have any proof of his steady presence in Congo since he left China?"

"I don't know. I'll see if I can put together some pieces for you in the next few days. I'll have to look."

Chief Wang Lideng was still contemplating the picture, then finally put it down. "I have to go now." At the door he bowed respectfully, straightened up, and added with a smile, "It was a pleasure meeting you."

She closed the door behind him.

The guest's unexpected presence troubled Gong Xiyan. To refocus, she sat down at the dining room table to pick up her work, which consisted of stringing real pearls and creating geometric patterns with them. But she didn't start right away.

What was going on with Zhang Xia? He always told her everything. She didn't understand these questions, nor what offense her husband could have committed to justify the visit by a figure such as the chief of Public Security. And how could Zhang Xia have risen from simple employee to being administrator of this Eternal Dragon company? She knew very little about Mr. Liu Kaï other than that he was the first one to have offered her husband a responsible job. He had made him his foreman. Zhang Xia was a gutsy and disciplined worker, and it was he whom Mr. Liu had picked to come with him to Africa, to a country named Congo.

It was now almost a year ago that they'd left Chongqing. And four years since they were married. They'd come a long way together. Zhang Xia was a gentle soul. They both came from the north of Szechuan. They had met during their time of wandering, when they left the countryside and found themselves having to face the city, homeless and unemployed. Thereafter they'd managed to get some small jobs. Employment wasn't the problem; construction was mushrooming. But it wasn't until Zhang Xia met Mr. Liu Kaï that their insecurity had stopped and they were able to rent a little apartment on the edge of the city. They were married, and a year later Gong Xiyan brought Zhang Yu into the world.

Every week she waited for messages from her beloved. He always wrote that everything was fine, but she realized today that perhaps he'd kept some things hidden from her—unless all of this was merely a misunderstanding. The chief seemed to believe her when she said that she knew nothing. In any case, it was important that she keep a cool head; she had a child to raise and work to get done. Gong Xiyan had received pearls in every color from a client; she was to string them according to a predetermined model. The patterns were then made into wedding belts and exported to a variety of Arab countries. She also sewed plastic cowries on small leather squares to make trinkets for tourists in Burkina Faso and Senegal. The work didn't bring in very much, but it suited her perfectly; it allowed her to get away from her everyday life, which was filled with interminable waiting.

She spent another moment dawdling, then her eyes fell on the clock above the kitchen door. It was time to pick up her son from his nursery school. She took a lightweight jacket hanging from her chair and went out, her head full of questions. She promised herself never to be separated from Zhang Xia again; it was too painful. Outside she went down the few steps to the street level below. First the absence and now this story about the company, his presumed presence in China—it was all too much for her. Zhang Xia was not a criminal; this whole business would soon be cleared up. Chief Wang Lideng had had an empathetic look, but she hoped she wouldn't have to see him again. A bus arrived. She raised her arm. The driver was slow to stop, and Gong Xiyan had to hurry to the door of the waiting bus, its motor purring patiently.

● ● ● ● ●

Chief Wang Lideng was at his post in the skyscraper of the Office of Public Security of the city of Chongqing, with three-quarters of the staff gone. Wang preferred this atmosphere to any other. In this calm ambiance he could think, without being interrupted every other second by the phone or any number of visitors he had to satisfy when they came to him for an analysis, the reading of a report, or a signature. He liked this time right before nightfall: the light filtering horizontally through the wide bay window; the panorama composed of a series of buildings decked out with telecommunication antennas, spitting steam jets; the façades, tall as mountains, squared off in glass and metal; in the distance, that rusty hue covering all the structures, scaffoldings, tanks, chimneys; and then, too, the cement dust whose particles could be seen saturating the atmosphere, choking the city, like the veil of a much too jealous mistress. He, the chief, loved it; it was China's setting and he wanted to contribute to it. Above the landscape, at the level of where he sat now, the sky had just finished glowing. Some clouds to the west still showed a few flames, but the main hue was dark blue. Looking even higher up, you could see the stars, one by one beginning to put on their evening gowns made of precious stones to show that whatever you did, the universe would always approve of everything, without restriction; it simply participated in the course of events.

The chief worked at least twelve hours a day. It didn't bother him and was essential to the smooth running of the city, which was growing in importance in the hierarchy of the cities of the People's Republic of China. Besides, this influence could not have existed without him. Without him—and, most of all, without the new governor, Bo Fanxi—this new expansion would not have happened the same way. Before being propelled to the province, the latter was already seated in the highest bodies of the Chinese Communist Party. Shortly before, he'd been named as head of Szechuan, and he had accumulated one success after the other ever since. Together they began to drastically lower the crime rate in the city, once Wang Lideng was chief of police. Before, it had been rather messy, and well-organized crime caused major investors to flee. With the complicity of police and high-placed politicians, triads had flourished. At that time, building sites emerged anywhere and in any way—it was just a matter of knowing whose palms to grease—while authorizations and licenses were within arm's reach. Entire sections of the city were contaminated by corruption. But all of that was over and done with—he and the governor had seen to that.

It hadn't been easy, but as soon as Bo Fanxi was installed, the new governor immediately summoned Wang Lideng very late one night. He had been frank with him and revealed that he'd been reviewing his file for a while now. He noticed that where solved cases were concerned, of all the high-ranking police officers Wang Lideng's achievements were by far the most impressive. In doing his research, the governor had soon remarked that, paradoxically, Wang's files were also those most frequently ignored or, if they did make it to the public prosecutor's office, almost always ended up being dropped. Either it was a matter of incompetence on his part or there were people sabotaging him. The new governor was inclined to believe the latter.

That wasn't all. The scrutiny of Wang's career showed that he'd climbed up the ladder, certainly, but less rapidly and less effectively than many of his colleagues. Wang Lideng admitted to himself that it had, indeed, been quite a few years that he had stagnated in the same position without complaining. The governor added that as far as he was concerned it was a question of jealousy.

The light was deliberately low and soft in the office. It reflected on the paneled walls, on the few contemporary paintings, and on the avant-garde furniture but barely touched the faces of the two protagonists sitting in the semi-dark. Every now and then a minuscule spark of white flashed from the surface of Wang's glasses but didn't go far and stayed inside a circumscribed closed circle.

Then the governor turned friendlier. "Frankly, what do you think of the organization of Public Safety in this city?"

They were walking on eggshells here. Wang Lideng hesitated to answer. Having felt throughout his career that he was consistently dealing with envious people, he had always avoided pointlessly exposing himself by trotting out any old thing. At this moment, he told himself that for once he should just take the risk. Face-to-face with the most powerful man in the province limited this risk somewhat, since his response—whether he told the truth or not—would either make him or break him—there was no middle ground. The interview taking place in the semi-dark left him to believe there was a level of trust between them, of the kind that might exist between conspirators, for instance. Wang Lideng decided to jump in.

"Mr. Governor, I do not usually voice any criticism concerning the departments or functioning of my administration, but to tell you the truth, it isn't great. But who could do any better under the current state of affairs?"

"The current state of affairs. I was expecting an answer like that, and I thank you for your honesty, Officer. In the near future I will need someone on whom I can count. I believe I was right to call on you."

The two men then began to speak ill of the head of the Public Safety Bureau, criticisms that were directed more at the individual than at the person in charge of a crucial component of the state, at the end of which Wang Lideng admitted to the governor that he had files on just about everyone, among which was the highest-ranking police commissioner. Thereafter it was easy. Included in the material that Chief Wang had been gathering for years was a video of the unfortunate commissioner with a girl of at most seventeen—in other words, the complete scenario of a sexual scandal-to-be in the news of a country that by itself had more than a billion potential TV viewers. To put in place a new safety strategy in the city, they inevitably had to cut the head off the department in question without too much gossiping, to be able to establish a new one, better adapted to the present context and more reliable above all. It wasn't necessary to display the amorous prowess of the high commissioner of police to three hundred million homes with a television; he didn't wait long to implode on his own, like an old-model screen. After him, Wang Lideng decapitated all the heads of administration, of justice, of companies, by connecting them with all sorts of affairs, one more disgraceful than the next.

Finally, when one of the most sensational trials ever took place in the People's Republic of China since the public trial of the Gang of Four, the triads no longer benefited from the protection that had been theirs for a long time. The reputation of the governor and the new police chief traveled around the country, and thanks to the freedom of speech and information that the constitution guaranteed, the news of their exploits in Chongqing and Szechuan was aired on nearly four hundred television channels; by more than two thousand newspapers, whose distribution consisted of a hundred million copies daily; on three hundred radio stations; by the Xinhua news agency and its hundred or more branches; by websites, blogs, the three thousand digital channels, the thousands of tons of magazines, by CCTV 1, 2, 3, 4, 5, 6, 7, and so on, broadcast live by Fox News in the United States, and then in many other of the world's communities. From Heilongjiang to Yunnan and from Xingjiang to Jiangsu, passing through Qinghai, Hong Kong, and Taiwan, no one spoke about anything but the most gigantic blitz ever run within, and even beyond, the Great Wall toward the autonomous region of Tibet or the northern limits of the captive Diaoyu archipelago.

● ● ● ● ●

Despite the victories amassed, the chief of the Public Safety Bureau, Wang Lideng, never for one moment lost his head. Mindful of the fragility of the human condition, he always managed to keep his composure—until this Eternal Dragon business. A strange feeling had come over him as soon as he had lifted the cardboard cover of the file, to the back of which the photographs of Liu Kaï, Zhang Xia, and Gong Xiyan were pinned. He was instantly attracted to the image of the young woman's face. He spent many long minutes absorbed by the expression of tender melancholy her features exuded. He knew that a photograph was, by definition, just an instant in anyone's life, but an expression didn't come out of nowhere. And there, in those eyes, he read that kind of sadness generated by what fate sometimes keeps in reserve for a person. He had seen it on the face of the actress Gong Li, shedding tears in close-up in *The Forbidden City*, the marvelous film by Zhang Yimou. And this woman, Gong Xiyan, had the same features—exactly the same—as the adored actress. The same light emanated from both of them. Wang Lideng was almost bowled over by it.

Ardent desire had driven him to pay her a personal visit. He wouldn't put anyone else in charge of this inquiry. He owed it to himself to approach her. She had the same high, proud cheekbones; that mysterious hair that cast a shadow on her temples; that full lower lip, disillusioned, capable of enchantment and comprising the most burning emotions; those straight, severe eyebrows; and those eyes. Wang's intuition turned out to be completely right when he was close to her in the small living room, for she, too, didn't do more than glance at her interlocutor, out of modesty surely, as if she were aware of her ability to turn souls to ashes. There was such fever in her, visible in that limpid lake bordering her lashes, in which Wang felt the desire to drown himself so he wouldn't have to feel the pain beating like a pulse, because of his organ that had hardened more than *huaimu*.[1] Ever since then the sensation inevitably returned each time he started thinking about the very beautiful, tormented Gong Xiyan.

1. Very hard and solid Chinese acacia wood.

Congo Inc.

9

COMPROMISE OF PRINCIPLES
连累

The sun was definitely beating down too intensely, and when you spend your day running around the city in every direction there comes a moment when you need to take a break, preferably in the shade with a cool drink in your hand. Isookanga took Avenue Tombalbaye to Kiro Bizimungu's office at the building housing the Conservation Service of Salonga National Park. Bosco the soldier escorted him to his commander.

"Glad to see you again, my fellow countryman," the former rebel greeted him. "Are you well?" he continued after sending the bodyguard out to get a Fanta and a beer.

"Not bad," Isookanga replied, taking a seat.

"I'm glad you came by. Since we last saw each other, I've been thinking a lot about those ancestral technologies you told me about. Do your practitioners really know how to cure a sick tree?"

"Absolutely. And they can cure human bones the same way they cure trees: they fix them when they're broken; they straighten them when they're crooked."

"Have you seen them do it?"

"Of course."

"Well, then, Little One, if those people can treat a tree, they should also be able to make it sick."

"I don't think so, Old One. My uncle Lomama knows only one thing: the forest. And he knows everything you need to know to help it flourish and survive. He can make it rain when the vegetation needs it. He's a rainmaker; he knows how to juggle stratonimbus clouds like nobody else, Old One."

Bizimungu leaned over to inspire trust. "Tell me, with the help of specific substances, couldn't you find a way to determine the type of soil you've got so you know whether it contains something like coltan or diamond? You know, the same thing you do to test for gold. You take a stone from the Salonga, you rub it on a piece of metal, bring it in contact with one of the substances your uncle is acquainted with, and see if it changes color. Isn't that possible?"

"I don't know, Old One. I'd have to find out."

The door opened and Bosco came in with the beverages. He took the caps off with his teeth, put the bottles on the table, and vanished without a word, looking gloomy, impassive as if he were made of cobalt. Isookanga took a swig straight from the bottle. Kiro emptied his glass in one gulp and poured himself another one.

"Little One, it's difficult," he said shaking his head. "But if your elders are capable of such things, then why are they not called on to plant new trees in Chad, for example, or in Saudi Arabia? They'd make a lot of money."

"Fortunately, nobody listens to them. Can you imagine? I saw some of them move whole swarms and send bee colonies to pollinate entire territories."

"I've heard of that," the former rebel interrupted, disappointment in his voice. "Early in the war, when we carried the RCD sign,[1] some of the comrades-in-arms were blockaded for months in Kabinda, in the Kasaï, bees pestering them from morning to night. Firing at them was pointless; they thought bullets were their cousins who'd come to play with them."

Bizimungu chuckled. "We never could take Mbuji-Mayi and its diamonds. Tried everything but we had to give up. Were your chiefs responsible for that? Really, some serious sorcerers you have there!"

---

1. RCD stands for Rassemblement congolais pour la démocratie (Rally for Congolese Democracy).

"Obviously. If I could help you get rid of all those trees for us, Old One, I'd do it. But they didn't teach me how to break that ecosystem. I was initiated to become a future chief, but my training wasn't completed. If only they had taught me to locate oil, diamonds, cassiterite, at least, I'd feel like a veritable potentate, powerful, looking to the future. Yet I'm forced to be content with this," Isookanga said, holding up his thumb, vaguely pointing to the posters behind him. With *Raging Trade*, at any rate, you don't have all these problems, you do what you want."

"*Raging Trade*? What's that?"

"It's a video game you play to put your hands on raw materials, Old One. In Gondavanaland."

"And what kind of land is that?"

"Gondwana. When Pangaea still existed in the Paleozoic era. South America, Africa, India, Australia, all of it was one landmass—ore aplenty."

"How do you know this game?"

"I'm an internationalist, that's how. Anything that has to do with mines or oil interests me. Even in the village I already had a laptop. That's where I learned it. It's diabolical. Lots of us in the world are playing, and for now I'm almost master of the situation."

Indeed, under the tag "Congo Bololo" Isookanga now knew how American Diggers increased its points. It was GGAP, Skulls and Bones Mining Fields, and Kannibal Dawa that snuck off on the sly. All three of them had succeeded in opening secret accounts where they stored whatever they wanted: points, vouchers for weapons, offshore companies. Congo Bololo figured it was time to break up some of these agreements. Thanks to his sophisticated weapons, he had managed to repel Skulls and Bones into the same zone as the Goldberg & Gils Atomic Project. Suddenly their alliance had shattered in a gruesome way. The corner where they must have assembled their troops was bursting with gold, diamonds, and cobalt. What was bound to occur actually happened. To control the wealth, they started firing at each other. From the distance, Congo Bololo had witnessed the carnage and snickered.

"In this game, Old One, I'm a raider. I recently annihilated everybody but one, Kannibal Dawa, who maliciously caught a second wind despite the losses I made him suffer. He did some wicked lobbying and has now procured a non-permanent member seat at the United Nations Security Council. He can do anything there. He can acquire depleted uranium arms at market prices, order satellite photos, build himself a steel dome if he feels like it, but most of all he can influence resolutions. According to what I read on my screen the last time I looked at him, Congo Bololo had just copped an embargo on the weapons because of that bastard Kannibal Dawa. They upbraid me for recruiting women to fight. You realize how unfair that is, Old One?"

"Really, Little One, you're in deep shit."

"Don't worry on my account. They haven't heard the last of me yet. I still have an arsenal of stealth weapons hidden here, there, and everywhere and I expect to use them. I'm going to put pressure on them."

"Good. Take heart, Little One. I need to get going now. I'm going to have a bite to eat. Come by and see me again. Salonga is your home even if I'm in control of it." Bizimungu managed a dismal smile.

Isookanga emptied what was left in his bottle, got up, and went to the door. "See you soon, Old One. As you know, I keep thinking about the raw materials."

And he was back in the street.

"Mr. Isookanga!"

The young Ekonda had no time to turn around before Aude Martin already had her soft arms around him. "How are you?" he said.

"I'm so happy to run into you. My research is done and I really wanted to see you again before leaving. Come pick me up tonight if you can; we'll have a drink together. I'm still on Avenue de la Libération."

"I'll try."

"Promise you'll come. It means a lot to me."

"All right, I'll be there. But I have to go now. See you soon."

"Very soon," Aude Martin answered, a little breathless.

She left the young Pygmy with an ecstatic look and walking on air.

● ● ● ● ●

It must have been around two in the afternoon when Waldemar Mirnas was at a table by himself in the Inzia restaurant in the shaded Gombe district. The many customers under the large thatched roof consisted of Congolese and Westerners, most of whom were experts in culture, humanitarianism, or conflict resolution—subject matter that the autochthones didn't seem to practice as they should. Consequently, the international community had mobilized and dispatched entire legions of experts to compensate for these serious omissions.

Where culture was concerned, young people came to initiate all sorts of projects, ranging from music to theater, graphic arts to dance, both to promote and capture heartbeats, original scansions, ancestral pantomimes, and riffs on the *satonge*.[2] The result would increase the perspectives and revenues of subsidized organizations, of artists categorized as contemporary, of confidential and Africanist labels. To propagate holiness around zero latitude, humanitarians in their immaculate vehicles were distributing rations of sanctified cookies throughout the land and attempting to comfort poor genuflecting souls, muttering dogmas they'd memorized in the humanities departments in the northern hemisphere. As for those in charge of conflict resolution, rather than silencing the guns, they struggled to identify the acronyms represented in the east of the country—RCD, CNDP, FDLR, FNL, etc.—their observers' eyes focusing on a line that an inescapable United Nations resolution had drawn.

Dressed in black, the restaurant staff went from table to table, putting down *malangwa* with sorrel, *fumbwa*, *lituma*,[3] fried sweet potatoes, catfish in banana leaves, turtle with squash seeds. The patrons seemed to enjoy their dishes: clanging of cutlery accompanied by cheerful murmuring floated above the diners' heads. Waldemar Mirnas prized the local cuisine and would occasionally eat here. He liked the flavors he had discovered, so different from what he was used to in Vilnius.

The officer had entered the Lithuanian armed forces when they were created more than ten years earlier, after the separation from the Soviet bloc, which hadn't happened all that smoothly. Since he had an engineering degree, he'd been recruited as second lieutenant, had climbed the ladder to the rank of major, and was now wearing the blue helmet of the UN operating in Congo. He'd arrived three years earlier and worked with contingents of all kinds: Senegalese, Moroccans, Pakistanis, Ghanaians, French . . . It wasn't an easy task. He had to intervene, negotiate, open fire if necessary. Over time it had all become quite tedious.

Yet, he wasn't growing tired of the country, and the ever present sun had something to do with that. Vilnius's grayness, the very low temperatures in

2. A one-stringed instrument.
3. Fish, peas and beans, mashed green plantains.

winter, the muck that muddied the landscape during the thaw wouldn't have to be his for the rest of his life, Mirnas decided upon his arrival. He was the only Lithuanian officer at MONUSCO—the UN mission for the Consolidation of Congo. He'd been in Afghanistan on behalf of NATO and didn't really like it. The unbearable heat in the summer, the almost Lithuanian cold of the winter nights, the men and vehicles packed with explosives that could detonate at any moment, and the Taliban, above all, so hard to identify since they resembled the man in the street just as drops of water are alike. You could easily become paranoid over there. Kivu, where he was sent next, wasn't a whole lot better, but the climate was nicer and the land of the Pashtun didn't conceal any coltan, cassiterite, or diamonds. Afghanistan was fine for yokels.

At least in Congo anything was possible, and with a little effort you could even change your life and climate. It was enough to lay low a bit, cash in, and go off to what were certainly more temperate lands such as Kuala Lumpur or Phuket, for instance; some place where the picture-postcard image might be hiding things that were far more intense than they seemed. And it was precisely in Congo that Waldemar Mirnas had met up with this intensity. Paradoxically, it was not on a battlefield as was to be expected, but, more prosaically, it was while wandering the streets of Kinshasa at night, driving through the Great Market area, when he first noticed the street kids, those girls with their outrageously arched tiny posteriors. Little girls, afraid of nothing, vulgar almost to the point of indecency. One night in the shadows he spotted Shasha la Jactance, the child whore, and from that moment on his blood had not stopped boiling in his veins, especially in those that flooded his head.

Kivu stood for violence but also for abundant riches—until the incident in Kamituga. A section he commanded had fallen into an ambush on a mining site and its members were massacred. What were they doing there? the UN functionaries in New York had wondered—all the more because, thanks to their satellite telephones, the massacre had been followed live from the offices on Millennium Plaza, on the bank of the East River between First Avenue and Roosevelt Drive. Apparently, they had not yet identified the perpetrators of the attack and were still looking for the motive for the crime. There were armed groups everywhere in that area, and the investigations came up against all kinds of difficulties, considering the murkiness of the situation in that part of the world. With the six victims whose death throes were heard in real time right there in Manhattan, Major Mirnas's command became questionable. In order not to stir up too much unrest, he was called back to

Kinshasa and promoted to other duties. From then on he handled logistics, a much cushier job with respect to his abilities. Sending armaments and munitions to the MONUSCO troops at the front was part of his new assignment.

But since the famous peace accords, the enemies he had once fought were walking in the city in suits, and the Lithuanian had a hard time putting aside the events that had taken place in the square in Kamituga. More often than not with a disdainful smile, he had from time to time run into some warlords.

As he was stuffing Nile perch in tomato sauce into his mouth, his face lowered, someone tapped him on the shoulder with a finger as hard as tropical wood and said, "How are you, Major? It's been a long time."

Kiro Bizimungu towered in front of Mirnas's table at his full height. "May I?" And, motioning to one of the waiters, he sat down.

Waldemar Mirnas frowned. If the recycled rebels were milling about town, the bloodthirsty commander Kobra Zulu was clearly the last one he wanted to meet. The Lithuanian forced a smile. "Well, Commander. I didn't expect to see you here. Have you been in Kin' long?"

"Yes, actually. But I don't go out very often. You know what it's like—you have to adapt, become integrated . . . But I rather like the city. And you, are you passing through?"

"No, I've been transferred here. I had a problem with one of my sections and lost six men."

Seeing Kiro Bizimungu's astonished face, Mirnas added, "Don't act so surprised. You must know about that, right? Wasn't the guy with whom my men had a run-in one of your sector commanders?"

A waiter approached and handed Bizimungu the menu.

"Don't bother," he said, "chicken with *moambe*[4] and steamed green plantains will do. Thank you. And a beer."

The waiter was barely gone when he continued: "Obviously, I was told about it. After all, I was in charge of the territory."

"Exactly." Mirnas's voice was bitter with controlled anger. "And I really doubt you had nothing to do with what happened."

"True, we haven't had time to talk about it yet, but you must admit some of it was your own fault."

"My fault!" The blood rose in the officer's face.

---

4. A sauce made with palm nut pulp.

"Me, I know nothing, good God! But from what I've heard, the men were nervous that day. The delivery was not what it was supposed to be. That's not acceptable from your end. You promise one thing, you bring something else. They felt they'd been ripped off, and they fired. And besides, your men didn't negotiate as they should have. When you have a difficult case on your hands, you should talk; we're not animals, after all. Is it true that you're in logistics now?"

"How do you know that?" Mirnas asked, feeling ill at ease.

"We have people at all levels, as you well know. It seems, in fact, that you're responsible for delivering weapons and munitions to the front."

"Leave me alone, Bizimungu. You've caused me enough trouble already."

"Don't be that way, you know we're allies you and I. We're like comrades-in-arms in a way, aren't we? Do you think that because I'm here in Kinshasa, the rest down there in the bush have been laid off? You're wrong. This is business. When they sign peace accords everything is liquidated, they file bankruptcy like any other company, then they recreate the armed group but with a different acronym; that's how an economic system functions when it wants to forge ahead. We, we'll always need equipment to do our work well, and as for the materials, I still have some and can pay you the same way as before; all you have to do is say the word. Your job is to ship, isn't it? Some of it to MONUSCO, some of it to my guys. What do you think?"

"Listen, I want nothing further to do with you, is that clear?"

"Calm down, Mirnas, I only want what's good for you."

The Lithuanian was beside himself but trying hard not to show it. He emptied his glass of beer in one gulp, wiped his mouth with the back of his hand, and leaned over to Bizimungu. "There's an inquest in progress," Waldemar Mirnas retorted. "I'd hurry back where I came from if I were you. If you believe . . ." The man stopped, made a face.

"What's the matter?" Bizimungu asked.

"Nothing," he said, touching his belly. Then he continued: "If you think you can get away with it, you're sadly mistaken. Six of the peacekeeping force killed—that's more than the UN can accept, and you're just about the only one on the list of suspects. I don't know how far they've come with their investigations, but I don't think they'll condone it this time."

"I have nothing to do with that business of yours. Besides, the sector commander who was in charge of everything has been dead for a long time—

a grenade. And don't try to implicate me, because should it turn out badly for me, I can't guarantee anything for you."

Waldemar Mirnas stared at the former rebel for a moment, then put his blue beret back on. He stood up, leaned on the table, a little weary, still holding his belly.

"Maybe, but nobody can accuse me of any violation The Hague will find reprehensible. You've heard of the International Court of Justice, haven't you, Bizimungu?"

With those words the officer disappeared, handing dollars to the waiter who was coming over to settle the bill and bring the former rebel his beer.

"I'll be in touch soon," the latter added before the blue beret vanished.

While waiting for his chicken and sipping his beer, Kiro Bizimungu started to think. "He's fighting back," he told himself, "that's to be expected; he's worried. But why?" Kiro couldn't find any reason. Until now, he, his men, and all the others had created havoc in the country, and what had happened? Nothing. How long had they been slaughtering? Who had ever tried to stop them? Everybody needed their services.

Having been at this all these years, Kiro knew how valuable and useful their work was. The multinationals had no choice. The minerals they needed so badly were in Kivu, nowhere else; he and his men controlled the region so that sooner or later they were forced to reckon with Commander Kiro Bizimungu. And it wasn't because he wore a necktie these days that they had to act as if he didn't exist. Thanks to his intermediaries, Commander Kobra Zulu was aware of Waldemar Mirnas's new assignment. They had done business together. In exchange for gold ore or diamonds, the Blue Berets delivered armaments, ammunition, and a little information. It was an exchange of friendly services and that was it, no harm in that at all.

Except that one of the deliveries had gone wrong. According to what he'd been told, the Uruguayan soldiers who were in charge hadn't provided the complete order of merchandise, and during the discussion shots were fired and it had turned into a massacre. It was not what Bizimungu had wanted. Nevertheless, his men had behaved logically. No problem where the ammunition crates were concerned, but of the twelve RPG-7 launchers that were ordered, four were missing. Not to speak of the rockets that were part of it. If the promised weapons weren't there, then where were they? Sold to whom? Certainly not to friends. They didn't do anything for free over there. The incident had happened, too bad, but that was no reason for the earth to stop spinning.

Right then a delicious aroma preceded the waiter who arrived with the food, and Bizimungu decided to think about other, more pleasant things. The case of Waldemar Mirnas would be studied later. The chicken *moambe* had nothing to do with it, and Kiro decided to give it his full attention.

• • • • •

As promised, Isookanga went to pick up Aude Martin that evening on the Avenue de la Libération. Expecting to be going out, he insisted on dressing elegantly. He was wearing his Superdry JPN jeans and a Jimmy Choo T-shirt that said, *This is not a Jimmy Choo & it's not available by H&M.* His NY pendant sparkled on his chest, and on his forehead he was sporting his Dolce & Gabbana glasses like a headband.

They walked through the streets of Lingwala and found themselves in a tiny bar where the décor didn't matter, since in the darkness you couldn't see the walls. Demands were made only on one's hearing and one's nerves in this sort of place. You didn't really go there to converse, but still the young researcher made an effort to be heard despite the guitars, bass, and drums of the music by Wenge Musica and Werrason, the King of the Forest. Spilling over from the dance floor, men and women surrendered themselves to violent movements of the pelvis, thrust forward in a rhythm that pulsed like the blood flow of someone in a manic frenzy. Isookanga and Aude were sitting on a bench, each waiting for the beer they'd ordered. They clinked glasses and emptied them in one gulp because of the stifling heat, then right away ordered another.

"I wonder what the Congolese would do without their music," Aude Martin said. "It's all you have, but what a treasure!"

"*Eboka, Motute! Eboka, Motute!*"[5] Werrason chanted.

And the dancers on the floor went even wilder. The guitar nearly seared their flesh in its attempt to influence basic metabolism and the cerebral hemisphere in control of willpower. Everyone on the dance floor, hips unencumbered by any psychological deterrent, succumbed to the music, faces impassive or, conversely, eyes closed and completely transported.

5. "Mortar, pestle!": a sexual allusion.

Congo Inc.

"It's my last night here." Aude Martin shouted to be heard. "I'll never forget this stay in Kinshasa. Thanks especially to you I've been able to learn about the complexity of this continent."

"What did you say?" Isookanga asked, unable to hear because of Werra's band.

They ordered another round. A tall, strapping man, dark as the night, held out his hand to Aude Martin and pulled her firmly to the dance floor. His pelvis thumped against hers boldly, powerfully, but controlled. She moved as sinuously as a cobra, her arms above her head, her eyes closed, ecstatic. The electricity she felt around her initially made her anxious, but the muscular bodies surrounding her didn't provide her with the alternative of shying away from their unyielding presence. The redolence of the armpit odors around her were beginning to go to her head. The women dancing showed her what to do, rubbing their rumps and pubic areas against the hard male organs, ostensibly unimpressed; you would have thought it was an Alain Mabanckou novel.

Aude let go and felt blazing flesh on every side, muscles taut, fluids shifting, obdurate looks, breath on the nape of her neck. At one point, in a spin, she couldn't take it anymore and dropped down on the bench, not even knowing who had dragged her onto the dance floor. She emptied her glass and put it back on the little table with a clang, pushing a long lock of hair out of her eyes.

"My God, I've never felt such ferocity. All these men! Even when they dance it's as if there's renewed suffering inside them. You sense that some kind of rage could erupt at any moment. How do you live in this powder keg?"

Isookanga felt something like a boa awakening inside his Superdry JPN jeans. What was she talking about now? The prejudices Aude Martin bombarded him with nonstop were beginning to get on Isookanga's nerves. What suffering was she talking about, that little white girl? All she had to do was ask the UN or the IMF.[6] All she had to do was reread the terms of the structural adjustment programs. Had she come to Congo to do an audit or what?

Fortunately, at that moment Wenge Musica Maison Mère changed moods and the lament of "Nicky D" was heard in the monumental baffles around the club. Everyone's heart melted at the beauty of the melody and Isookanga's was no exception. He ignored the concepts of social anthropology and, opting for peaceful coexistence, pulled Aude Martin onto the dance floor. He held

6. IMF stands for the International Monetary Fund.—*Tr.'s note*

her at a distance, leading her at arm's length so the difference in their height wouldn't be too noticeable but, most of all, because the boa that had raised its head just before was starting to move as if it wanted to force its way through.

Yo obendi nzoto pe distance, Nicky D
Ndima yo otikela ngai souvenir po na bosana te ke
nazalaka na chérie na ngai Nicky D
Awa, yo nde, bolingo ya sincère
Oh, oh, oh, ngai na yo likambo te
Na lingaki na bima na yo dimanche, na Inzia, na sambwi
Souci na ngai suka te.[7]

All very well and good, but evidently Wenge Music and the King of the Forest, its leader, would never change. Without a warning they heard *"Eboka, Motute!"* blast again, and this time the basses were even louder. Hips went wild again. It kept going for a very long time. Beating relentlessly.

Following Batwa choreography, Isookanga, his feet firmly planted on the floor, was making micro-movements, but a phenomenal energy was unfolding. His open hands wide around the young white woman didn't touch her but were mysteriously transmitting a current through her entire body. He moved his right shoulder forward. Legs lithe, fists tightened, he flattened the ground with imperceptible stomping motions, throwing his pelvis forward every other beat, performing a hyper-classic shadow-fuck. He moved his left shoulder forward and, without stopping, repeated what he'd been doing. Eyes closed, face turned to the play of light, his Dolce & Gabbana glasses on his forehead throwing lightning flashes all around like magic spells, goading the young woman's libido.

The music, sweat, and alcohol had taken hold of Aude Martin. She no longer knew which way to turn. She felt her panties were at risk and thought she'd been bewitched; something ancestral would prevent her from freeing herself from this fateful charm. She'd heard about that. They said it was like a gris-gris that would cause the downfall of women from colonizing countries when they showed themselves to be foolhardy and frivolous.

---

7. "You broke off and took your distance, Nicky D / Please leave me a souvenir so I won't forget / I have my darling whose name is Nicky D / You are sincere love / Between us there's no problem / I wanted to go out with you on Sunday to Inzia / There, I'm filled with shame / My worries are never-ending."

"Let's get away from here," she whispered to Isookanga, suddenly worried. "I want to go home."

Before the piece was finished Aude insisted that the young Ekonda bring her back to her apartment. She was afraid, she said.

• • • • •

In the taxi they didn't speak. She was holding on to his arm, pretending to be asleep, but Isookanga noticed a trouble-filled tension between them. All evening she had been making stereotypical comments on Africa and Congo, and because of it the python nesting in his Calvin Klein underwear—feeling threatened—was now hatching a muted rage. Isookanga tried to quiet it down mentally. He had always avoided women. On the rare occasions that he had undressed in front of one of these creatures, he could mislead them before the act, but once they got going it was always "Hey, *mosutu, ééh! Nalingi lisu'u te!*"[8] It was the kind of shriek that horrified Isookanga. And all because of his mother's negligence. Now he was facing insults from the whole feminine sex in Équateur Province. "She's just like all the others; she's not going to get any!" Isookanga swore to himself vindictively.

The taxi arrived; in a rush to get back to her sanctuary, Aude Martin tossed a wad of banknotes to the driver as she opened the door. She produced a stream of words that Isookanga didn't hear, as his resentment and the alcohol they'd imbibed prevented him from noticing anything that was going on outside his underwear with the initials C. K. Aude Martin had to struggle for a moment with the lock, but then they were in the bedroom, on the edge of a bed that occupied almost the entire space.

"When are you Africans finally going to grab your chance, once and for all?"

Isookanga heard it as if through a sort of fog.

"When you think of what this continent has to endure, how does a Pygmy handle it? With the energy you all have, why always such resignation?"

Phrases that went too far. Indignant, Isookanga turned his back on her. He reckoned he'd leave her then and there, but she clutched onto his Jimmy Choo T-shirt and clung to him.

8. "Hey, you're not circumcised! I don't want to anymore!"

"I want only one thing: to share this suffering," she said. It was like a cry from the heart. "I beg you, don't leave me!"

The most obtuse python in creation—the one with just one eye—had been ruminating his loathing of the Africanist's condescension for a while now. At this last cry, a forceful torsion made itself known inside the Calvin Kleins. They fell onto the bed. Isookanga lost complete control as his Ekonda hunter's spirit took over.

With astonishing speed, he unbuttoned his Superdry jeans and with a tight fist grasped the boa right below its head in an attempt to control it, but it was shaking like a paddle working against the current. Isookanga was familiar with the phenomenon, having read about it on a health blog. He knew that the testosterone being secreted in a high dosage because of this madwoman's words was now acting up inside him, triggering feelings of rage, certainly, but at the same time activating an irrepressible erection, magnified by a need for resolute conquest. The explosive mixture was the reason why his body went directly counter to his own will, even though he in no way wanted to satisfy the woman's appeals nor go against his abhorrence of showing his shameful sex. The boa's head was looking for a victim and Isookanga felt trapped, the full weight of his body thrown onto Aude Martin.

He forcefully grabbed the young woman's legs and pushed them up on his shoulders. She had already removed any obstacle by swiftly taking her jeans off one leg. Before Isookanga knew what he was doing, without even needing to look, he had pushed back the edge of her panties and felt his sex plunge down into a bush of moist hair and then, without transition, into a bottomless well, a delight to die for. The moorings almost broke loose, were it not for the raucous cry the young woman let out from the depth of her chest, which tormented Isookanga's nerves even more. He began to hammer away at her with his pelvis, banging aggressively against the bottom of a well that seemed unfathomable to him.

The Pygmy was unaware of the extreme sensitivity of the woman's mucous membranes. Propped up on his knees, he didn't know that each thrust he executed was—for her—like the whipping his ancestors had suffered at the time of slavery; that each assault between her thighs was as merciless as the hand-severing axe, as the stump Leopold II and his descendants had inflicted; that each penetration of his organ provoked a turmoil worthy of a riot for independence; that the grunts coming from his mouth were reminders of those uttered by the Belgian Gerard Soete[9] during the dissection with a saw of Patrice Lumumba's body; that each jolt inside her sensitive belly resounded like the salvos fired off by vicious neocolonialists, like the diktats of the International Monetary Fund, like the resolutions of the UN, like a reprint of *Tintin au Congo*,[10] like the speech by an ill-informed French president in Dakar, like the propaganda of racist sentiments on Twitter.

Living through this nightmare, Aude no longer resisted. Ripped apart, she felt like the victim of dagger blows tearing through her; she felt like those raped women of Kivu, abandoned by everyone, despised, tortured, mutilated, persecuted, exiled, taken hostage, reduced to slavery, defiled, defiled again, but still struggling. Then there was a never-ending explosion inside her that might have matched the fire deployed during the wars of Independence, of Katanga, of the Rebellion of 1964, of Shaba I, of Shaba II, of Liberation, and of the one they call Unjust that is still going on, and on, and on, and on, and on. Her cry—which, incidentally, Isookanga no longer heard—echoed in her innermost consciousness, exploding into an enormous spray of white light, of indescribable purity, which decomposed into innumerable sparks, resembling what might be redemption when seen in myriads of flakes shaped like stars, sparkling unto death.

"*Likambo nini awa? Yo! Ozosala ye nini?*"[11]

Knocking on the door intensified and several people could be heard, fighting to speak.

"Who is it?" Isookanga shouted, rolling over on his side, his pants halfway down his calves.

"Open up!" was the authoritarian response.

Aude Martin still had one of her jeans legs on, but her panties lay at the foot of the bed, torn to shreds, fragrant, pure as a dove on the altar of the holocaust.

"My God! My God!" she kept repeating, pulling the shirttails of her blouse over her heavy breasts, which were the color of milk with wide, dark brown areolas.

---

9. Police commissioner, executioner of Patrice Emery Lumumba.
10. *Tintin in the Congo* by the Belgian cartoonist Hergé.—*Tr.'s note*
11. "What's going on here? What are you doing to her?"

Before she could say anything else, the door flew open as if a hurricane had hit it. In her agitation, the young woman had forgotten to lock it.

"*Yo! Ozo nyokola ye pona nini?*"[12]

"*Nasali nini?*"[13] Isookanga asked, now standing and trying to button his pants.

Her orgasm brusquely interrupted, Aude was on the verge of a nervous breakdown. Sitting on the bed she was crying her eyes out, her shoulders shaking with sobs.

"What have you done to her, you? *Basalaka mwasi, boye te!*"[14]

The neighbors were there, awakened by the uproar that Isookanga, colonialization, and its aftermath had incited. They wanted to be sure the young white woman wasn't being assaulted by the *kuluna* gang running rampant in the district. Their fears seemed justified, as she appeared to be in real danger. And besides, the guy looked suspicious. Starting with his size.

"Don't worry, Mademoiselle; this individual won't harm you again," one of them said.

Isookanga tried to defend himself, but it was useless. He was like a dictator about to be overthrown: half a dozen men and women were pushing him to the exit, shouting all kinds of things.

Still in shock because of the dirty-headed python, Aude Martin was too traumatized to say more than a few words. "He castigated me," she finally managed to divulge.

They covered her half-naked body with a *pagne*.

"It wasn't my fault," she sobbed in lieu of a denial.

The researcher didn't understand the aggression perpetrated on her body. As if a transfer had occurred. "He raped me."

Surrounding her with soothing words and caring arms, her protectors tried as best they could to console her. The emotion had been horribly violent, her approach had taken a beating, but had she adequately paid to settle the debt her ancestors had incurred so long ago with these people? she wondered with a delicious sense of guilt.

---

12. "You, why are you torturing her?"
13. "What did I do?"
14. "That's no way to treat a woman!"

• • • • •

Holding his breath, Old Lomama stopped as he pushed a branch aside. At eye level with him, a soft green mamba snake was moving its minuscule head back and forth, flicking a menacing tongue. The old man remained motionless until the reptile, its body tense, slithered down to a lower branch and silently vanished into the undergrowth. The forest had swallowed up the Ekonda chief at dawn; he sometimes made his way on the ground, sometimes over the natural bridges and pathways formed by branches and lianas. He was wearing nothing but his breeches of crushed bark. He carried his bow across his back, a quiver wedged under his right arm. Other than the song of birds there was no sound. Taking flight every now and then, one of them would break the stillness with a rustling in the trees that stood upright in all their majesty and strength, searching for light at all costs, firmly rooted for centuries to a land that had been generous enough to make its omnipotence available to them so they could fulfill their quest.

Old Lomama was looking for game. He'd been following the tracks of a wild boar since the late morning, and from what he observed, he knew it was a large male. Old Lomama liked feeling the shiver of pursuit, confronting his expertise in the natural world. He could have been content to hunt a monkey on the edge of the forest, but feeding himself wasn't the only thing: it was much more satisfying to know that his neurons were functioning well inside a body capable of slinking into the foliage. But his search was taking far more time than he had anticipated. To some extent Old Lomama expected it, but not to this point. He had left to check on what for now was only an intuition. It seemed to him that game was becoming scarcer or had changed location, withdrawing farther into the forest.

Old Lomama knew what was responsible for this state of affairs. For him it was the telecommunications pole those barbarians with their flying monster had planted among the trees. Obviously, the animals had fled without a murmur. Why shouldn't they? Since it had been put up, that bit of metal had brought nothing but trouble. First of all, it had caused harm on the level of social peace, because it had its detractors among the majority of the Ekanga population as well as its supporters, who were thrilled to finally join the modern world. Although one could ask in what way the antenna could possibly be of service to them—phone whom? surf what?—they would defend the iron tower as if it were a member of their own family. Then there was the matter of subsistence; sustenance had turned on its heels. Now they had to go for miles to flush it out. Some people simply didn't look any farther than the end of their nose.

And his own nephew Isookanga was one of them. Nothing but nonsense. Modernity, modernity. Can you eat modernity? Yet, until his adolescence Isookanga had been well trained, but then within the space of a few years he'd become rebellious, starting to defend ideas that had nothing to do with the Ekonda and the preservation of their biosphere. A kid talking about pipelines and oil wells has a problem and should be taken to the fetishist.

And where was he now? Since their separation, he and Isookanga hadn't really talked. The old man was pining for his nephew. The young man often did exactly as he pleased, but Old Lomama missed him. He hadn't been able to convince him to stay, and he bore that as a failure that had been gnawing at him for months. What was his nephew doing? Was he all right? Did he have enough to eat? Where was he sleeping? The old man was worried about his sister's son. The little guy was meant to succeed him as chief, but Old Lomama didn't even know whether he was going to come back one day.

The sun was high in the sky, the heat and humidity saturating the air. Only a few rays of the daytime star were visible as they managed to pierce the dense, leafy screen and were reflected on some of the trunks, where they scattered into small patches of light. Old Lomama stopped in front of some suspicious tracks on the ground. The characteristic smell of a corpse hovered in the air. He moved forward again and noticed that the earth under his feet was churned up as if two elephants had been fighting. He looked around more intently and examined the broken branches in the immediate area. Tufts of hair he recognized were stuck here and there. Old Lomama identified it as leopard's fur. The carrion odor he smelled must be coming from one of its victims. But normally, Old Lomama thought, a leopard kills to eat and doesn't usually abandon its prey.

Lomama wanted to find out where the stench was coming from. He didn't have to look very far. An enormous leopard was lying on its side, chops bared over impressive fangs, face frozen in a bitter grimace. Old Lomama would have recognized that fur among thousands. This was Nkoi Mobali,[15] lord of

15. Male leopard.

the site, who made the laws for miles around. What had happened to him? Lomama sat down on one knee next to the remains. The animal had deep lesions across his entire body—bites and tears like furrows. What enemy was this, capable of such a fierce attack on a leopard? With what kind of power was it endowed? The old man didn't understand. One or several jaws had bitten Nkoi Mobali's neck and hindquarters. The jugular had been severed and the big cat had bled out, a dark stain spread out underneath him. He'd been dead for about two days, Lomama figured. All sorts of insects had infested the body. Squadrons of ants, beetles, and carcass-eating creatures were engrossed in a gargantuan feast.

Old Lomama left the corpse to study the tracks left by one or more aggressors. On the soil he found the footprints of an animal with two nails in the front like those of a wild boar. They were similar but smaller, less massive, carrying something lighter. A herd of young boars? Impossible. Because it seemed Nkoi Mobali had been faced with a large number of individuals. Lomama kept searching. He reexamined the branches. Looking carefully, he found nothing but the leopard's coat. Long brown-black hair, undoubtedly from his mane, and tatters of dirty, gray-covered skin were present at the crime scene. It was a villainous crime without any real motivation. One didn't kill someone like Nkoi Mobali. After all, he was at the peak of the food chain. Nature knew how to regulate her own operation and counted on the leopard for that. He was one of her crucial elements, in fact. Furthermore, it concerned a noble animal.

He and Old Lomama had known each other a long time. They had actually met during a wild boar hunt. The old man was tracking a solid male when he and Nkoi Mobali came face-to-face. The animal stood steady on a low branch, its long tail whipping the air. He growled once. Surprised at first, Old Lomama no longer budged. He pretended to be looking elsewhere and had started talking.

"Nkoi Mobali, I humbly ask your permission to pass. I truly know that you are the king of this region. I haven't come to quarrel over your power. I'm here to find food. The wild game here is yours, I know, but you could eat some of it and leave a little for us. Over there in the village the children are counting on me. Even if you don't like getting married, would you let your children starve? I'm tracking a boar right now. Let me have him, and I'll pay you back."

While the old man was talking, Nkoi Mobali stopped moving his tail and kept staring at Old Lomama with his piercing, cold eyes. From his throat came a sound that could pass for acquiescence. The animal had jumped to the ground very close to Lomama and, turning his back, left to vanish lithely as if absorbed by the shade of the forest.

The old man remembered his bearing, his volume, and couldn't understand what was at the root of the drama that had transpired here. The Ekonda immersed himself again in analyzing the indications. He took a bit of the other hair in his fingers. The animal—or, more likely, animals—that had singled Nkoi Mobali out for such treatment had a bushy mane. Old Lomama brought the strands of hair to his nostrils. He knew what he was holding but couldn't draw any conclusions from it, for the animal with this characteristic hairiness didn't live in any adjoining area. It came from far more open country. Despite anything Old Lomama might think of this, what he was holding between his fingers came from the skin of a warthog—there was no doubt. It was insane, but the facts were there, Nkoi Mobali was unquestionably dead. Old Lomama tried to reconstruct the event.

If the lands belonged to the Ekonda as administrators, Nkoi Mobali was king. His reign was absolute. There was not even a queen who lived with him. He was hard on everyone; he was hard on himself. He regulated the demography and distribution of the fauna. He had the power of life and death over all the vertebrates within his range. Nkoi Mobali needed to know what was happening in his territory and, thus, crisscrossed it daily from one end to the other. He didn't have to hunt every day, eating on occasion was enough for him, but he had to show himself to make his power known, display his yellow eyes and his fangs, which were as long as two human fingers. He left the imprint of his claws on the tree trunks and paths and marked his territory with urine.

The intruders Nkoi Mobali challenged that day were not familiar with the established rules, and a fight had broken out. In view of the leopard's downfall, they were inevitably mismatched. Warthogs moved in large groups, had an irascible character, and their tusks could cause nasty gashes. Like their brothers the pigs and wild boars, they sank their teeth in and pressed down so their jaws would meet and break the bones, or not. They liked to feel their teeth make contact. And, indeed, the leopard's body was riddled with bright red patches where the flesh had been bitten and ripped off. Judging by the ravaged area, the fight must have gone on forever. The big cat must have fought with all the power of his royal rank, but in the end he'd been brought down.

Then Old Lomama spoke: "Ah, Nkoi Mobali! Immortal hero! I shall always speak of your dignity, your noble bearing, now and forever. Nkoi Mobali, I shall speak of your courage and strength, but of your magnanimity above all. Because of your demise, people will know that the end of the world is near. Heroes die first because they're destined to show us the way. I'll take your skin, Nkoi Mobali, and display it so everyone will know what's going to happen to us, to show that what was not possible at one time has now become possible."

After these words, Old Lomama took his knife and began to skin the animal. Despite the appalling smell, he continued his task to the bitter end. When he was done, he wrapped the skin in several layers of leaves larger than two human hands and tied it up with a bit of twine. He no longer felt like hunting and went back to the village, his head full of questions, beginning with the presence of warthogs on Nkoi Mobali's terrain. The metal pole had certainly played a role in this tragedy—Old Lomama was sure of it. How else could the disappearance of ordinary caterpillars from the area be explained, or the fact that warthogs were venturing this far in? Old Lomama knew that signals were transmitted from Kinshasa, and to remedy the problem he'd have to go to the source. The antenna could kill. The skin he was carrying wrapped around his waist was an irrevocable witness to that. Rage molded by revolt stirred inside Old Lomama. He had to let the country's leaders know that Nkoi Mobali was dead, the victim of a cowardly murder by a coalition of warthogs. It might seem unimportant, but it might also be a sign of the early stages of an event, like the end of the world or something similar.

🔟

PLEASE READ THE ATTACHED NOTE
请阅读附上的说明

Since the Hundredfold Law had been introduced, the Church of Divine Multiplication was always full. The Sunday after the account of Paradizo Ltd. was opened the reverend informed his congregation: "Dear brothers and sisters, I have prayed and to me the Lord has revealed the following: 'Jonas Monkaya! Your faith is still not great enough. I am going to put it to the test before proving to you with copious blessings that I am the Lord of lords. You must intercede with me on behalf of everyone by fasting and praying for a week. I want to see what you're capable of. Follow my directives, do what I ask, and glory shall be yours. You will also challenge your faithful to see if they believe in you. Ask them to write their name on an envelope; I shall multiply its contents a hundredfold. Thus, they will see that I am the Lord of hosts.' That, dearest brothers and sisters, is roughly what the Lord said to me."

There was an explosion of praise. "He lives / the King of Kings. . . ," the congregation sang.

A week later, as soon as the faithful had stopped shoving one another to deposit envelopes filled with their contributions, from behind his lectern the reverend, face raised to heaven and eyes closed, interrupted his song to speak:

"I see . . . I see three checks coming directly from heaven. There are names on these checks. Names of true, wholly virtuous Christians. These people, they did not hesitate to give to the Church. Deacon, go get the checks!"

Brother Kasongo went behind the curtains and returned holding rectangles of watermarked sheets of paper.

"Brother Kas, read what's written there! But before anything else, tell us who issued them."

The congregation held its breath.

"It says, Paradizo Limited."

Inquisitive whispers and gesticulations followed. Everyone was calling his or her neighbor to witness.

"Now, Brother Kas, read the names and the total amount entered."

The music was playing softly, instruments making themselves unobtrusive, although drum rolls could be plainly heard. In a loud, clear voice, the deacon read, "Malundana Crispin, two thousand dollars!"

Incredulous exclamations. The deacon continued: "Bahati Amisi, five thousand dollars!"

The cries swelled, and applause began.

"Sister, *ya poids*,[1] Mokobe Hémeline, ten thousand dollars!"

Total frenzy ensued. Now booming, the orchestra accompanied the shouts of joy. The choir abidingly struck up some harmonies across several octaves. The flock was stamping its feet and dancing as it had never done before.

In the pulpit the pastor was relishing his triumph. His eyes ran over the audience, in full agreement with the generosity of spirit that, thanks to his intervention, reigned supreme. His glance came to a halt on Adeïto Kalisayi. Her eyes were raised, she was deep in prayer. The expression on her face didn't seem to share in the pervading joy. The pastor had noticed this woman before. There was something restrained and incredibly dignified about her. He knew nothing about her except that she always came with bodyguards who would wait for her at her car. She must be the wife of someone important—that's what she looked like, at least.

Then, not knowing what came over him, he closed his eyes and started speaking into the microphone. In the middle of prayers, the assembled clearly

---

1. Sister who carries her weight (financially, in influence, or physically, as you choose).

heard, "I see . . . I see a woman dressed in a bright pink suit, with gold earrings and real pearls. Her shoes are by Christian Louboutin, the great Cameroonian designer. She has appealed to God, and it seems to me she has not been heard as she deserves to be. She is sincere, her heart is full of light, and yet she feels as if she is tied up with ropes. May she come to see me in my office after services, I shall pray for her. If we must provoke the eternal fire to sever the bonds that shackle her, we shall do so and the chain shall be reduced to ashes. Oh, Almighty God!"

The rest of his words got lost in the brouhaha engulfing the place. At that moment the entire structure of the Church of Divine Multiplication was shaking, like a rocket heating up its nozzles before taking off toward an extragalactic firmament with the reckless, inspired Reverend Jonas Monkaya as its captain.

• • • • •

After giving instructions that he was not to be disturbed any further, the pastor sat down at his desk. Mama Reverend had gone home and all was quiet. While he waited, he picked up a Bible, opened it, tried to give his attention to a verse, but as he read the third word his mind was already elsewhere. He tried again but couldn't concentrate and decided to close the book. Watching the young woman just a few minutes earlier, he had sensed a troubled soul that needed permanent succor, lavished by a deeply compassionate man. An anointed man. That would be the very least by which to gain access to this kind of woman. One needed pure hands to touch the skin that the reverend presumed was there beneath the short fuchsia-colored silk skirt. If he had noticed the quality of her pumps, it was because of her ankles, in perfect harmony with the roundness of her knees and thighs. Standing behind the lectern was a good spot from which to observe the dazzling speed with which legs are crossed and uncrossed in the front row.

Since he'd noticed Adeïto Kalisayi, an idea had entered the reverend's head even before reaching his office. Business was taking off marvelously. Soon he would need an additional colleague to do secretarial work and bookkeeping, duties that were part of Brother Kasongo's work until now. Kas could hereafter be in charge of ministering to the faithful. That way the reverend would have more time for himself. The young woman, assuming she was free, of course, could very nicely take on the role of assistant. So he could let his gaze wander over her as he pleased all day long. He had set himself up across from her at the table where they were now counting the money. She could accompany him on his trips. Why not? He'd make her his deaconess. That's as far as his thoughts had led him when there was a knock on the door.

"Yes," he answered.

Adeïto came in. She sat down on the chair the pastor offered her.

"Welcome to my office, my sister."

"Indeed, it is the first time I'm paying you a visit, Reverend. Usually I don't stay after the service."

"Not a problem; I understand. Would you tell me your name, please?"

"Adeïto Kalisayi."

"You know, Sister Adeïto, this church is your home; it belongs to you. If by any chance you feel a need for comfort, human warmth, if you wish to unburden yourself, we are always here to welcome you."

"I don't know if I can accept all that, Reverend."

"My sister, prayer helps a great deal, believe me. Come more often. I will organize an evening of intercession just for you alone. I will do a laying on of hands for you."

"My husband doesn't let me go out much. He controls everything I do, and at night he prefers to have me nearby."

There was a knock on the door. The reverend frowned and was about to snub the intruder, but before he could open his mouth a giant in fatigues had already stepped into the office, a Kalashnikov over his shoulder. Gruffly, Bosco announced, "Madame, the commander called. He wants to see you right away."

"Very well, Bosco."

She turned back to the pastor. "I'll try to follow your advice, Reverend. I have to go now," she said and stood up. "May the Lord bless you."

"I am going to pray that—" was all the pastor could answer.

The door closed in the middle of his sentence, cutting him off brusquely. Stunned by the abrupt intrusion, he, the man of God, no longer felt so well. He felt a little like anyone else right after an unforeseen coitus interruptus. It was nothing; he would manage, he told himself, waiting for it to pass.

● ● ● ● ●

On the thirty-second floor of the United Nations building in New York, a frowning Chiara Argento was studying the Kamituga file. She closed it with a deep sigh. She removed her tortoise-shell glasses, removed the clip from her thick black hair, shook her heavy locks, and formed them into an easy ellipse at her neck. Then she leaned back in her seat more comfortably and reached for the cup of coffee on her desk. This couldn't work, she told herself. You couldn't have an army that functioned with troops coming from so many different places under various commands. Ever since the fall of the Roman Empire, people still weren't getting this. Today, again, the failure of the system had become clear. On the one hand, through the intervention of accords ratified by the international community, there were the armed forces of the DRC, infiltrated by rebels of indeterminate nationalities who could revolt whenever it suited them; on the other hand, you had an intervention force, also consisting of disparate troops, each with its own notion of things. And all of them assembled in the same country. The result was here: catastrophe for a long time to come.

Chiara Argento didn't even get incensed anymore; where Congo was concerned she had definitively adjusted to the state of affairs. They needed to move ahead, but methodically, as when you walk on glass with bare feet. The massacre of Kamituga wasn't easy to explain. Everybody was lying; you never knew with whom you were dealing, who was behind whom. It was the same at the French National Assembly, one hidden agenda replacing the next. Chiara was in charge of maintaining the peace in one of the largest vipers' nests history had ever produced, so vast that it managed to smother the screams of its millions of victims.

On the other hand, where the six Blue Berets were concerned, she had listened carefully all the way to the end of their death throes. She had summoned her collaborators as soon as the phone call from Kivu was received. Through the speakers scattered around the spacious office everyone was able until the very end to hear the crackling of the machine guns, the desperate shrieks of the soldiers, and the bark of the RPG-7. The six Uruguayans were stuck in a recess and resisted as best they could, but the assailants outnumbered them and Chiara had helplessly witnessed their extermination. She would never forget it. From that moment on, action was called for. The incident had shredded the institution's image, and to have it restored the perpetrators had to manifestly be arrested. Killing soldiers working for peace was like a crime against humanity; the guilty would not avoid trial by the International Criminal Court. But in the complicated game of the alliances in Congo, charging someone was one thing, but catching and incarcerating him was another kettle of fish. They had to act cleverly and with sangfroid, and until now that's what Chiara Argento had been striving to do.

The young woman rose, briefly arching her back to stretch her muscles. She was slender as a reed, wearing a short black dress, and her silhouette stood out against the backlight of the large window. Thirty-two floors below her, the East River was teeming with pleasure boats, barges carrying materials, ferries that from the distance looked like particularly well made miniatures. On the other bank was Long Island. To the right, beyond Belmont Island, you could see the steel arches of Gantry Plaza Park and the huge Pepsi-Cola sign, languid as a streetwalker waiting for the night to display her red neon lights.

Those responsible for the massacre were well known. Before they died, the Uruguayans had mentioned their names: Bizimungu and Commander Bob, the sector leader. But they had to be collared first—hard to do when the commonly accepted principle entailed sacrificing justice for peace. But to make peace it was often necessary to know how to wage war. Chiara Argento needed months of perseverance to wage hers. In narrow cohesion with her closest collaborator, Celio—an enigmatic Congolese who was keenly interested in mathematical concepts—they had done outstanding work: with false declarations, emails, and fanciful communications, they had managed to make Bizimungu a key player in the inter-Congolese dialogue. They'd succeeded in finding him a position in Kinshasa. The fish was finally drawn into the net. It was now a matter of closing it gently, of making as few waves as possible until the bastard could be transferred to the criminal court in The Hague. Still missing was a motivation for his actions. The fact that the incident had occurred in a place where they mined gold was certainly not irrelevant. Chiara sensed there was something shady going on, but, never mind, she would take it all the way, even if it would tarnish her administration.

She picked up the phone. In a soft voice, almost a whisper, she said, "Celio, could you set up a video-conference for me with Kinshasa? I'd like to speak with Mirnas. I'd like him to clarify one or two things for me. Could you arrange that? See you later. Whenever you want. Thanks."

• • • • •

Isookanga had just finished his day and sold his whole supply of Pure Swiss Water. He needed to increase the production again, he thought. With a surplus balance, he and Zhang Xia expected to look for additional partners soon. Isookanga was thinking of Little Modogo and Trésor. Even if it meant carrying boxes of merchandise for the others, it was better that Isookanga stimulate their enterprising spirit by granting them a franchise on Pure Swiss Water. He would suggest the plan to them when they returned.

One of them wasn't long in coming. As if ejected by the crowd, Modogo suddenly appeared exactly where Isookanga had just put down his cooler beside Shasha, who was cooking. She called out, "What's wrong with you, Modogo? Did you finally meet up with the devil?"

Before the boy could answer, Mukulutu Blindé, one of the nastiest *shégués*, came running after him, looking less than pleased. He rushed forward to grab Modogo. Fortunately, Isookanga, Shasha la Jactance, and Gianni Versace—testing his new approach in front of Marie Liboma—were present, or the kid would have had a rough time of it.

"Hey, calm down!" Isookanga commanded, arms spread wide to keep the fighters apart. "What's going on?"

"*Vieux na ngai.*[2] You know where I'm coming from?" Mukulutu raged.

"Explain, but calmly."

"From jail, Old One! Because of him!"

And Mukulutu Blindé shoved his fist in the direction of Little Modogo, who dodged him and snapped, "*Lââs perses, si elaï!*"[3]

"You see?" the fighter railed, beside himself. "Because of his curses I just spent a day in a jail cell."

"How come?" Isookanga asked.

"This morning I was going out to sell my ready-to-wear. You know very well, Old One, there's no one in all of Kinshasa who sells secondhand pants with the same fine names as I do. So this morning, just before I left to sell my stuff, this little asshole flung one of those spells he's used to casting on people in my face. So I said to myself, 'Mukulutu, stay calm.' I controlled myself and said nothing. But as soon as I got to the Avenue du Commerce, the cops and some business agents were all over me and hauled me off to jail. They said I had no vendor's permit and took away everything I had!"

"But what's Modogo got to do with that?"

"He's a sorcerer, Isoo! Don't you hear how he talks? He put a curse on me!"

---

2. "Old Man."
3. "The last person you'll see alive," from *Scream 1, 2,* and *3.*

Isookanga had mixed feelings. Mukulutu was exaggerating, but perhaps, yes, Modogo's words might have a harmful effect on someone who knew how to listen. When a rating agency speaks, maybe nothing happens right away, but the butterfly effect will be immediate. Everyone starts giving you funny looks, loan maturities are suddenly fraught with astronomical interest rates, and sometimes, even before you can seek any financial protection in a fiscal paradise, you could easily—like Madoff or Mukulutu[4]—find yourself in prison without a parachute, without anything, ruined. Mukulutu was right: depending on who uttered them, words could sometimes bear a disastrous weight and have an even greater effect than the shock of a photograph of oneself in handcuffs, unshaven, unkempt, on the front page of every newspaper.

"Yo, Modogo!" Shasha la Jactance called out, back on her stool. "Stop with those evil maxims of yours. Can't you see you're beginning to scare everybody?"

"I'm sick of it! Just wait till I'm grown up. I'm going to be part of the *kuluna*. Every gang wants me: the Benghazi, the Bétons Noirs, the Chinese, the Tcha-Batchuba; they're begging me to join. The Maï-Maï have water to defend themselves against bullets, the *kuluna* told me they'd have me—me and my dialogues—for protection."

"Do whatever you want; I'm going to see Zhang Xia. Mukulutu, the cops don't need anyone else to give you a hard time. Modogo, I'll see you in a bit. I have a proposal for you."

With these words Isookanga cut through the crowd, still dense in the late afternoon, and headed for the Avenue du Commerce.

Along the way he was thinking about *Raging Trade*, which was bothering him more and more. Lately Congo Bololo was having nothing but problems. He was no longer able to make any headway. The levels were constantly increasing, and he was paralyzed by the UN decisions because of maneuvers by American Diggers, Skulls and Bones, and the GGAP, all of whom were allies of that son of a bitch Kannibal Dawa. They were after his head; that was clear. Negotiations were in progress with Hiroshima-Naga, Blood and Oil, and Mass Graves Petroleum, to counter their strategy, but that would take time. Each was in it for himself.

---

4. Bernie Madoff, sentenced to 150 years in prison in 2009 for swindling through the establishment of a Ponzi scheme, the financial pyramid.

Isookanga thought of a different, faster solution: reinforce his aerial capacity once again. He knew that Uranium and Security had managed to break the codes of his aviation by default and had developed a new version of the Rafale plane. Substantially improved, it was a variant of the real Rafale: baptized Rafale 2.0 it had the original characteristics pushed to the extreme. The virtual mode was selling like hotcakes on the Internet and—in all kinds of video games—equipping the armies of those who wanted to maintain supremacy in the air and destroy anybody and anything in air combat. He had managed to penetrate most of the defense lines, and his antimissile protection safeguarded him from the majority of the projectiles. As for his maneuverability, it was like a wasp's at Mach 1.4 speed. Isookanga had to obtain some of these technological wonders. He would check the Net later to find out how to proceed.

"Old Tshitshi, how's it going?"

"Fine, Little One."

Old Tshitshi was busy sweeping the slab he used as a lookout post. Zhang Xia was sitting on the chair, the cooler by his side. Having crisscrossed the center of the city all day long, he was resting his legs.

"How's everything, Zhang Xia?"

"Fine, Isoo."

He sat down on the ground next to his friend.

"You have any news from home?"

"No, nothing. What I do know is that I should be there, with them."

"No doubt, Zhang Xia, but sometimes you have to make sacrifices."

"Easy for you to say. You don't have a wife, you don't have a child, you don't understand."

"I don't understand? *Kolela ya mbisi na kati ya mai, emonanaka*? Do you notice when a fish cries in the water? Please know that I'm quite capable of loving. If I don't have a wife, it's because they're only interested in my body, and I'm not circumcised, Zhang Xia. The worst possible curse for a man. And all because of my mother."

"Your mother? She did that to you?"

"When I was very little she forgot to take me to the circumciser, and now women disparage me. It gives me complexes. And that's very serious, so I've read; white people, when they have them, are never cured. I'm sure that this Oedipus Wikipedia talks about must have been in the same predicament as I.

His mother surely must have abandoned him when she forgot to have him circumcised—even though that's not what it says there. It made him very strange, though."

"Isoo, don't think about your mother like that. You know what Prozac is?"

Isookanga shook his head.

"If you keep this up, it's the medication you'll need to take someday. It's like a drug that makes you forget."

"But the women in Ekanga will never forget. So how does it change things?"

"Precisely! You'll be like those Westerners with never-ending psychological problems. It was simple before, with the great Mao Tse-Tung; they sent everyone like that to be reeducated. They came back cured. With scientific socialism we've accomplished miracles as well."

"Mao had healing gifts? More effective than Freud's?"

Isookanga considered this for a moment. "Tell me, this product . . . its producer in the West must be making tons of money. How many millions over there are unloved and uncircumcised? Just figure out the number of doses a day. It's like Pfizer; you know them?"

"I've heard of them."

"They're something else. You realize that with a molecule they call Viagra they managed to commercialize erections? Those pharmaceutical groups will end up by imposing their law on our behavior, Zhang Xia. I believe we should think about reducing the psychotropic drug market and investing in other areas—in personal development, for example. In any event, affected or not, I don't care. If I have a daughter, I'll call her Antigone in protest, like the daughter of Oedipus. She'll be the lineal heiress to Pure Swiss Water and not just foolishly sentimental like the other one.

"Well, Zhang Xia, there's no point in adding that what I've told you about my anatomy is strictly between us. All of it just to explain to you that you're here for the welfare of your family. Stop dreaming. You're like everyone else: you need Congo to develop yourself. In fact, there's something I want to talk to you about."

"Go ahead," Zhang Xia answered tersely.

"Commander Bizimungu, the visionary in the field of minerals I told you about, remember? They've given that guy control over my region, and he's as ready as I am to get rid of a lot of trees to exploit that part of the land legitimately."

"Exploit the minerals?"

"Yes, but that's not all; they'll have to build roads, establish infrastructures."

"Wait, I may have something for you." Zhang Xia pulled up his T-shirt. He wore a small plastic bag around his neck containing documents and a red passport with Mandarin ideograms on it. He took out a CD-ROM showing the same kind of characters. "See this? Everything you want to know about the location of minerals is here, on this disk."

Isookanga's eyes opened wide. "You're kidding! And you had that on you, all this time?"

"Of course."

"But Zhang Xia, that's worth a fortune! You can buy yourself a ticket back to China with that."

"You think I could trade it in for a ticket?"

"I'm sure Commander Bizimungu would be happy to pay just to find out what's on that disk. With that information he'll know exactly what's underneath every tree."

"Isoo, I think you're imagining things about that guy. I don't really feel the same way. He's a warlord. I know them well. It's in China that they went to work for the first time—and in the service of the same imperialists as in Congo. These people have a very short view of things. While they wreck the country, they still find good reasons for doing what they do. Anyone can make a mistake in the belief you're taking the right path. Even the Great Helmsman was wrong at least once.[5] Wanting to free himself from Soviet socialism, he tried an alternate route. That cost China millions of lives as a result of famine and malnutrition."

"Are you sure there weren't any plusses at all?" Isookanga tried to play it down. "Surely the nation must have benefited from the experiment somehow, because from then on you've been able to accumulate one success after another and build the new Chinese socialism."

"I don't see it that way. Nothing can rationalize the suffering that was inflicted; you can't justify disaster."

5. The Great Helmsman was one of the names for Mao Tse-Tung.—*Tr.'s note*

"Fine, we'll go see the commander. You who are in public works, you could do construction in Ekanga. In the meantime, you don't have to hang out with him. He trusts me. He knows that I'm up on the ancestral technologies, that because I'm familiar with the trees, I also anticipate what's below them. I'll tell him I know how they spot manganese, for instance. With your disk and my computer, I'll know where. I'll tell him that, and he'll pay us to get more information. We can make a lot of money, Zhang Xia. In the underground in the East he was involved in strategic matters. He's a pro, a major player in globalization."

The young Chinese couldn't stop thinking, "Globalization is crap to me."

● ● ● ● ●

As the sun began to set, relative calm had returned to the Great Market. Shasha was in front of the nook engrossed in her cooking. She was preparing antelope meat, *moto moko*,[6] on two braziers, *bitekuteku*,[7] and steamed fresh manioc. She was being especially meticulous, for the dishes were meant for Waldemar Mirnas, the peacekeeper. The two of them had something like a contract. Once a week she was his. He would come for her and take her to his house in Gombe. They had met one night in the rainy season, when the air was sticky and thick with humidity. She'd been oddly impressed with his immense height, but also with his hair, the color of dry straw. As for his icy blue eyes, until now she hadn't been able to gaze at them yet.

When they arrived at his place, he had been considerate and even treated her with kindness—until the moment when he ordered her to take off her clothes and put on a white apron, the kind maids wear. He came from the heart of the Baltic and had arrived in Congo with the same clichés that live in the collective unconscious of a large part of the planet with regard to African docility—both male and female. In view of the notorious insubordination of the people with whom Waldemar Mirnas was made to rub shoulders, he quickly realized these ideas were a bit obsolete. The malleability of the Congolese eluded all analysis. The major wanted to understand and had picked Shasha as a sample of the population. She had the temperament of a lynx, and Waldemar Mirnas wouldn't rest until he'd molded her according to his

6. Lightly smoked so the meat remains tender.
7. A vegetable.

wishes. Dollars were the appropriate tool for this purpose, and his money managed to ease the doubts one might have about oneself.

Forced to be naked and on her knees, Shasha's heart gave birth to an implacable hatred. She'd had her fill of tragedy and humiliation. The slaughter of the people in her village, the martyrdom of her parents, the escape with her little brothers, the death of the younger one, the trek on foot with Trésor to Kisangani, the compromises she had to agree to all along the way. And then the boat, the river, the arrival in Kin', the hunger, the street life, the prostitution at age fourteen.

Fortunately, it was as if Shasha was beside herself at the time. She would go on and on to someone; she wouldn't stop, not until the other person withdrew. If you were a pain in the ass, she was formidable, which is why the *shégués* had named her Shasha la Jactance, Kolo Eyoma.[8] By tooth and nail she had created a place at the Great Market for herself and Trésor. She needed dollars, but, simultaneously, her hate for those who gave them to her was mounting with each passing day—and that hate was focused specifically on Major Waldemar Mirnas, UN officer, on a mission of intervention in the Democratic Republic of Congo.

That particular night he came after sunset to pick her up and take her home with him. On the days she was with him he gave his domestic staff time off so he could be alone with her. When she entered his villa, she followed an established ritual and went straight to the kitchen to put down the dishes she had prepared. She knew what came next. He would sit down in an armchair and take off his shirt, exposing his bare torso. The man was a giant, more than one meter ninety-five tall. At forty, he'd grown corpulent. When La Jactance came back to the living room, she went directly to him. Still seated, he started taking off her clothes, one by one, the way you remove petals from a rare flower. When he came to her panties, he removed them slowly, to let the pinkish-hued bud in the center above her skinny thighs appear like a sunrise. Then, like a blind man lost in a labyrinth, he felt her body. He wrapped his hands around her bottom, hard as ebony, and inhaled the air around her. Then he put the little apron on her, which reached to just above the triangle of her sex. At that point she served him dinner. He took his time eating, savoring each mouthful, sensing the flavors, assimilating them, while creating images

8. The boss of damage.

in his mind: proteins, lipids, mineral salts, trace elements, iron, aluminum, coltan, manganese, germanium, cobalt, copper, uranium, bauxite, niobium, platinum, chrome, helium 3, beryl, soil with a high silicate content.

Standing near him, as always with lowered head while Mirnas enjoyed his meal, Shasha was flooded with shame. At first, as his hands were running all over her body, she felt as if she was burning beneath her skin; she thought she would get used to it, but the sensation of an acid bath persisted, despite everything. The peace workers came to her in 4 × 4s marked "UN," with the list of their earthly fantasies: dark, silky skin; smell of pepper seeping from armpits as intoxicating as cocaine; firm, supple flesh resisting any insistent pressure; hips moving like an unleashed wave, expert at leading you to perdition and abandoning you in the storm, the way billows would with an adrift castaway. In this ambiance, Shasha la Jactance felt like the lifebuoy that has sunk after use. Her hatred of the Lithuanian had turned so cold that the man, blinded by the whirlwind Shasha's body created during his oneiric travels, was aware of nothing.

Mirnas would have given anything for the dizzying journey to never stop. While he was thinking this, after a final forceful thrust, a lightning wave sharply tore his flesh and a gigantic crash ravaged his entire being, hurling him toward a kind of immateriality. Confused, he heard himself shout out a long lament while the child whore—legs bent, his palms around her bottom on the edge of the table—was pounding away with her pelvis locked around him. The head of his penis sunk deep in the blaze, Waldemar Mirnas was forced to surrender, realizing with each second what was happening to him: the never-ending reply of a surrogate eternity.

● ● ● ● ●

The MONUSCO office building was easy to spot. Given the floodlights, sandbags, cement obstacles, and the barbed wire surrounding it all the way to the top of the walls, it was obvious that it contained an organization unwilling to take any risks but at the same time making many enemies. Guards in blue helmets were on duty. The gate opened to let a 4 × 4 go through. Waldemar Mirnas entered his office and turned on his computer right away as he checked his watch. Almost time. It had to be close to 10:00 AM in New York. He sat down and waited.

Waldemar didn't like the conversation he was about to have. The inquest into the events at Kamituga continued. What was it they wanted this time, there in New York? There was no shortage of dead people in the country. Six more or six less wouldn't change a thing; this war was destined to continue. For once, everyone's interests coincided—except for those of the Congolese, of course. Everything was working out well for everyone in this conflict. Nothing ideological or political about it. It was simply a matter of being in control of the largest reserve of raw materials in the world, and may the best man win.

"Good morning, Miss Argento."

"Good morning, Major. Let's get right to the point, shall we? I wanted to talk with you about something of great concern to me. I've spent some time studying all the reports you've sent me. I really want to congratulate you; you've done fine work." Chiara Argent fell silent for a few moments. "When I look at the troops' assignments," she went on, "I can tell who was where and at what moment. However, if I check the workforce you had available in that sector, there are six soldiers too many."

"I don't understand," Mirnas responded ingenuously.

"Let's be clear, Major. The victims, were they really assigned to a reconnaissance mission, as your first report stated?"

Mirnas's face reddened. "Are you accusing me of lying?"

"I'd just like to understand. Their movements appear in the daily reports you sent to me. But if I count your men carefully, some of them supposedly participated in this reconnaissance mission as listed in your first report, but at the same time they were doing something else. There are six phantom soldiers, Major. Your numbers don't correspond to those we have in New York. But let's leave this for later, we'll certainly find the answer to this question. We're also waiting for the reports of the communications control in the region on the date of the massacre. It's a bit complicated, but we hope thereby to identify the activities of Commanders Bizimungu and Bob. I wanted you to be aware of that. Please check the movements of these six men on that day. I'll call you back very soon. That will be all for today, Major. Have a good afternoon."

And she hung up. The Lithuanian brooded for a moment, then banged his fist on the table and cursed. He promptly felt a cramp in his body and, leaning over, put his hand on his belly. For a while now the peacekeeper had been suffering from a pain that cut across his gut from all sides at once and would stay entrenched at the level of the plexus, causing him such ferocious heartburn that it took his breath away. He should worry less, he said to himself, pay attention to the ulcer. And that bitch in New York with her pathetic questions wasn't helping matters in the least. She should leave him alone with her reports and her insinuations. Six poor bastards had been buried long ago, over there in Uruguay; let them rest in peace.

Nausea overwhelmed him, his mouth filled with saliva and a taste of metal. He took a handkerchief from his pocket and wiped his lips. There was blood. He cursed. He should see a civilian doctor. The physicians treating his unit had found nothing, but something wasn't right: the atrocious pains, the bleeding—it wasn't normal.

• • • • •

"So what do you think, Celio?"

"Hard to say. He seemed pretty undaunted where the staff assignment was concerned. It's logical he would be defensive. When he feels a little more cornered, he can always claim there was a mistake in the report. And since there aren't any direct witnesses anymore, he can rest easy that he won't be linked to anything at all."

"You're forgetting Bizimungu," Chiara responded. "Commander Bob is just an underling. It's Kobra Zulu who's responsible for the massacre, but with impunity so prevalent in Congo that it's normal Mirnas wouldn't get flustered. He must be telling himself it will all blow over."

"You really think he's hiding something? After all, it may have been some business between Bizimungu, Commander Bob, and the Uruguayans, who were acting on their own. That's one hypothesis. But, as I think about it, this guy is not a professional in what he's being suspected of. His system must have some flaws. If I were you, I'd take a look at his accounts. A transfer always leaves tracks."

"I'll say a word or two about it in my reports to the International Criminal Court. I'm convinced he's actively involved in this affair—why else would he falsify any documents? To cover his men? What were they doing in Kamituga? Why this massacre? The rebels in that area don't usually open fire on our men in the context of their operations. They certainly went beyond that of a classical operation here. We're dealing with something else. There was an outburst."

Chiara Argento blinked briefly. Elbows on the table, she pointed a pen in her partner's direction. "There are far too many interests in Congo, Celio.

They all want to line their pockets. It's the only purpose of the rebellions; all of our reports prove it. Our Blue Berets act like everyone else—it's that simple."

She leaned back in the leather chair. "Haven't you noticed how slowly we've been made to do this inquest? Spokes in our wheels at every turn? Even though it concerns the murder of our men. As soon as I have the information I need, I'll try to move very fast. I suspect that sooner or later they'll tell us to stop the whole thing and deposit our files in the same cabinet where they dumped the black boxes of the Falcon that crashed on April 6, 1994, in the sky over Kigali."

11

CHANCE ELOKO PAMBA[1]
运气，没什么

Standing in front of the main station with a parcel under his arm, a suitcase at his feet, Old Lomama was gazing at a view of the Boulevard du 30-Juin that flowed majestic as a cement river lined with buildings taller than a *wenge* tree and two or three *lifakis* put end to end. The telecommunication poles stood in a row here, one every hundred meters, and the rooftops were crowned with satellite dishes and antennas. On this river, cars were making a hellish racket, calling out at one another with their roaring motors and honking horns. The people were like an ant or termite colony, about to invade the shops that made up the architecture, too ostentatious for Old Lomama's taste.

He cried out to a street vendor selling cigarettes, tissues, disposable razors, and organic aphrodisiac roots. "Young man, do you know Isookanga?"

"Isookanga who, Old One?"

"Isookanga Lolango Djokisa."[2]

"Don't know him, Old One, sorry."

---

1. "Luck is nothing."
2. "Isookanga Wounded Love."

Old Lomama called on another vendor, carrying neckties, some of them folded and draped over his left arm, while with his right hand he waved the others above his head like a viper's nest. "Tell me, son, you know Isookanga?"

"Isookanga who, Old One?"

"'Isookanga who, Isookanga who'? Does nobody in this city know my nephew, or what?"

The street vendor moved on, telling himself that the elders sometimes really thought they owned the world. And the mosquitoes after them.

Old Lomama tried his ploy three or four more times. Then, although he'd always known Kinshasa was a vast metropolis with many people, he realized he hadn't suspected that regarding a tight social fabric, that wasn't really the point. Nobody knew anyone.

Old Lomama was swept up in the flow of the crowd and found himself walking down the Avenue du Commerce, suitcase in hand. He approached a young man dressed in a Gucci sweat suit, headset on his ears, holding a digital pad, busy selling mobile phones stacked up in a messy pile on a small table. There were clones of all sorts—Samsung, Nokia, LG, Blackberry, iPhone—which, thanks to the technology transfers demanded by the government of the People's Republic of China, had been duplicated and mass-produced somewhere in the periphery of Wuhan or Nanjing.

"Son, do you know Isookanga?" he asked again.

"Isoo who? No, Old One."

"He's my nephew and I'm looking for him. He left the village a long time ago and I'd like to find him."

"If you really know him, there's a way. What's he like?"

"My nephew? He loves technology and everything modern. He's a determined man, my nephew, and a true Ekonda. Isookanga Lolango Djokisa—it's the name his mother and the ancestors gave him."

"That's it?" the vendor asked. "Wait, I'm looking." He tapped lightly on the touch screen of his pad, chanting, "Isookanga, technology, modernity, determined, Ekonda."

He punctuated his formula with two or three light touches of the tip of his middle finger, waited two seconds, then caressed the surface of the instrument three times, the way one does to the neck of a cat in the hope of flattering him.

"There! Read this, Old Man." And the young vendor handed Old Lomama the screen.

"Read it to me, please. I don't have my glasses."

"There's a story from AFP on Google sent by *Le Potentiel*:[3] 'Street Kids Riot at the Great Market.' Here it says, *'At a given moment the spokesperson of the shégués went to meet with the city's governor. Young Isookanga, native of Équateur Province, a pure Ekonda with a profound interest in technology and modernity, gave a determined speech,'* et cetera, et cetera."

"*Shégués*, who are they?"

"Old One, you don't know the *shégués*? You, in the village, you don't know anything. They're the street kids. Many of them live at the Great Market, not far from here. If you go see them, you'll find your nephew; he's their spokesman, that's what it says here," he said, showing his multimedia tool. "The screen never lies."

"Thank you, son. Which way is it?"

"That way, Old One. That will be a total of five dollars."

"What? Young man, don't you know the law of first birthright? Five dollars! You want to disrespect me?" And the old man left to avoid having any further dealings with the young boor who didn't know tradition.

"You, you Batwa, you're all the same. You don't know how to communicate. You'll never be on Twitter!" the vendor shouted as a curse.

As the old man walked to where the street children were, the service that the backlit mirror-like thing had provided left him speechless nevertheless. A little dismayed as well. "I asked people," Old Lomama said to himself, "nobody knew anything. But some little guy with a reflective screen manages to answer my question. Does that mean a machine is meant to replace mankind? Will people no longer look at the eyes of their human brother or sister, and soon refer only to a surface that generates images, numbers, and letters? And won't those who own such instruments be tempted to dominate others, the way this brazen young man just did, expecting to get five dollars?" The old man was skeptical. As he saw it, the modernity that loomed was to be feared. It wasn't with strings coming out of one's ears and with letters touched on a mirror that people would understand each other.

• • • • •

3. Agence France Presse.—*Tr.'s note*

"I'm looking for the *shégués*."

Old Lomama was addressing a saleswoman on whose colorful stall rows of mangoes were displayed, avocados, papayas, guavas, mangosteens, star fruits, and beef heart cut in half to show the white, creamy flesh.

"The *shégués*? Those sorcerers! Papa, you don't want to be looking for those kids. They're bad news; no one knows what to do with them."

"Papa, don't listen to her, they're just poor children," said a woman in a neighboring stall who was selling exactly the same things. "God is sending us trials and tribulations to show we're approaching the end of the world. Luke 21:23 says. '*But woe unto them that are with child, and to them that give suck.*' People no longer trust in Jesus. '*He has sent me to heal the broken-hearted,*' Isaiah 61:1. It's the fault of the parents; they're heathens—they no longer respect the Word of the Lord. Life itself has made these children the way they are. They're sacrificial lambs, innocents in the mouth of the lion of Judas."

A commotion began, the spectacle of a table collapsing and oranges and grapefruits scattering over the ground like tennis balls in a Roland-Garros Grand Slam tournament. Two boys, one tall and one short, trying to strangle each other, were stuck in a wrestling arm lock. Adults had to separate them and force them to pick up the citrus they had knocked all over the place.

"What did I just tell you, Papa? They're devils!"

"Son." Old Lomama was talking to one of the wild boys, now crouching down to pick up the oranges and wiping them with his filthy T-shirt. "Do you know Isookanga?"

"Old Isoo?" Little Modogo answered. "Absolutely!"

"You know where I can find him?"

"You have to ask Shasha la Jactance. She lives over there," he said, pointing in the direction of the recess in the administrative building.

"Thank you, son. But tell me why you're fighting with someone bigger than you? It's not good; you should respect your elders."

"Respect Mukulutu? Never! He started it. I was just passing by, doing nothing, I only said, '*Yowaa nex!*' And he hit me. But I'm not afraid of him; I have a *toungle*," the little one said, showing a sharpened screwdriver from a crease in his jeans. "When I grow up I'm going to be *kuluna*. They all want me!" he added like an oracle.

Old Lomama left the urchin to gathering the spilled fruit and continued his search.

People were constantly going in and out of the market's office. Running the site was no picnic. In addition to protecting its security, cleaning up, and distributing the vending spaces and daily permits to do business, the place was busy because it's where one had to obtain a spot, a table. Those who worked there were courted from morning to night; it was never empty. Over a few beers they talked about inflation and the rate of the dollar; they compared the volume of trade with Ankara and Rio; they speculated on a growth of more than six percent thanks to the Bandundu, among others, who had managed to profit intelligently from the manioc bubble; they discussed the need to bypass the embargo on the Schengen visas by intensifying close ties with Vietnam and India, after Dubai and China; a sister-in-law was making three or four round-trips a year going there.[4]

On a bench outside sat a guy, probably the attendant—he looked like someone who had no real reason to be there—his legs crossed, calm, staring at the sky, chin in hand.

"Son, I'm looking for Shasha something."

"There's no Shasha working here."

"They told me she lived here."

The man gave the Ekonda a closer look. "You mean over there?" he asked, pointing to the ground and a recess farther down. "Papa, the Shasha you're talking about is a street child. Is she the one you're looking for?"

"Yes," Uncle Lomama answered.

"Are you a relative of hers?" the attendant asked with a hint of disdain.

"No, but I'm looking for Isookanga, my sister's son. They told me I should ask Shasha."

The man looked Old Lomama up and down. "Are you Pygmy?"

"I'm Ekonda."

"Same thing. Sit down over here," he told him pointing next to him. "They're not there at this hour of the day; they're working their trade. But they'll be here soon. Just be patient. Besides, they have nowhere else to go."

Sitting on the bench with his suitcase at his feet, Old Lomama had nothing better to do than watch the activity around him. It was unbelievable; he'd

4. The Schengen visa allows one to travel throughout the Schengen area; this consists of twenty-six countries, twenty-two of which are part of the EU, the other four are part of the EFTA states.—*Tr.'s note*

never seen so many people at the same time. So this was it, the big city. And all that merchandise. What they used here in one day, in terms of textiles, kitchen utensils, hardware, stationery, tools, could have supplied his village for at least twenty years. And, the abundance notwithstanding, children were sleeping in the street; it was inhuman. Old Lomama didn't get it. To go so far as to abandon a child? To what kind of extreme were people driven to reach this point?

Old Lomama didn't understand the strange movement regulating society, which seemed akin to what happens between the two earthenware bowls used to distill *lotoko*.[5] The bowls communicate via a tin pipe, but one is full of manioc and fermented corn; assisted by the fire below it, it empties out into the other, one drop at a time, very slowly, as if there were never enough. As if the Danaids, showing up in hell filling perforated barrels with water, were becoming super-stingy.[6]

When Isookanga showed up in front of the administration building, he was so surprised that he dropped his now empty cooler. He rushed into his uncle's arms and embraced him.

"Isookanga, is that really you?"

"Yes, it's really me."

"It's really you?"

"It's really me."

"It's really you?"

"It's really me. Oh, Uncle, what a surprise! When did you arrive? How did you find me?"

"Son, I'm here. What did you expect? That I'd abandon you all by yourself in a city like Kinshasa that contains more hyenas and jackals than the entire lower region of Tshuapa? With what I've seen here so far I'm even less reassured. I just arrived by boat. I've been asking all over to find you, and it was a machine that told me where to look."

Isookanga didn't understand what the old man meant but didn't react, all too excited to find part of himself again.

5. Alcohol made of manioc and corn.

6. In Greek mythology, the fifty Danaids killed their husbands on their wedding night and were then condemned to carry water in a sieve for all eternity. It refers to the futility of any task that can never be completed.—*Tr.'s note*

"They told me you live over there," Old Lomama went on, indicating the recess.

Isookanga didn't answer.

"They also told me you're in business."

"I sell the finest water in Kinshasa, Uncle."

"Sell water! You forget that in the village anyone can knock on your door and ask for a drink."

"I'm involved in globalization; everything is opened up. I have an associate whose name is Zhang Xia. I'll introduce him to you."

"Zhang Xia, what tribe is that?"

"He's Chinese, Uncle."

"Ah!"

"I'm also consultant to a man who protects Salonga Park."

"That's good, but where is your house, Isookanga?"

"Uncle, Pure Swiss Water is enjoying a favorable trade balance right now. Soon I'll be able to have what I want. Zhang Xia and I are in the process of getting franchises. We already have two of them and there are more on a waiting list."

Old Lomama didn't understand a word of his nephew's gibberish, but what he did retain was the bit about protecting Salonga. That's why he'd come, after all. But he repeated his question: "Where is your house, Isookanga?"

"I don't have one, Uncle."

"Well, I for one have to find a hotel. Get me there."

Old Lomama and Isookanga disappeared into the city of Kinshasa through narrow alleys, expecting to see a hotel sign.

"Uncle, did you really come here to look for me?"

"I'm here for one thing, one thing only: to save the village. In the hope your stay here has straightened out your ideas, I would like to take you back so that you can accomplish your task."

Isookanga said nothing.

His uncle continued: "And I'm here because of that blasted antenna, too, which is going to kill us yet. Nkoi Mobali is dead already."

"Nkoi Mobali?"

"The big leopard. If we let it go, if we say nothing to the authorities, God only knows what more they're capable of shoving down our throats down there in the forest."

"How long are you staying, Uncle?"

"As briefly as possible, but however long I need to."

"Life in Kin' is expensive."

"Because you people here are poor. In the forest we're not. It gives me everything I need to deal with the big city. I'm afraid of nothing. I have my coffee plantation. We've been lucky lately. With the problems in Ivory Coast, the anti-FARC operations in Colombia,[7] the drought in Tanzania, the hurricanes in Central America, our coffee is selling higher than last year. Your friend Bwale helped me sell off a few bags and here I am."

Isookanga had forgotten. When he was still there, he hadn't imagined one could earn a dime from the local area. "Uncle, let's try it here."

The hotel receptionist who welcomed them suggested a reasonably priced room with twin beds.

"Uncle," Isookanga said, "you shouldn't. I can sleep with my friends."

"Be quiet, Isookanga! You're staying with me. Surely you don't expect me to let my nephew sleep in the open air when I have a room."

The young man didn't object for long. The hotel was at street level. They were given the key to a minuscule room at the end of a hallway, but it was clean, and, besides, the old man had brought *pagnes* with him. With a glance around, he put down his suitcase. "You still have business to do at the Great Market?"

"Yes, Uncle."

"Go deal with it. I'll be waiting for you. Here, take this," he added, handing him a few banknotes. "Buy us something to eat and drink on your way back."

"I have money, Uncle."

"I'll eat your money later on; I'm not retired yet. Here. Go now!"

"Damn! He's something else, the old man," Isookanga thought. "He managed to get to Kinshasa without asking anyone for anything. Then he finds me, too, and in no time at that."

• • • • •

Isookanga was happy with his uncle's presence. Despite his popularity he was still lonely in Kinshasa. From now on he had someone he could count on.

---

7. FARC stands for the Revolutionary Armed Forces of Colombia, one of the world's richest guerilla armies.—*Tr.'s note*

Then the memory of Aude Martin came back to him. The Africanist had sent him an email. She apologized for her behavior, saying she'd been carried away by emotions she still hadn't been able to identify. She regretted having gone crazy that last night. She was living with someone she loved in Brussels, and what had happened with Isookanga had been nothing but a misunderstanding. She was all torn up, she wrote.

"You can never overestimate the love of women," Isookanga thought, realistic but a little disappointed nevertheless. *"You don't love me, you just love my doggy style,"* Snoop Dogg declared to a girl in a video clip. The rapper never deluded himself; he was strong and completely aware of people's intrinsic nature.

Isookanga reached the market, where Shasha la Jactance and the others were getting ready for their nocturnal activities.

"Old Isoo, the great mediator, is back!" Mukulutu Blindé announced. "Shasha told me your uncle has arrived from the village, Old One."

"He came to get you?" Marie Liboma asked. "Hey, you're spoiled, Old Isoo. Me, I do all I can. I go to church every now and then. I pray. I try not to roam around on Sunday, but no one ever comes. You think luck has shafted me the same way my parents did?" the girl wondered, compulsively chewing her gum. "Yet, they say, '*Chance, eloko pamba*,'[8] but I still don't see anything coming my way, Old Isoo."

"*Mwana mwasi, soki akufi naino te, koseka ye te.*[9] Maybe you'll be a star, Marie. In Hollywood, at the festival of Berlin, in Cannes—they love girls like you."

"Are you serious, Isoo?"

"I'm sure of it. My uncle, he's a chief. He has powers. He has to know where his people are every moment of the day. He undoubtedly consulted a diviner to find me. But now," Isookanga added, "I'm a true Kinshasan and I intend to remain one."

The young man gathered up a few things hidden in a nook of the recess. "Gotta run, guys. I'm staying with my uncle tonight. At the hotel. See you tomorrow."

"Later, Old Isoo," the kids responded.

8. Slogan of the *shégués*.
9. "As long as the youth isn't dead, don't laugh about him."

Trésor, crouching on the ground, knees against his chest, was staring in the distance. The conversation didn't seem to concern him; his thoughts were with his parents and with what seemed like a cosmological void.

Isookanga headed for Old Tshitshi's slab. He had to speak with Zhang Xia. Since his uncle had arrived, his ideas had become even clearer. It seemed that Bizimungu trusted him. If Isookanga were to offer him a trade for what was on the disk, he was sure Bizimungu wouldn't hesitate to put money on the table just to get his hands on the information. He was going to make Zhang Xia a proposal. He absolutely had to make this disk pay off. How could he have kept it hidden until now? It was time for him to go back to China. Isookanga knew his buddy had a rather morose nature, but it was worse than usual right now. He needed to rejoin his wife and son as soon as possible or else he was going to snap—Isookanga could feel it coming.

When he came to the Avenue du Commerce, he again found a pensive Zhang Xia. The Pygmy knew what to confine himself to; he preferred shaking him up a little.

"How's it going, Zhang Xia?" he said, greeting him with undue enthusiasm.

"All right, nothing much," the Chinese answered.

"My uncle is here."

"Your uncle?"

"Yes, my mother's big brother. He arrived from the village today. I'll introduce you later. But that's not what I'm here for. I brought my computer. We're going to take a more serious look at your disk. Where is it?"

Zhang Xia stuck his hand under his T-shirt, pulled out the little plastic bag, and took out the disk.

Isookanga had already opened his computer and just had to press a button. He placed the disk in the machine and waited for it to load. A window opened and a map of Congo appeared, peppered with symbols in every color, matching Chinese ideograms. Isookanga couldn't get over it. He knew the country was rich but, no, not to this extent.

"Zhang Xia, just look at that! If heaven on earth wasn't created here, I don't know where it would be," he observed, suddenly creationist. "But where did you get this CD?"

"The day my boss let me go he sent me to drop it off at a compatriot's house. I couldn't find him, so I kept the disk."

"It's worth gold. How could the Chinese put such a detailed map of the minerals together?"

"We, too, have our rockets. And they don't just put monkeys in them; there are satellites and probes as well."

"Zhang Xia, you and I now know where the minerals are in all of Congo. Can you imagine? Listen. I'm going back to Bizimungu and I'm going to propose that he buy this map. He loves gold and diamonds. He'll be thrilled."

"Isoo, are you sure he's going to pay for that? Perhaps he won't believe us; there are many forgeries that come from China."

"Look." Isookanga bent over the screen, pointing a finger. "You see this here, close to Lower Congo? What does it say?"

"Tungsten," Zhang Xia read.

"You see? All I have to do is disclose this to him, for instance. He can go there if he wants and see for himself; it's not that far. He'll extract a few samples, have them analyzed, and he'll have proof that I'm not making this up."

"Making up, what's that?"

"Lies. Then we sell him only the map of minerals in Salonga. What does it say over there, near Monkoto?"

"Gold," the translator responded.

"Damn, there's plenty of it! How much do you need for a plane ticket? A thousand, two thousand dollars? That's not so much, he'll pay. Gold is what he loves most."

"Whatever you say, Isoo, we can always try."

"It'll work. You must get back to China. I can't stand seeing that sad face of yours any longer. We should get a Salonga map in French. With Photoshop that's easy. Let me study this a few more minutes. Hey, look! What is that sign there, on the Bateke Plateau?"

"Germanium."

The two spent some more time together while Old Tshitshi stayed out of the way, not wanting to interfere. Besides, the younger ones were deeply immersed, their heads practically inside the screen, in a universe that Old Tshitshi didn't really comprehend—too virtual for him.

After consulting with Zhang Xia, Isookanga went back to the hotel. On the way he passed a small market, where he bought some pieces of braised chicken, goat cheese, manioc rolls, and a few sweet drinks. He found Uncle Lomama settled in, his suitcase unpacked. They ate and drank.

As he was examining the ceiling through the glass bottle, the uncle asked, "Tell me. That visionary friend of yours, what has he done for Salonga? If you collaborate with him you could give him advice; you know the forest almost as well as I do. Look what I brought."

Old Lomama fished a package wrapped in a *pagne* out from under the bed. He unfolded a large leopard skin.

"What's that?"

"I already told you—it's Nkoi Mobali. Remember, I told you about him a long time ago."

"Vaguely; it does ring a bell," Isookanga answered.

"The village is having problems, Isookanga. At the time, you thought installing the telecommunications antenna was beneficial, but look at this skin. Look at the injuries. It's a disaster, Isoo. And you'll never guess what killed Nkoi Mobali. Warthogs! You realize that? Those animals don't live in leopard territory, and yet they ran into each other because for some reason or other the warthogs must have been forced out of their own region. In their confrontation Nkoi Mobali couldn't have been in peak condition and was brought down in spite of his strength. Don't forget that the leopard eats only every once in a while. Because food is becoming scarce—even for a superior creature like Nkoi Mobali—he must not have eaten for more than three weeks. I never imagined that in my lifetime something like this could happen."

"But, Uncle, how is all of this possible?"

"Something's happening in the ecosystem, Isookanga. Parameters are in the process of changing radically. If a force of nature like Nkoi Mobali can't be secure, then I don't hold out much hope for the skin of the Ekonda, my son."

"But, Uncle, we can't keep on living on the periphery of the world. We have to join it, or else it won't be long before we'll drop off the radar screen completely."

"Nkoi Mobali was part of the world; he was actually one of its crucial links. His death represents a serious imbalance. If you disrespect nature, she'll take revenge. Your friend, Salonga's protector, does he know about the leopard's death?"

"No, Uncle, I don't think so."

"A true leader has to be told about what goes on in his territory. I must inform him. As chief of the clan that's my duty."

Isookanga agreed. "I'll be happy to take you there, Uncle."

"Isoo, open another one of those sweet drinks for me, please."

"Another Fanta, Uncle? Of course."

• • • • •

The next day, the nephew showed his uncle the city: the countless decrepit cars, the emissions of mercury and lead from motors running on diesel, the merchandise piled high in shop windows and overflowing onto sidewalks, the gridlock of human beings in the streets, people calling out at one another as if their craziness were everyone's business.

When they reached the office building of the Conservation Service of Salonga National Park, one of the bodyguards received them. He didn't open his mouth, as usual. He escorted the visitors to the fifth-floor office of Kiro Bizimungu.

As they entered, the former rebel stood up and extended his hand warmly.

"Old One, I'd like to introduce my uncle, Old Lomama."

"I'm very happy to meet you," Bizimungu said. "Your nephew has told me all about you. Please have a seat."

"Pleased to meet you, too," the uncle responded as he sat down.

"I am your managing director. I oversee Salonga National Park."

"That's what my nephew said, which is why I wanted to meet you. Let me show you something." Old Lomama unwrapped what he had in his lap and placed the leopard's skin on the desk.

"And this is?" Bizimungu asked, somewhat surprised.

"This is Nkoi Mobali."

Then Old Lomama told Kiro Bizimungu about the sad fate of the great leopard. If Commander Bizimungu was a true leader, it was his duty to protect pillars of society such as Nkoi Mobali, his duty to try to understand what might have made the warthogs flee to find themselves so far from their own habitat. Had they fled from telecommunication poles? Could there have been some dangerous global warming that drove them to seek the coolness in the forest of the Ekonda? What were these rays the antenna sent forth that caused an animal not to respect the good order of things anymore and take the liberty to do just about anything, even kill a leopard like Nkoi Mobali? Couldn't anyone see that even someone as worthy as his nephew had been diverted from his duty because of the waves the tower emitted?

And the old man explained how the warthogs had turned mad because of the antenna. He showed the holes their jaws had made in the big cat's skin. He added that perhaps he was old, that maybe he knew nothing about anything, but, still, he was noticing that the laws ruling the world today were a great deal more merciless than the laws of the forest he'd known before. At the speed things were going, it would no longer be just warthogs eating leopards, but people would end up devouring each other one day as well.

Kiro Bizimungu listened carefully to the old man and thanked him for recognizing the importance of the situation. "I still have many people to see, I need to find out more. I have to visit the ministers of the Environment, Telecommunications, and of Scientific Research."

Since he had finished making his pitch, the uncle rolled up the skin again and stood up. "Isookanga, I'll leave you here with your friend. I have things to do. Don't move, I'll take a taxi. First I'm going to the UN office. People should know that Nkoi Mobali is dead and that his body was viciously mutilated. Commander, sir, I'm very pleased to have spoken with you. If you should come through Ekanga, do come and see me. You'll have no trouble finding me." And he left the room, the parcel under his arm.

"He's a tough one, your uncle," Bizimungu said, almost in a whisper. "Is he always like that?"

"Often worse. The old man talks too much. And when he talks, you'd think he's hoping the trees will grow even faster. It's incredible, Old One."

"All right, then. You have anything to say to me? About our last conversation? Your uncle didn't tell you anything new?"

"I have something better." Isookanga pulled his seat closer to the desk. "Imagine, Old One, I have an associate, he's Chinese."

"You, you have a Chinese associate?"

"Didn't I tell you I'm working as an internationalist?"

"Go on."

"So my associate has a CD-ROM that lists all the minerals in Congo."

"Little One, you actually have that? But it's what I've been looking for since . . . Bring it to me right away. I'll pay."

"Right away isn't possible."

"Why not?"

"Everything is written in Chinese; it needs to be translated."

"So? Your associate can do that, can't he?"

"Yes, but I have to work out a French version on Photoshop, and that will take a little time. And I also have to talk to him, make sure he's all right with selling it to you."

"Little One, bring it here. I'll pay a thousand dollars in cash."

"Two thousand, and I'll convince him to sell it to you."

"Have no fear. Translate it and come back with your friend."

They exchanged a few more words about those narrow-minded spirits who understood nothing about science, technology, and money, and then Isookanga went back to his business. He had to corner Zhang Xia to finalize this transaction.

● ● ● ● ●

Wang Lideng went back several times more to see Gong Xiyan. Each time, he refused the tea she offered him while his questions became increasingly more intrusive. What had she been doing on such and such a date? Whom did she see on a particular day, and what was she up to with this or that friend in a given place? She always answered, never hid anything, but it did make her understand that Public Safety was keeping a close eye on her, determined to check her comings and goings.

That specific afternoon, the man spoke even more harshly. He demanded additional proof of Zhang Xia's presence in Kinshasa, but all she could supply were printouts of the emails she had already provided before.

"These documents are meaningless!" he flung at her. "I'm beginning to lose patience with you. You're hiding the truth about your husband's activities, Madame. I won't let you go on like this. You must know that the business he's involved in is extremely serious. We've arrested his associate, this Liu Kaï you claim you hardly know. And yet, to the best of our knowledge, he and your husband are the chief administrators of Eternal Dragon. They've used this company to take advantage of the government's programs and have gotten their hands on very important funds intended for the creation of certain enterprises, primary of which are those dealing with energy, infrastructure building, and the supply of raw materials.

"Your husband and Liu Kaï understood that, but Eternal Dragon made the mistake of beginning its activities in Chongqing, where I'm the one who makes sure the law is applied. We think they left for Congo to escape their responsibilities but had to come back for reasons we don't yet know. For now, only Liu Kaï is under lock and key and has admitted everything. Your husband ought to follow his example, and we'll see to it that their entire network is brought down. There still are a few cancers spreading rot though some branches of Chongqing's autonomous city government, Madame."

Gong Xiyan felt numb, rendered powerless by a threat whose existence she hadn't even known about until very recently. Zhang Xia had never told her anything about Eternal Dragon's activities. In the modest living room the interrogation continued. The director of Public Safety and the young woman were sitting as usual—she in a corner of the sofa and he at right angles to her in the armchair. Despite the sternness he conveyed, this time was a first, for Director Wang had accepted the tea she was serving. During his previous visits a smile would sometimes escape from him, but this day his brows remained set in an imperturbable frown. The man was observing her from behind his glasses and sensed her profound dismay, her composure notwithstanding. Her head was down and she was once again avoiding eye contact. It was almost painful. It created a terrible tension in him; the only thing that could have appeased him would have been the possibility of looking deep into her eyes—he was perfectly well aware of it. Every now and then, their knees touched briefly and the director would feel a shiver run through the young woman.

"But, Madame, to obtain these funds, some people, unfortunately, resort to fraud and to corrupting functionaries. They facilitate the acquisition of subsidies, and the money is then divided among them. Within the scope of our campaign to clean this up, many have already been arrested. Surely you have heard about the trials that have recently taken place. The Chongqing government has decided to put a definitive stop to this kind of behavior. Too bad for your husband."

Gong Xiyan didn't know what to think. Why had Zhang Xia never told her anything, and what was he still hiding from her now? Indeed, she told herself, the whole business must be extremely serious if the chief of police was coming to her in person to lead the investigation.

"I'm only trying to help you, Madame," he whispered.

Gong Xiyan turned to the police officer. Through the reflection of his glasses she couldn't see his look, but something she couldn't put her finger on made her feel that he seemed to be softening. Hearing what the director had revealed to her, she felt she was losing ground. Her knee leaned against his for just an instant, and that brought her unexpected reassurance. Through that moment of their bodies' physical contact, it was as if her consternation had passed over to him to be mitigated there. Without raising her head, her eyes passed over his broad torso, which was leaning toward her. The man's chest looked like an impenetrable wall, but at the same time, paradoxically, she felt the urge to rest against it, if only for a moment. She moved her knee away from his. The room was silent. The warning lights of the electronic devices—television set, converter, the computer screen in sleep mode—were watching them, gently blushing without blinking. On various pieces of furniture, framed photographs were speechlessly staring at the strange couple, avoiding each other's gaze as best they could.

Wang Lideng continued: "There's nothing more I can do for your husband. As soon as the agents of my division get hold of him, he will be incarcerated. As for you, if you persist in remaining silent, I can only consider you as an accomplice and treat you accordingly."

Gong Xiyan leaned her head forward, her long hair covering her graceful profile. She did not respond. It lasted for a while. Wang Lideng breathed softly. She turned her face toward him. Her eyes were glistening behind a touching liquid veil, which managed to throw the director of Public Safety completely off balance. That very same instant a single tear rolled to the edge of the woman's eyelid and slid in slow motion onto her velvety cheek. It was as if a giant screen were illuminated right before Wang Lideng's face and the images of Gong Li in cinemascope in *The Forbidden City* assaulted the brain and entire being of Chongqing's chief of police. Before him he saw the empress, her routed army, its captains on their knees—awaiting their execution—and the emperor, triumphant, haughty, staring at the empress, whose passionate look expressed both resignation and sublime defiance.

Emotions surged up and submerged him, literally like a tsunami. He should never have become personally involved in this Eternal Dragon business, he told himself. Without premeditation, his trembling hand moved between the woman's knees. He felt something like a vise tightening abruptly around his right hand. He pushed on and right away the pressure stopped. As if slipping into a furnace of silk and heat, his fingers advanced to stop a little beyond the hem of her skirt. Wang Lideng wouldn't be able to say exactly what happened next. Outside in the distance, on the horizon, Chongqing's metropolis raised its skyscraper columns, which appeared behind a translucent screen, turning yellow from the microparticles of mercury and sulfur, from the various excretions that infused the hot, moist air of the Szechuan summer.

12

GAME OVER!

游戏结束！

A phone call wouldn't do. Discussing Kamituga legitimately would require at least a one-on-one conversation. Chiara Argento was sitting across from her boss, the assistant secretary general of peacekeeping operations. She had been waiting for telephone data for months. By calling on the State Department, especially when it concerned a criminal inquest, that should theoretically be easy to obtain. But, in fact, nothing was simple. They talked about defense secrets, about the greater interest of the United States, about noninterference in the domestic politics of a partner country. Chiara Argento had to go up six floors to try to unravel this tangled web.

"How are you, Miss Argento? We really haven't had any time to see much of each other lately. Files, files, and more files . . . You wanted to talk to me about that horrifying drama in Kamituga?"

"Yes, indeed, Mr. Secretary. I am missing a crucial element: the record of communications between Kiro Bizimungu and Commander Bob on the day of the massacre. I'd also like to know who else had any telephone contact with them, on that day as well as the preceding ones. Is that so difficult?"

"It's not a matter of difficulty, Miss Argento, but in the scope of Africom,[1] all of the region's telecommunications are picked up by the satellite antenna of Mount Karisimbi, which, unfortunately, is located in Rwanda. Consequently, we need to go through the authorities of that country. That's where it gets stuck; they stop short at giving us that information."

"Don't we have any way of forcing them?"

"Yes, we do. But the Americans need them for other things. They provide them with assistance for certain missions—in Darfur, for example. They're very useful, you know; the Rwandans are the foothold for the Americans in Africa, just as Congo once was."

"Let's give them something in exchange."

"Like what?"

"Satellite images of the Hutu positions of the FDLR, for instance, that would be useful to them. They've been looking for them for how long now? Ten, fifteen years? Suggest that they offer Rwanda a non-permanent seat on the Security Council, or have them promise to make Rwanda the fifty-first state of the Union. What do I know? Make them some sort of offer."

"You're awfully persistent, Miss Argento."

"Not persistent, just conscientious."

The assistant secretary general gave a short laugh. He held out his hand to the young woman. "I'll see what I can do," he promised.

Responding to his gesture, she got up.

• • • • •

Since that conversation, Chiara Argento's progress had moved ahead almost as she wanted it to. It still took some time, but in the end she had the information she'd requested, and its analysis was enlightening. Kiro Bizimungu and Commander Bob had definitely been in touch right before and right after the massacre, just as she'd imagined. Hence, she could easily back up the indictment from Mariama Fall, the public prosecutor of the International Criminal Court. By studying the data, one noticed that if one trusted the relay records, in addition to the two allegedly guilty parties, another phone call had been made from an unknown number within the same perimeter as the

---

1. African Command: the U.S. Army's command in Africa.

MONUSCO command. Chiara was sure there was a conspiracy between the Blue Berets and Mirnas. She had enough information to push ahead with the tightening of the net. They now had to influence the Congolese government.

"Celio?" she said, the phone glued to her ear.

"Yes," a somewhat shaky voice answered.

"I must speak with Mr. Kiamba. Right now. Let's hope he's done what he had to do. I have complete confidence in you here, but don't forget that if your contacts don't work, we'll have to start from scratch. I need some confirmation from Kinshasa. Is that possible?"

Chiara Argento wanted to know where things stood with the capture of Bizimungu. The operation required the implementation of a joint UN-DRC military intervention. And some people were dragging their feet. She didn't understand the apathy holding back the Congolese leaders just when it was time to neutralize those individuals who were destructive to them. True enough, the ramifications were endless and so complex that the whole thing resembled an immense game of jackstraws threatening to collapse if the right little stick wasn't moved. Everyone was linked by acceptable or unacceptable activities: small arrangements between friends, or worse, between enemies. In short, everyone had everyone else by the balls in this country.

The phone rang.

"I'm connecting you to Kinshasa, to the presidency," her Congolese colleague said.

"Thank you, that was fast. Hello, Mr. Kiamba? How are you? Yes, I'm calling for news. J-1? All right. So I can count on you? Good-bye."

Chiara hung up. A shiver ran down her spine. The ball was now rolling. The next night, Kiro Bizimungu would be neutralized and sent off to the ICC—as long as it went without a hitch and there were no escapes, of course. All she had to do now was give the green light and a UN plane would be waiting on the tarmac of Ndjili to carry out the transfer to The Hague.

There was one more person Chiara had to call. She picked up the phone. "I would like to speak with Mrs. Mariama Fall, please. Madame Prosecutor? Yes, this is Chiara Argento."

Though it was late after she'd made a few calls and written a report, Chiara felt perfectly fine, something that hadn't happened in a long time. The Kamituga file was practically closed. More than a year's work. She noticed the adrenaline running through each capillary of her body. A delicious feeling. She had lost some friends along the way. Some had rejected her because of her obduracy. The UN was going to be dragged through the mud, that was certain. According to elements in the investigation Mariama Fall had in hand, significant sums of money had passed through Waldemar Mirnas's accounts, considering what a peacekeeping officer earned. They had already been blocked, according to the public prosecutor. The Lithuanian was done for. Chiara wanted to relax, finally let herself go. Her glance fell quite logically on the telephone on her desk. She picked it up and dialed a number. As it was ringing, Chiara became aware of the long lament of a ship's siren on the East River, which was shimmering softly in the dark, like a fragment of the Milky Way.

"Celio?" she heard herself say. "Igor Stravinsky. Does that appeal to you?" she asked. "What are you doing tonight?"

Her voice was low. There was a silence. "No, just asking. No, everything's fine. Good night. See you tomorrow, Celio."

And she hung up. There wouldn't be any concert this evening. In any case, she wasn't going by herself. Her nervous system would simply have to adjust to it. Why had she called him? Chiara decided to walk a little and then take a taxi home, find some peace of mind and be back in the comfort of her Park Avenue apartment again.

• • • • •

At the wheel of his 4 × 4, Mirnas was driving mechanically, seeing nothing. Not merely because it was one in the morning but mainly because he was fiendishly preoccupied. Along Lumumba Boulevard music was playing on a few terraces to cheer up the lingering drinkers. Kerosene lamps shining here and there showed a few vending women still busy keeping the drunkards going with grilled chicken thighs and hot *pili-pili* sauce.[2]

Mirnas fretted as if jinxed by the little lights that enchanted the Kinshasa nights. He had other things to worry about. By chance he'd passed by the airport to take a look at a load of munitions and transmission gear leaving for Bunia. He was very surprised to note the presence of another plane he knew well, one that was used during delicate UN missions. The aircraft was waiting, standing slightly apart from the other planes. The Lithuanian had grabbed his phone and made a few calls. Apparently, no one in his department knew

---

2. *Pili-pili* is a standard African (very) hot sauce.—*Tr.'s note*

that one of their jets had just landed. They should have told him: he was in charge of everything that had to do with the logistics of MONUSCO.

His mind began to race. The flight was obviously trying to be as discreet as possible. As a MONUSCO officer, Waldemar Mirnas had certain prerogatives. He called the tower and was told that the plane's final destination was Schiphol Airport in the Netherlands. So a prisoner transfer shouldn't be ruled out, and the only one who might be the object of a careful investigation recently was Bizimungu.

Things weren't looking good for Mirnas. Thanks to Congo he had managed to collect a nice little nest egg; the anticipation of the former rebel under lock and key meant he, too, needed to be concerned about being arrested, sent back to Lithuania, forced to face trial and be disgraced, and in the gray gloom of his homeland contribute to the unemployment statistics for all time. There went the endless beaches of Rio, the Bay of Phuket, and the Manila sidewalks.

Next he had phoned his Congolese contacts and from them found out the worst. The military was about to arrest Bizimungu at home that very night. They expected a scramble to occur during the changing of his guards. Those who were expected for the night wouldn't appear, having been rendered harmless long before. While Waldemar Mirnas was driving around like a lunatic, unaware of all that was awaiting him, the trap was tightening around Kiro Bizimungu, also known as Commander Kobra Zulu.

• • • • •

For the hundredth time Waldemar Mirnas tapped his telephone: Bizimungu was still not answering. "Damn, what's he doing? How can he sleep with that conscience of his?" the Blue Beret wondered. He tried again. Just before the answering machine started, Bizimungu's voice was heard. "Hello?"

"This is Mirnas. Get a move on; they're coming for you!"

"What are you saying? You know that's impossible. And why should they?"

"Why?" Mirnas was stuttering with rage. "You're done for, Bizimungu! And I tell you, I'm the only one throwing you a lifeline right now. Take it, there's still time. It's all over, everyone has dropped you. If you don't believe me, take a look outside and see if your bodyguards are there. There'll be nobody to protect you tonight. They've already been neutralized. I'm coming from the airport; there's a plane waiting to take you to The Hague. I'd be far away by now if I were you, but it's up to you. Good night, Commander."

Phone in hand, Bizimungu tried to come down to earth. Like a robot he went to the door and called his men. "Déo!"

Indeed, no one was there. What had Mirnas said? That the military was coming to break down his door and grab him? That a plane was waiting at this very moment to take him to The Hague, to the International Criminal Court?

Bizimungu should move, but an immense weight kept him from doing so. It seemed as if his warrior's reflexes were no longer functioning. He knew the syndrome. His instructors had warned him about it long ago. He had seen it in the eyes of his enemies during the different wars he'd lived through. Kiro Bizimungu was aware that fear had entered him and that he needed to get rid of it as quickly as possible. Many before him had felt it and he hadn't liked the deplorable display.

He should flee, now, as his Tutsi brothers had always done these past decades. First, when still a young boy, he had had to flee Rwanda with his parents during the umpteenth slaughter and find refuge in Congo. They'd settled in the Masisi Territory. The serene life in the green hills, like those in their own country, had lasted a few years until 1994, the year of the genocide. Bizimungu didn't have time to finish his first year at the University of Kisangani.

In neighboring Rwanda, the Tutsis were once again in danger, and the dead were already being counted by the hundreds of thousands. Since April, for three months a genocide had been in progress. They needed men over there and declared that Kiro Bizimungu was capable of delivering those who'd been seized inside the circles of hell. The accounts of the survivors who had managed to flee to Zaire were straight out of Dante. The Hutus had abandoned their reserve and decided to apply a final solution to the Hutu-Tutsi problem. A blood pact was made. Then, under the false pretext that the glittering bird that had exploded in the sky was a heavenly sign, an entire people had turned on one another, and the inhabitants of the hills began to systematically kill their neighbors, their spouses, their children, everything that could possibly be likened to a Mututsi.

People were hounded and slaughtered with machetes as if they were cattle. They were chased into the deepest marshes. Every surface of the territory was swept to drive them out and exterminate them. They were compared to something even more foul than vermin. Their dismembered corpses were tossed into latrines. In the churches flesh and blood grew to be plentiful enough for diabolic libations. Not a single one was to be left. Those among the Hutus who didn't want to share the cup of blood with their brothers were killed on the spot—tens of thousands of them. The entire country had become an immense slaughterhouse, where the object of the holocaust was human flesh, preferably Tutsi flesh. They had to be eliminated to the last one. And it was going to be easy.

Dashing down a hill after a few days walking across Burundi, Bizimungu and those with him had come upon a squad of uniformed men in rubber boots. The soldiers of the Rwandan Patriotic Front. They quickly taught Bizimungu how to handle an automatic rifle. Retaliation was on the march; it was a matter of life and death and reigned supreme in a country that was no more than a vast field of corpses. The counteroffensive was merciless. The RPF moved ahead like a steamroller. Bizimungu might have been paralyzed by what he'd seen along the way, but the hate that rained down on him there was such that, despite everything, his body and his Kalashnikov managed to vent themselves. With rage and violence. Preceded by unrelenting firepower, he and the others crisscrossed the country like exterminating angels.

Ahead of them the population fled by the hundreds of thousands. With women, children, weapons, munitions, central bank, administration, and all of those who had shattered skulls with bludgeons, torn flesh apart with grenades, slaughtered entire families with machetes, cut shins to prevent anyone from fleeing, and disemboweled pregnant women, in order to confirm their willingness to go as far as they could, all of those who had wanted to purify the country with Tutsi blood, suddenly realized that the sign Imana[3] had sent them in the very beginning didn't mean what they had thought it meant. That he had revealed the falcon's prophecy to them only to curse them better. Like Cain, they then began to flee, straight ahead—toward a hypothetical salvation and toward a frontier that now demarcated heaven and hell. They hastily sped straight to the Zairian border. Hoping that there, at least, they would reach some sort of purgatory.

Bizimungu, too, wanted to leave the Rwandan soil where he had been forced to walk over corpses to keep moving. The images he'd put up with during this death march told him to leave the country. With his battalion, they pursued the Hutus to the rampart the Zairian forces had built at the border.

---

3. "God" in Kinyarwanda.

The Rwandan armed forces and the Interhamwe,[4] their backs up against the wall, were forced to counterattack. Lost in his memories, Bizimungu remembered that night very clearly: mortars, never-ending cannons, Katyusha rockets, surface-to-surface missiles began to roar, and in a hellish racket the sky was set ablaze. Both sides deployed all the firepower they had, and tons of white-hot metal traversed the firmament, which turned scarlet. Many came very close to going mad because of the continuously thundering cannons, mercilessly churning up the hills together with the men on them. A tropical Armageddon but with no redemption this time.

Telephone calls flew back and forth between Paris and New York. At that moment, the magic of the Whites intervened. One could see a cloud of turquoise hue envelop the assassins to protect them, and the border suddenly opened up like a gate.[5] Surrounded by the bloodthirsty Rwandan armed forces, more than a million Hutu refugees poured into Kivu like a flow of toxic sludge. At the frontier, demobilized and dressed in civvies, Bizimungu was nevertheless identified as an RPF combatant and arrested. He told the Zairian military that he was from Masisi and that he had nothing to do with what was happening on the other side, that he wanted to go home. He offered them his services.

To gain their leniency and try to halt the looming epidemic, young Kiro had had to help the soldiers retrieve the hundreds of corpses that were drifting on Lake Kivu during the night. In the morning he brought out the bodies of his brothers who'd been killed in Rwanda. What weighed little arrived first. At dawn the young man was forced to plunge his hands into the lake to pull out the placentas floating in the water. Soon after came the newborns and the fetuses, forced from women's bellies with daggers. Only then did the adult bodies appear, whitened because they'd been in the water so long. When he pulled them out, they disintegrated in his hands. Even the soldiers felt sorry for him then. They gave him back his freedom and without stopping he ran all the way home to North Kivu.

When the question arose of establishing the AFDL to bring down President Mobutu in Zaire and introduce themselves into the country's machinery

4. Militias, perpetrators of the genocide in Rwanda.
5. Operation Turquoise was led by the French according to Resolution 929 adopted on June 22, 1994, by the UN Security Council.

through the Banyamulenge concept,[6] they came looking for him again. But not only that. That season under the ancestral canopy, shielded from the objectives of surveillance satellites, the forest was secretly filled with the sound of skulls being bludgeoned, with the death rattles of victims of decapitation, and with the screams of those on whom they now took vengeance: men, women, children, all of them. For they had to hunt down and eliminate the Hutus, who had kept on doing their filthy work on Congolese soil and who might return to Rwanda to pursue the never-ending cycle of revenge. Next came the rebellion of the RCD, the CNDP,[7] and more blood, more carnage, always more. They would go through several other acronyms—those weren't in short supply—making Kiro dizzy.

The algorithm Congo Inc. had been created at the moment that Africa was being chopped up in Berlin between November 1884 and February 1885. Under Leopold II's sharecropping, they had hastily developed it so they could supply the whole world with rubber from the equator, without which the industrial era wouldn't have expanded as rapidly as it needed to at the time. Subsequently, its contribution to the First World War effort had been crucial, even if that war—most of it—could have been fought on horseback, without Congo, even if things had changed since the Germans had further developed synthetic rubber in 1914. The involvement of Congo Inc. in the Second World War proved decisive.

The final point had come with the concept of putting the uranium of Shinkolobwe at the disposal of the United States of America, which destroyed Hiroshima and Nagasaki once and for all, launching the theory of nuclear deterrence at the same time, and for all time. It contributed vastly to the devastation of Vietnam by allowing the Bell UH1-Huey helicopters, sides gaping wide, to spit millions of sprays of the copper from Likasi and Kolwezi from high in the sky over towns and countryside from Danang to Hanoi, via Huế, Vinh, Lao Cai, Lang Son, and the port of Haiphong.

During the so-called Cold War, the algorithm had remained red-hot. The fuel that guaranteed proper functioning could also be made up of men.

---

6. The term propagated in the fall of 1996 to legitimize the Congolese nationality of the Tutsis settled in Congo and demand that nationality through warfare. It was created by connecting the Kinyarwanda prefix "*banya*" ("who comes from") to Mulenge, the name of a Congolese village.

7. National Congress for the Defense of the People.—*Tr.'s note*

Warriors such as the Ngwaka, Mbunza, Luba, Basakata, and Lokele of Mobutu Sese Seko, like spearheads on Africa's battlefields, went to shed their blood from Biafra to Aouzou, passing through the Front Line—in front of Angola and Cuba—through Rwanda on the Byumba end in 1990. Disposable humans could also participate in the dirty work and in coups d'état. Loyal to Bismarck's testament,[8] Congo Inc. more recently had been appointed as the accredited supplier of internationalism, responsible for the delivery of strategic minerals for the conquest of space, the manufacturing of sophisticated armaments, the oil industry, and the production of high-tech telecommunications material.

While Commander Kobra Zulu was cornered, they had continued to perfect the algorithm somewhere between Washington, London, Brussels, and Kigali. Kiro Bizimungu, now stigmatized in the international community as a Monyamulenge,[9] had become a simple active coefficient, an ordinary strategic datum, a mechanism of the most common sort.

● ● ● ● ●

The man was feeling tired but this was not the time for fatigue. He went to his room.

"Adeïto, wake up, we're leaving!"

"What are you talking about?"

"They just alerted me: UN soldiers and the FARDC[10] will be here in a few minutes. They're coming to arrest me. Move!"

Adeïto jumped out of bed and quickly stuffed two or three things in a bag. She hurriedly threw on a skirt and a red silk blouse, *babouches*—Moroccan slippers—on her feet. Bizimungu also grabbed a bag and crammed it with banknotes he kept in his wardrobe and a pistol. They went out. The ex-commander had to open the gate himself. They got into the 4 × 4 and drove off immediately.

Neither of them spoke a word. The only sounds were the purring of the motor and the friction of the tires on the asphalt. They were each absorbed in their own thoughts. The landscape slipped by. Bizimungu hadn't thought

8. See the epigraph to this book.
9. The singular form of "Banyamulenge."
10. Armed forces of the DRC.

of any specific place to go; they had to get out of town first. His instinct quite naturally led him toward the east. They took Lumumba Boulevard.

"We'll go to the church," Adeïto announced.

"Listen, this is not the right moment."

"Yes, it's exactly the right moment. That's where we'll take refuge. Nobody will think of looking for you there. If they don't find you at home, they'll watch every road. We'll wait at the pastor's house until things settle down."

Kiro Bizimungu clearly loathed the Church of Divine Multiplication, but he had no choice and Adeïto was right, of course.

The night had actually begun well. Bizimungu's body had miraculously regained stamina that evening. Adeïto's prayers hadn't had the same effect as usual. His skin had barely touched hers when his strength came back. He hadn't heard the phone ring when Mirnas called. Desperately focusing on his pleasure, the only things he had noticed were his own blood pounding in his head and the sudden sensation of emptying out from below into her body.

"Take a right here," she said.

Bizimungu turned the wheel onto a shabby little street. It was dark. Garbage and stones were strewn over the ground. The 4 × 4 began to sway.

"Go straight," Adeïto ordered.

The former rebel was driving carefully, trying hard to go as fast as possible. They rolled on for a moment. Suddenly, there was a dull knocking followed by the characteristic brief hiss of a flat tire.

"Shit!" Bizimungu swore as he braked. "We have a flat. Is the church far?"

At that very moment, without any warning Adeïto opened the car door and started running straight ahead down the winding alleyway.

"Hey there, wait!" Bizimungu yelled, jumping out to follow her.

Adeïto only heard the wild beating of her heart. She had hiked up her skirt, dropped her *babouches*, and made off so fast she could hardly breathe, in bare feet, with tousled hair.

"*Moyibi*,"[11] she shouted into the night. "*Moyibi!*"

She ran as fast as she could, ripping the blouse she was wearing with her hands. In the outlying neighborhoods the police were rarely present. Throughout the country they never did what they were expected to do. And so, instead of patiently waiting for the law to take over, people would take

---

11. "Thief!"

care of matters themselves. Lights were turned on, doors opened in the darkness. They picked up manioc pestles and iron bars, rubble and worn-out tires. When Adeïto suddenly turned up at an intersection just before the church, the number of onlookers was already large. The young woman stopped amid the people. They were all looking at her as if she were an apparition. She spread her legs, slipped a hand under her skirt, pulled it out, and held it up, shimmering with a gelatinous substance.

"*Botala eloko asali ngai!*"[12] she screamed, showing her fingers tainted by Kiro Bizimungu's sperm. "*Auti ko violer ngai!*"[13]

Dripping with sweat, the offender had reached the intersection as well. At the woman's words the people froze. The word "rape" she uttered had long since branded the Congolese conscience, and they no longer tolerated it. They threw themselves on Kiro Bizimungu. When he understood what was going to happen to him, it was too late. Everyone wanted to make him pay for his hideous crime.

"She's my wife," he managed to get out.

But his voice was no more than a whisper. He was overcome with fear. It had settled down in him, and he could no longer react; his body and his mind simply no longer obeyed him.

Bizimungu's entreaties didn't seem to impress the crowd. They were vying for the honor of placing a tire around his neck and setting it on fire. Many had come out of mere curiosity but weren't averse to lending a hand should it be needed. Trying to arouse some compassion from a possible compatriot, Bizimungu tried to speak in Kiswahili, but no one in the elbowing crowd seemed to pay any attention to what he was saying. On the contrary, it only intensified the anger and hate of those who didn't speak that language. Kiro Bizimungu was all too familiar with that situation and fully cognizant of the necklace torture. He'd heard people talk of it. Apparently, what nobody ever forgets are the screams of the tortured begging for water and the appalling smell of burning flesh.

Cutting through the crowd, some youths showed up waving old tires above their heads and shouting threats. It was a motley crew: men, women, children, swaggerers, good-for-nothings, abused girls, two or three *kulunas* who had simply been bored, but among them there were also survivors of

12. "Look what he's done to me!"
13. "He just raped me!"

ethnic cleansing as well as their sympathizers. An immense free-for-all had overtaken the intersection. The former warlord was held tightly by the throng around him that kept him from moving. All he could do was weep and beg, but who could hear him?

Since his arms were jammed flat down alongside his body by his countless executioners, he couldn't keep the first tire from being pulled down over his head, which was now girding his body more efficiently than any strap. A desperate "Ah!" was heard. Despite his attempts at any gesticulation, two more tires were added to the first one. Managed by an expert hand, one of them remained at the level of his neck. Drums sounded in the distance, a chant floated through the night. *Halleluiah, Halleluiah, Amen . . .* Nocturnal praises from the Church of Divine Multiplication carried all the way to the crossroads. Some of the faithful who had heard the ruckus came to see what was going on.

"Sister *na ngai, likambo nini?*"[14]

Adeïto didn't answer. It was as if she were paralyzed.

Soon the pastor arrived. "Sister Adeïto, what are you doing here at this hour?"

She remained silent, distant. Her torn blouse exposed a heavy chest, glistening with sweat. At the same time, the people around Bizimungu were growing restless, wanting to add still more tires. The man himself could no longer look at his wife, his gaze forced to stay riveted on the menacing hands fluttering around him like a swarm of bats.

"Adeïto, who is that man?"

The young woman clung to the reverend's shirt, sputtering into his ear, "He says he's my husband, but he never was!"

The Reverend Jonas Monkaya turned toward the crowd in anger. He raised his arms, wanting to say "My brothers!" and adding a few verses of mercy, but the words wouldn't come out of his mouth. All he could manage was "Wait!"

Not loud enough, however, for anyone to hear him. They had just sprinkled Bizimungu with gasoline. Since the siege of Kinshasa in August 1998, the inhabitants of Ndjili knew the drill. They'd learned how to burn an aggressor. Suddenly, all at the same time, they moved away from their victim. One broke

---

14. "Sister, what's happening?"

free and with an elegant gesture tossed a burning paper torch. With a small explosion, the fire caught instantly. Kiro Bizimungu fell down.

He struggled on the ground, letting out heart-rending screams, restrained by the burning tires that released the roar of a furnace. Flames licked the sand around him. After his clothes melted, his skin began to break up in large pinkish patches. A characteristic, exceptionally heavy odor of grilled meat wafted through the air. The former warlord was still stirring but soundlessly now. His teeth showed through his lips, burnt to ashes. The flames buckled his body until the moment when he finally adopted a curled-up position, arms folded against his chest like a monkey that's been smoked. Fat oozed and slid to the ground in swift little flames like lizard tongues. His sex organ was the last member to move. In one enormous erection it lengthened and swelled for a few more seconds, arousing regret among some of the women present and provoking jealousy in a few of the men.

And then there was almost nothing left of either the tires or of Kiro Bizimungu, aka Commander Kobra Zulu, except for a dull carbon monolith, smoking and smelly, whose alabaster eyes were questioning the crowd. The onlookers stood idly by, watching the spectacle a little longer. When they realized there was nothing exciting happening anymore, they left the scene, leaving it to the emaciated dogs that now approached the unexpected banquet, still sniffing it with a great deal of suspicion.

Then the Reverend Monkaya took off his jacket and draped it over Adeïto Kalisayi's shoulders.

"Come," he said.

She let him lead her away.

"The church is your home and I am here. I've been praying incessantly. Don't be afraid of anything anymore; the ties have just been severed. The eternal fire has been powerfully displayed. Listen."

Drums were beating, praise songs were drifting over the neighborhood, the night had grown tranquil again.

• • • • •

Isookanga and Zhang Xia had purchased a folder to hold the CD-ROM as well as a hard copy in French by way of a graphic Adobe software program. The Pygmy put on his black T-shirt with the skull and crossbones again. His chain gleamed at his chest. The two friends entered the building where Bizimungu had his offices. Since the bodyguards weren't around, they took the elevator to the fifth floor. The office door was open; Isookanga went in, followed by Zhang Xia.

Before they could even begin to understand the situation, a large number of police officers grabbed each of them by the belt of their pants while others pointed their Kalashnikovs at them.

"*Likambo nini?*"[15] Isookanga cried out.

"Watch out, he's dangerous. I know him." Colonel Mosisa had just spoken. "Well, Mr. Isookanga, since we're seeing each other again . . ."

"Tell your men to let go of us!"

"What are you two doing here?"

"I came to see Commander Bizimungu. I'm entitled."

"When did you last see him?"

"A few days ago, but I called him yesterday."

"You called him?"

"We were supposed to see each other to talk about Salonga. I'm a consultant."

"Do you know where he is?"

"We had an appointment right here."

"We're looking for him, too, and he may have been found, but we're not sure. His 4 × 4 was seen abandoned in Ndjili, but there's no trace of him. They did pick up a burnt body not far from there, but they can't formally identify it. Okay . . . Take them away!"

"Hey!" Isookanga shouted.

"I'm innocent!" Zhang Xia resisted.

"Yes, Governor, it's the same little guy, and the Chinese teacher is with him. I'll spell his name for you: Z-h-a-n-g and then X-i-a, Zhang Xia. All right." And Colonel Mosisa hung up.

It didn't seem real, he told himself. The spokesman for the *shégués* had crossed his path once again, but this time the officer had no intention of letting him off. He was going to try hard to lock up the Pygmy for a long time, at least for being complicit in a crime against humanity. Orders from above had come in; they were looking for traces of Kiro Bizimungu all across Kinshasa and beyond. The command was that he be captured at any price. Colonel Mosisa was still waiting for the identification results of the body found at

15. "What's going on?"

Ndjili, but in the meantime he and his men had entered the office to carry out a search, and both the Pygmy and his accomplice had appeared like rats at the bottom of a mousetrap.

His phone vibrated. "Yes. Oh, good! But, Governor, this guy doesn't deserve any attenuating circumstances whatsoever! All right. It will be done. But only because you say so." He hung up again.

"Shit!" Colonel Mosisa cursed out loud.

On the governor's orders the guy had to be set free. They were afraid the *shégués* would start to riot, and there was no point in inviting any antagonism from even just part of the population. Letting the Pygmy go was yet one more of those bloody stupid things that prevented Congo from moving forward as it should, Colonel Mosisa was thinking, but politics were politics, orders were orders, and he simply had to go along with it. As for the Chinese, he needed to be detained; the Immigration Service would be coming for him later.

• • • • •

Shortly after his brief incarceration, Isookanga headed instinctively for the Great Market.

"Hey, Old Isoo, we heard you'd been taken to jail by some cops together with Zhang Xia," Shasha la Jactance called to him, returning to the recess with Modogo.

"I was the one who saw you, Old Isoo. I saw how they were hauling you off in their cars. I tossed off a magic formula so their cars would break down a little further down, but it didn't work; you were going too fast."

"Not to worry, guys, I'm here. I was able to get out. The governor himself had them let me go."

"And Zhang Xia?" Shasha asked.

"He wasn't as lucky; they kept him, but I don't know why. We didn't do anything wrong; we were just going to pay Old Bizimungu a visit. I'll give them until tomorrow. If they haven't let him go by then, I'll get him out myself."

"Old Isoo, I'll go with you if you want," Marie Liboma whispered. "You know how sharp I can be."

"And we know your strength, Old One," Jacula la Safrane added. "We know your negotiating power."

Indeed, Isookanga knew how to bargain, but he had a bad feeling about Zhang Xia. He had tried pleading on his behalf but in vain; the colonel didn't want to hear a word. He wasn't going to let the Chinese go. And there was nothing pleasant about the cell they'd been made to share with a dozen other guys; he had a hard time imagining his friend spending one night, or more, in there.

• • • • •

In the dark jail Zhang Xia was crouching in a corner. Nobody had bothered him and Isookanga when they came in, but they did have to pay for the candle burning in the center of the 6 × 4 meters room. He and his pal had discussed their immediate future, created several hypotheses about what might have happened to Bizimungu, and assessed the relationship with him and the problems he may have run into. However, Colonel Mosisa's information about the burnt corpse that was found in Ndjili worried them.

After two solid hours a cop had come for Isookanga, but Zhang Xia was made to wait, without a clue. Since his boss had disappeared he felt that events were increasingly getting away from him. It's true that when the wind blows the grass inevitably bows down. Hence, the premonitions he'd been having lately were no mere flukes. Zhang Xia had tried to keep going with the illusion, but having illusions is believing that what you wish for is true, that what you hope for is true.

He just hoped that everything that was happening to him wouldn't be connected to what his wife had written him about the man who had visited her. She hadn't said so specifically, but he assumed it concerned a police officer. What could he possibly have done to justify a police investigation at his house in Chongqing? Zhang Xia was getting lost in speculations. He, who so fervently wished to go home to China, now caught himself dreading a possible return.

• • • • •

"You can't keep going on that way, Isookanga. No one in our family has ever gone to prison. But since it did happen to you, it's because you're supposed to learn a lesson from it. *Mayi eninganaka pamba te.*"[16]

16. "Water doesn't move without a reason." A proverb meaning that an event may conceal a hidden cause.

As usual, Old Lomama took advantage of the incident to offer his opinion. "This is the city and the laws are different here; they're pitiless. They're not for you. It could also mean your destiny is a different one, my son."

Isookanga was listening but only with one ear, because the decision of going back to the village was beginning to force its way into his head. And for that he didn't need any uncle. He was ready. As soon as Zhang Xia came out of jail he would go home to his family, no doubt about that. And the young Ekonda couldn't see pursuing a career in Pure Swiss Water all by himself. In a city like Kinshasa, where money reigned supreme, it shouldn't be too difficult to find someone who eventually might want to buy the map of minerals now that Bizimungu had vanished. The capital city was all good and well, but the life one led here didn't offer a lot of security as Isookanga was slowly beginning to realize. As they say, *Esika okoma te, mapata ekweya.*[17] In the village there was the telecommunications antenna; there was shelter and food. He had just acquired a solar USB charger from Amin Jamal, an Indian Shiite, and he owned the map of raw materials burned onto a digital disk. What else did an internationalist need to live the way he should?

"Uncle?"

"Yes, Isookanga?"

"Did you know there's gold, bitumen, and diamonds in the Ekonda soil?"

"Of course, Little One. Way back when, how do you think those who chose to hunt with a rifle managed? Lead couldn't always be found, but mystical stones and nuggets were there for the taking. They used those in the cannons they fired, and it worked just fine."

"But why didn't you ever tell me this before? Especially since you never stop saying that a traditional chief must be the same as Goldman Sachs: he must know everything."

"First of all, you're not a chief yet. And furthermore, men being what they are, if you tell them about such things, good-bye calves, cows, pigs: nobody will want to work anymore. Little One, have you ever heard of gold fever? Of those addicted to by-products? Of those who throw themselves out of Wall Street buildings because they bet on a rising market? 'Insider trading,' you know what that means? All that is lethal, believe me—me, your uncle here

17. "There where you didn't make it, clouds fell down." A proverb meaning you have illusions about what you see from a distance. You think that over there it's heaven on earth—in other words, "the grass is always greener."

before you. My son, I think it's high time for you to get your ideas together and find a satisfactory wife who loves you and takes care of you."

"That, Uncle, is not possible."

"Isookanga, it may hurt a little, but with a good circumciser anything is possible."

"But, Uncle—"

"I don't want to hear it! While you were gone, your mother sent me a letter. She told me that it's never too late to do the right thing."

"But, Uncle—"

"Be quiet!"

• • • • •

Early the next day, Isookanga presented himself with leaden feet at the headquarters of the Rapid Intervention Police. It was a series of one-story buildings in front of which lines of people came asking for news about a member of their family or a friend who'd been arrested. And they were many. In addition, there were men in navy uniforms everywhere. Isookanga asked for the office of Colonel Mosisa and waited a long time before he could see him. The officer arrived, escorted by his assistant, a second lieutenant, tall, doe-eyed, with a disdainful look and an arrogant bosom barely held together by a blue woolen shirt.

"Well, now, Isookanga," said the colonel when he noticed the young Pygmy among the petitioners.

"My respects, Colonel."

"I suppose it's me you've come to see?"

"I'm here for news about Zhang Xia, Colonel."

"Ah? But you're too late, Little One. They came for him during the night. He must be flying across the Red Sea as we speak. They sent him back to China."

"Don't say that, Colonel. I really have to see him!" Isookanga exclaimed.

"Little One, your friend is uncivil. We received information about him from his embassy. He's dangerous and being sought by the police in his country. A firing squad is almost certainly waiting for him there. He has corrupted functionaries, and in his country corruption is officially outlawed. The governor intends to maintain a good relationship with the Chinese. They asked us politely and we've extradited him. There's nothing to be done; we have to defer to the international laws or else where are we headed?"

Congo Inc.

Inhaling deeply, the second lieutenant smiled approvingly. Before the buttons on her female uniform could pop into his face, Colonel Mosisa cut short the conversation: "Well, Little One, behave yourself from now on; stop the petty crime. Here in the DRC it's different, we have human rights here. Did you notice how kind I've been to you? Where your friend lives, it's no joke; there's the law. Fine. Have a good day, Little One."

The colonel stepped aside to let the aide-de-camp pass. She preceded him into the office with a deadly sway to her gait, one of those no one would have dared teach in a police academy worthy of its name.

● ● ● ● ●

The day had been especially bitter for Isookanga. Zhang Xia was gone, and it seemed to the young Ekonda that he had bequeathed him part of his gloom. His friend had to go back to China, but the circumstances were a little rough, he thought; they'd been unable to separate as true brothers by promising to see each other again, face-to-face one last time, bowing deeply. The Pygmy felt as saddened as a trader when a speculative bubble bursts just before Nasdaq closes on Friday afternoon. Isookanga's gross domestic product was at its lowest and his heart was heavy. He wandered through the city for part of the day, then sought refuge in the hotel while Old Lomama was trying to get an audience with some ministers. Isookanga had been staring at the ceiling for hours, remembering his times with Zhang Xia. All he hoped for now was that his friend would reach China safely and that nothing untoward would befall him. Surely the colonel had exaggerated a little; Zhang Xia was no criminal.

At sunset he went to the Great Market to see his friends the *shégués*. Gianni Versace presented Marie Liboma with a very rare label, signed Jean-Paul Knott, which he had just sewn onto the sleeve of a secondhand jacket. Shasha la Jactance was sitting on a small stool, cooking. She was busy chopping something on a flat stone with a machete, something Isookanga couldn't identify right away.

"Shasha, what's that? What are you cutting up there?"

"Nothing, Old Isoo. I'm making dinner for my MONUSCO guy. I should feed him properly. After all, he came to defend Congo's civil population, didn't he? He should get what he deserves, Old Isoo. He should be seasoned, he and the dishes he eats."

"But Shasha, what are those hairs you're chopping up?"

"Nothing. I'm telling you, Old Isoo, it's just between that white man and me. We're *shégués*, no? They even call us child sorcerers. But you know my name, Old Isoo; it's Shasha la Jactance, Kolo Eyoma. *Alukaki, azui.*"[18]

Isookanga didn't persist. But he was familiar with the practice. In the village he'd heard that scorned concubines killed their lovers this way when they misbehaved. The woman wronged would mince buffalo hairs into quasi microscopic bits, which she would mix into his food. That hair wouldn't dissolve in the stomach. It wasn't biodegradable and would end up causing incurable ulcers that—after months of spitting up blood—would lead to a painful death a little more than a year later.

Isookanga had seen Mirnas in his 4 × 4 coming to pick up little Shasha. Those were evenings when the intense heat went hand in hand with a black night, when for this reason an almost organic electricity emanated from bodies, creating unfortunate interferences in the neurons of some people. But this was not how Isookanga envisioned globalization. One couldn't dump on people to that extent, for in the end they would inevitably want to take revenge.

It's only logical: when the balance of payments turns out to be problematic, it becomes imperative that, via charges and gains, accounts be balanced first by getting the people dealt with. Where the Lithuanian was concerned, Shasha wasn't doing anything different. It's a regular practice in a liberalized universe. And the megalopolis is the place par excellence where people's concepts and madness are telescoped with extreme violence, generating energies as dense as those of black holes. The new century is a consumer of these, and the Democratic Republic of Congo is there to obtain them.

Besides, "*Mabele elisi,*"[19] the funeral lament sung by the Bamongo confirms it. In an environment polluted by the deadly waves of uranium, cobalt, columbite-tantalite, what can one expect from any individual who has passed through the centrifuge and is developing in the context of a next-generation nuclear reactor? Permanent radiation doesn't bring innocence back; it leads to rage. And too bad for the sensitive souls if the place of concentration and fission is Kinshasa, laboratory of the future and, incidentally, capital city of the nebula, Congo Inc.

18. "He was looking for it, he's found it."
19. "The earth is rich (with our dead)."

EPILOGUE

A non-stop China Airlines flight from Dubai dropped Zhang Xia off in Chongqing. After they officially served him notice of his guilt at the airport, a police squad took him away, bent over, hands tied in back, to the Public Safety Headquarters in the center of town. After a forty-eight-hour interrogation he came into a courtroom, dazed, where they sentenced him to a six-year prison term, two of them suspended, for corruption of functionaries and embezzlement of corporate assets, perpetrated by an organized gang—the most serious counts of indictment. Liu Kaï, moved to the rank of mere accomplice, was given two years, one of them suspended. Zhang Xia planned to appeal, but his court-appointed lawyer asked him to produce proof of not having been in China at the time that his signature was appended to all kinds of documents. It was the only way by which to introduce a new file.

That was basically what Isookanga thought he understood as he decoded the email Gong Xiyan had just sent him in a French she'd found on a translation site. She mentioned an article, a photo in a newspaper, a revolution, street children. Isookanga was sitting on the bridge of a barge sailing toward

Mbandaka. They had already passed Maluku, and the network signal was beginning to fade. The young man turned on his computer, wanting to take advantage of it before the batteries were completely dead. He had to open the message in simplified HTML format, because the reception was that poor. On his hard disk, Isookanga saved an article scanned from the daily newspaper *Le Potentiel*, in which they described the *shégués* riots and showed a photo of Zhang Xia and himself taken from far away. He tried to send the file in JPEG format but without success—too large. Zhang Xia's appeal proceedings were set for two weeks later.

The boat was taking its time, and for lack of a nearby telecommunications antenna it was impossible for Isookanga to access the Internet and even send any links. He was watching the stream of water, gladly letting his mind wander while a strip vanished from the battery's warning light. For *Raging Trade* it was all over; it didn't have enough network left, not enough energy to make anything get off the ground at all, certainly not any stealth bombers hidden a thousand miles from anywhere in places to which no one had any access except by passing through ever more complex levels. He would think it over once he was in the village. Zhang Xia had advised him to read Sun Tzu's *The Art of War*. The situation could be remedied at that moment, and in a strong position he could propose agreements to Kannibal Dawa. That risked turning out, painfully and with difficulty, the *diktats* of American Diggers, and its satellites still weighed too heavily on the territory of Gondavanaland. *Run nigga, run nigga / Run, mothafucker run*, Old Snoop Dogg kept singing, unruffled. Isookanga wasn't that serene anymore, of course, but the fateful rhythms comforted him with the thought that the gangsta was not only a relevant spokesman but also an exceptional visionary, because nothing in the near or distant future could have actually contradicted the lyrics of the famous song "Vato."

The sun had completed its course, and the banks consisted of nothing more than the silhouettes of foliage. A little orange and red remained between the shadows bordering the river. While finishing its path the sun had refrained from revealing that several time zones away, one of its rays hit Wang Lideng's glasses as he sat frowning in the armchair in the living room. A lightning flash struck, and that was enough, once again, to startle the sensitive soul of Gong Xiyan, sitting with her knees brushing against those of the chief of police in the modest apartment on the edge of Chongqing, in Szechuan Province.

Congo Inc.

Uncle Lomama was wrapped in a blanket to protect himself from the mosquitoes. Like his nephew, he was busy thinking about the Ekanga village, nestled in the depth of the forest. Both of them were thinking of it, but in different ways. The old man was remembering the drama of Nkoi Mobali and reflecting on a way to stop the pollution the antenna produced by covering it with a thick coating of mud. Termites knew how to do that. The old man planned to prepare them as soon as he was back in the village. He knew intuitively that the ministers and officials he'd been able to see wouldn't be of any use to him.

As for the young man Isookanga, he had nothing in his head but the vast dark green surfaces that, unobtrusively, contained gold-bearing layers beneath thick vegetation but looked like nothing special. *Kabotama Mongo, elengi, o!*[1] he thought to himself inwardly. With the disk that contained the map of minerals, Isookanga was truly going to occupy his place as chief—as soon as his uncle would let him take over, obviously. It turned out that going to the city had been useful: it had allowed him to find out that he wouldn't merely reign over *kambala* and pangolin but over more down-to-earth values as well,[2] the kind that were easily attributed to any monarch with a bit of glamor. Why not to him—Isookanga Lolango Djokisa, young Ekonda and an internationalist besides?

1. "What a pleasure to be born a Mongo!" a saying.
2. Kambala is a type of African buffalo.—*Tr.'s note*

In Koli Jean Bofane was born in 1954 in the northern region of what is today the Democratic Republic of Congo, and currently resides in Belgium. His first important publication was the novel *Mathématiques Congolaises*, published in France by Actes Sud in 2008 and the recipient of the Grand Prix littéraire de l'Afrique noire and the Jean Muno Prize from the Société Civile des Auteurs Multimédia (SCAM). *Congo Inc.: Le testament de Bismarck*, published in 2014, was awarded numerous prizes, including the Grand Prix du Roman Métis in 2014, and in 2015 the Prix des Cinq continents de la Francophonie, Prix Coup de coeur Transfuge/Meet, Prix littéraire des bibliothèques de la Ville de Bruxelles, and the Prix de l'Algue d'or (prix du public).

Marjolijn de Jager is a trilingual (Dutch, English, French), award-winning translator of works by, among others, Werewere Liking, Tahar Djaout, Ken Bugul, and Assia Djebar. She also translated Gilbert Gatoré's *The Past Ahead* (2012) for Indiana University Press's Global African Voices series.

Printed and bound by CPI Group (UK) Ltd, Croydon, CR0 4YY

09/06/2025

14685937-0002